OUTER CIRCLE

OUTER CIRCLE

IAN RIDLEY

www.v-books.co.uk

Twitter: @VBooks10
Facebook: vbooks10
Instagram: vbookspublishing

Cover design by Steve Leard
Typeset by seagulls.net
Back cover picture by Alex Ridley

ISBN: 978-1-7396396-0-0

For Vikki.

If you judge a book by the cover,
then you judge a look by the lover…

The truth was a mirror in the hands of God. It fell, and broke into pieces. Everybody took a piece of it, and they looked at it and thought they had the truth.

Jalaluddin Rumi

PART I

MONDAY
AUGUST 13TH
2012

1

SAUL

THE problem with having the time of your life, Saul thought, is that you don't realise you're having it. Only later, sometimes much later, only after comparing other experiences, does it dawn on you that those moments really were the time of your life. Except for today, except for these past few weeks. Saul was of an age to know that this had indeed been the time of his life, the time of all our lives. If only as an onlooker, albeit a contributing taxpayer, he recognised that he had been part of something joyous, magnificent and uplifting, something he might never sense or savour again. As for the life of a beloved friend or an admired acquaintance – not that he could cite many of either these days – he felt grateful that it had happened, sad that it was over. And when things were over, he was also old enough to know they left a void that needed to be filled. For good or evil.

London certainly felt pleased with itself as it basked in sunshine and pride this Monday morning, so different from the usual start-of-week commuting drudgery. The capital liked itself, was at peace and ease with itself. He could feel it sitting here in Regent's Park, absorbing the summer's sights and sounds and smells as he sought rest from his long walk, and shade from the rising heat of mid-morning, in the covered shelter just off Chester Road at the top of the Avenue Gardens.

Saul had a routine on the treatment days. He liked to walk down Primrose Hill from his flat, cross the bridge over the

Regent's Canal, then follow the path around the back of the zoo, hearing the animals and the delight of the children, before linking up with the Broad Walk at the drinking fountain. From there, as the mood took him, he would take in either Avenue Gardens or the sweet scents of the Queen Mary's Rose Gardens on Inner Circle, the interior one mile-round road at the hub of the park. After that, he would head to Clarence Gate and Baker Street Station. It was around two miles and not the direct route but it was the pretty way and he wanted to do it to prove he could, early in the day before the tiredness took over.

He took out the page proofs to read from his battered leather shoulder bag but he was too absorbed by the gorgeous scene to read much. Young lovers sauntered past hand in hand, heading north up the Broad Walk having taken in the formal beauty of the Italian Garden and the adjacent, wilder English Garden, still glorious though a month past their best, blazing reds the predominantly planted colour this year. Among them, middle-aged couples concealing affairs sought to avoid being captured in the photographs and videos of tourists recording this re-energised city. The Internet's posted images, Saul mused, made affairs so much more difficult and tiring these days.

He gazed up to see a plane heading for East London to make its turn along the Thames to land into the prevailing west wind at Heathrow. Looking back down, a half-smile came to his face reflecting the glimmers of humanity he had lately been redis-covering as he watched a scene passing most people by in the pre-occupation of their activities. The tattered old man he often saw here was usually berating passers-by, to the amusement of the park's regulars and the alarm of visitors. Today he wielded a bunch of twigs tied with string into a broom and was sweeping leaves into the shape of a heart.

Saul had not smiled much for some while but the sheer cele-bration of the human spirit exhibited through London's Olympic

Games and its closing ceremony last night had drawn him out from his cell of self-absorption and into the exercise yard of hope. He had choked back tears, sometimes unashamedly shed them, but this time they were not of sadness nor fear. They told of pride in the country he took for granted at the show of itself it had put on and admiration for the men and women who had dedicated lives to fulfilling the sporting talent they had been gifted. They had beautifully diverted the country from its economic recession and consequent privations.

Before, he had more often been weeping tears of fear as first light poked through the bedroom curtain, not howls of self-pity, but sobs of sadness that his life was now threatened, and of regret that he had not yet accomplished what he had hoped, or shared such as he possessed. He feared that after this time *of* his life, time could be called *on* his life.

'There are,' his old tutor Russ had once told him, 'the three S's of a life: survival, success and significance.'

Well, Saul had somehow survived his youth of only-child solitude and his mother dying young, and had had a modicum of success in publishing in his highest earning years. But significance? The books he had edited in a career with a publisher before redundancy, and these days corrected and proofed as a freelancer, were adequate enough – crime novels that eased boredom on long flights or enlivened afternoons on foreign sunbeds – but they were not life-changers. What would be the legacy of 59 years of just, well, trying?

'You've been no trouble,' the owner of the St Ives bed and breakfast had told him in the spring on his regular week enjoying that special North Cornish light. He smiled, thanked her, and said he might ask for that on his headstone. Beneath the pleasantries, though, he didn't want that to be the best that could be said of him.

Saul had always imagined that he would have noticed if – or rather when – he had cancer. God knows he had spent long enough worrying about it. A headache was a brain tumour. An unidentified fleshy mass in his scrotum was most assuredly a testicular lump. He thought there would be pain. He didn't expect such a silly, random set of symptoms to add up to the disease that for so many dared not speak its name.

At first he guessed that getting up twice a night to piss was just the result of drinking tea in bed as an accompaniment to *The Daily Telegraph* crossword and *Today In Parliament* before the midnight news, then falling asleep to the soothing strains of the shipping forecast. Then, when it got to three times, he thought it just the tedious transition from middle age – with its emotional crisis that had done for his marriage five years ago – into the physical deterioration that would accompany the final third of his life. Only when he found himself standing over his trickling stream of urine wishing it would hurry up so he could get back to bed did he suspect that something might be amiss.

It was then that he recalled his dead father's lament, as he stood next to him in the pub urinal that time. 'Can't fucking start and can't fucking finish,' Dad had said, shaking his penis furiously, to Saul's embarrassment. And it was then that he thought he should get checked out for the prostate cancer that had ultimately killed his father, who had been too fearful – and too late – to discover it before it slithered cunningly into the pelvic lymph nodes and beyond to the morphine-medicated agony of the bones.

His GP, Dr Bhagwan, couldn't be sure and thus was he sent to the Royal Marsden Hospital for a biopsy that would confirm traces of cancer in 95 per cent of his prostate. It always made him smile to himself, when he recalled the procedure. It consisted of Saul donning indignity in the guise of a hospital gown that tied up at the back and out of which hung his arse, then lying on his side on what resembled a massage table while a doctor inserted first a syringe with a long needle up the anal passage and into the prostate to inject an anaesthetic. It was followed five minutes later by some kind of extended probe. What it looked like, Saul had no idea and did not want to know. About the only benefit of being in this situation was that it was all going on behind him.

There would, he was told, be 10 shots from the probe, which turned out to be more of a gun, into 10 different areas of the prostate to take samples from all angles. And so he lay there, waiting for the click from the gun, which felt like a snake's tongue flicking out venomously at someone or something that had riled it.

He sensed each one, not as pain but shock, his buttocks stiffening against the anticipated impact. Thankfully a pretty young nurse was sitting, observing, in his eyeline, there to monitor screens but also to engage him in distracting conversation.

He found himself, though a private man, wanting to talk rather than be talked to. To cover his embarrassment at the whole absurd situation, he asked what a pretty girl like her was doing in a joint like this. He was old enough to get away with it not being construed as a chat-up line. She smiled. 'It is part of my secondment,' she said. 'I am very interested in the rectal wall.'

Try that one on a first date or over a curry with a boyfriend, Saul thought. You certainly wouldn't have wanted to share Bombay mix with her.

'That's five samples taken,' said the doctor after the fifth flick of the snake's tongue. 'We're halfway there.'

Does he really think I'm not counting? Saul thought to himself. He didn't say it, of course. A fondness for sarcasm that he was trying to curb did not sit well with all people and he definitely didn't want to upset these ones. He was, after all, at the mercy of a man with a very large probe.

At the procedure's conclusion, he slid himself off the bed, trying to make light of it, smiling at doctor and nurse, but he felt faint and noticed red droplets on the floor beneath him.

He wobbled as he walked to the door, blobs of blood marking his path as they fell from his anus, and the nurse quickly sat him down. Soon she had returned with an adult-sized disposable nappy. Not long after, she came back with a cup of tea and a digestive biscuit. He had hoped afterwards to get the tube back to Baker Street, comforted that he could usually get a seat these days as nobody batted an eyelid when he plonked himself into those reserved for the aged, infirm and pregnant, and then walk back home through the park. Even with an hour's rest and tea-drinking, though, he was in no fit state. A £20 taxi fare back to Primrose Hill it would have to be.

Where once he would have winced – at both the ordeal and the cab fare – today, infused with the mood of the nation, he smiled at the memory of the whole absurd procedure from two months ago. He checked his watch and saw that the time was approaching for him to leave for today's session of radiotherapy.

It was just as he gathered up the A4 pages he had been reading into his bag and was about to rise to his feet that the young man sat down on the seat along from him. He was just another kid, tall and lean, in skinny brown jeans and plain white trainers, on a day when the park was full of them, but there was something different about him as he huddled in his garishly coloured hoodie. Who needed a hood up on such a warm day? And his was not the joshing demeanour of other kids in the uniform of youth, nor did it chime with the atmosphere of the day. Beads of sweat lined the bone of his brow. Saul could see he had brown, ample hair but could not tell the length. His gaunt face was pale and his hands shook as he rolled a cigarette.

He looked up at Saul, who smiled routinely at him, as Londoners had grown accustomed to doing over the last month in spite of themselves and the city's usual unwritten code of blank faces and aversion to eye contact. Saul, who often struggled to contain his irascibility, had always fitted in well with that; he was solitary by nature, detested loud conversations and the vacuous mobile phone monologues of those lacking self-awareness.

In return, the lad could muster only a weak pursing of the lips amid the wispy facial fluff. Saul was quickly transported back to the pre-Olympic days of suspicion and, turning it round to when he was in his early 20s, as this kid seemed to be, he too would have found it strange that a grey-haired bloke in Marks and Spencer chinos and short-sleeved shirt wearing outdated trainers was smiling at him.

Then, like a fallow deer in a road startled into alertness by the approach of a car engine, the boy's shaking stopped as the increasing whine of a police siren shattered the summer scene. Saul was puzzled by the rigidity of his sudden stance, roll-up locked in his lips. He stared fearfully, pleadingly, at Saul for maybe five seconds. Saul saw pain in the boy's eyes and felt a hurt all of his own.

He wanted to reach out, to ask him what he could do to help, but suddenly the lad was walking briskly south in the direction of the Euston Road, down the Broad Walk towards Outer Circle, the three-mile perimeter road that protected the park and its comforting confines from the fevered reality of the concrete cityscape.

The boy turned around briefly to see if Saul was watching him, to see if his guilty reaction to the siren had been noted. When he saw that he was still being observed, he broke into a jog. Even if overdressed for it, he fitted in with runners here.

Saul did wonder about the kid and what had spooked him. But this was London. There was a lot of anxiety about, even if the current mood was masking it. Everybody had somewhere to go, usually for something pressing, in the anonymity the city had always thrived on and probably would do again one day soon.

Saul looked at his watch and broke into his own jog. He had better get a move on. The radio beams were beckoning.

2

RASHID

THE organisers of a family fun day at the London Central Mosque in the northwest corner of Regent's Park had gone to their beds relieved men and women on Sunday night. For a long time, the 12-member Board of Trustees of the landmark golden-domed building, designed by Sir Frederick Gibberd and built in 1978, had come under criticism from the more vocal among the capital's Muslim community for doing little for younger people. But they had responded finally and all had agreed it was a huge success.

They had not declared it an official festival to mark Eid and celebrate the end of Ramadan as some wanted because this was just a first year, a trial, and they wanted to see how it played. It was more than good enough for most, however. There was a souk of stalls in the courtyard, selling clothing, books and toys, perfumes and oils, and ones doing henna and face painting. There was a chance to learn the calligraphy of generations. There had been a barbecue and cakes and games and a bouncy castle. Thousands had come, attracted by the weather and a chance to relax and enjoy themselves after the privations of Ramadan. East had met West and all had gone home to northern and southern points of the capital, too, in a vibrant mood.

The reason the Board relaxed their opposition to such an event after some years of being pressed was not just because they had moderated their views about such frivolity on so a holy site.

Instead, they had been convinced that security for the day was feasible and affordable. The mood of the nation this glorious summer had been one of tolerance. Security around the city had been tight, the intelligence services were on top of any threats, and domestic suspicion of the Muslim community had eased amid the embracing, even celebrating, of each other's differences. The threat from rogue elements among the more militant practitioners of their religion was low, the threat to them as a retaliatory result lower still.

Until today.

As he stood at the entrance to the prayer hall and surveyed the scene, tears of helpless rage welled in Rashid's eyes at this vision of hellish carnage. How ironic that their holiday of Eid was supposed to be about charity, forgiveness and gratitude. His ears were simultaneously assailed by the twin wails of police and ambulance sirens. As piercing as they were, they were preferable to the sounds that had previously, obscenely, assaulted his ears.

They were the screams of men whose bodies were aflame.

He had been working in the bookshop when the guy walked into the Mosque, wearing blue overalls and a black balaclava with a small flag of St George embroidered on the nape. That little detail stuck with Rashid. The man carried a black backpack and a long tube as from a portable vacuum cleaner in his black-leather-gloved hands. Rashid was naturally startled at the sight but dumbstruck and static for a few moments. The focus of his disbelief, indeed, was how the man had moved unchallenged through the reception area and into the prayer hall, past the row of shoes at its entrance, to where men had gathered in anticipation of midday prayer, milling, talking or sitting alone in chairs around the perimeter of the space the size of a basketball court.

By the time Rashid was ready to persuade his shocked limbs towards the prayer hall, the victims were already on fire. He saw three, no four, as he scanned the room. Make that five. He stood and took the buffeting to his right shoulder then to his left as men escaped past him out into the courtyard and from there into Park Road via the main entrance to the complex.

What had this balaclava'd man done? How had he done it? And where had he gone? Rashid had not seen him amid the throng that was rushing past him.

Momentarily, something – shock, fear – stopped Rashid moving forward or back as he surveyed the scene. He could see bodies writhing in agony as the flames spread up and down to heads and toes and back. It was the screams, though, that would leave the lasting impression. A few men remained, their instincts telling them to stay rather than run for escape, and sought to beat the flames with their prayer mats. From a distance it looked as if they were assaulting their brethren, but the violent, desperate acts were the token deeds of the help-less. Too late would the hall's automatic sprinkler system act. The ceiling was high, two storeys high, to accommodate the magnificent chandelier at its centre, and the smoke had taken too long to activate the detectors.

Stunned, and without knowing what he was doing, Rashid stumbled back out through the reception area into the court-yard. Men, as well as women who had fled from their own prayer room, had been drawn together, some in speechless silence, some in tears, others in gabbled, heightened speech, monologues rather than conversations.

The morning's activity of clearing and cleaning up all the accompaniments to yesterday's fun day had been brutally halted. The souk was half-dismantled, the bouncy castle partially deflated. Suddenly, in the open air, the stench of burning bodies from inside the building filled Rashid's nostrils, drawing up into his throat and mouth the food left in his stomach from the indulgence of the previous night that had marked the end of Ramadan. Just 15 minutes earlier, people had been cheerily going about their business, be they Muslim companies hired for the previous day and who had been tidying the scene this morning, or those who were here early for the second of the five prayers of the day, the *Zuhr*.

Rashid realised that there was nothing to be done out here and that he should go back to help those in the prayer hall. This time he hurried, starting to come to his senses as he heard the echoes of the training from the life he had rejected, but which seemed to keep coming back for him; as head and heart, intellect and instinct, vied with each other. By now the sprinklers had gushed into action, by now the burning men were soaked. The killer had gone for those wearing the cowing white *galabiya* but they were no longer white, just blackened tattered rags, some seared into the now-matching skin of the lifeless bodies beneath them, which were strewn across the blue carpeted prayer hall. Alongside, the few men left inside who had tried to help, those wearing jeans and regular shirts, were sitting in shock, making no moves to evade the waterfall from upon high, as if it might cleanse them of the horror they had witnessed.

Rashid was too late. He was aware of a something deeper than sadness but could not name the feeling. He noticed, in the southwest corner of the hall, an open door, a fire escape, and felt drawn to it. Oblivious to the sprinklers drenching him, he moved swiftly towards the sunlit opening, gazing down at the prone bodies in his path, past a weeping man sitting in a chair at the side of the hall, and out into the grassy area where the late morning light caused him to squint. He heard two shouting voices and picked his way through the trees that offered shade and a chance to accustom his eyes to the daylight before pressing on towards the back entrance to the Mosque. It was wide open. Normally a padlock and chain fastened the two black wrought iron gates but the chain now lay useless on the ground, like the shed skin of a snake.

He realised that the metal had been sliced, and his attention was suddenly attracted by the roar of a car engine accelerating south along Outer Circle. He looked across the road to the entrance just past the traffic lights at Hanover Gate and thought he saw a running man disappearing into the park. He was wearing something bright.

Rashid crossed the two-lane Outer Circle, apologising to a driver who had angrily sounded his horn as the lights were now green. He staggered into the park in the slow motion of the witness to an atrocity and unsteadily walked towards the children's paddling pool. Parents watched with fear this dazed figure wearing a soaked blue *kurta* tunic, fawn cotton trousers and brown sandals, and immediately grabbed the hands of their children. Rashid fell to his knees on the path and began to weep. When he fell onto his side and curled into the foetal position, all dispersed around him.

He lay there and closed his eyes, disappearing into the obscenity of his mind's eye, for how long he did not know. The next thing he knew, he was hearing the voice of a young woman standing over him. He looked up and saw a police uniform and a young woman's face staring down at him. 'Are you all right?' she asked.

Rashid did not know if he was all right. He was not burned, he knew that at least. He couldn't tell what he was feeling. Shock? Anger, or even rage? Sadness? All of it was in there somewhere, along with something else. Something he was beginning to identify from that vague feeling at the back entrance to the Mosque. Was it guilt that he had not been able to help save a life? He would not be alone in that but he didn't know it now. There would be many seared internally with lasting scars, even without the fatal external burns that had clearly killed some of his brethren.

'You've come from the Mosque, yes?' the police officer asked.

He nodded faintly. He was in his own cocoon, dredging his own memory pool. What had happened? A bomb? *They have caught us off our guard*, he thought, *taken advantage of our openness*. But if it was a bomb, why was there no explosion? The golden dome of the Mosque, these days partly tarnished to bronze by time and weather, and the white minaret tower were intact. Where had the fire, the smoke, come from?

He gazed back towards Outer Circle, to the Mosque. Now he could see fire engines, ambulances and police cars and vans parked. Some had gone to the front on Park Road but the park and the back entrance offered quicker access with less traffic to interrupt them. Police were cordoning off a section of Outer Circle between Hanover Gate and the Macclesfield Bridge over the Regent's Canal a few hundred yards around the corner. To the terror of the authorities, that area contained the American Ambassador's residence at Winfield House. More armed men than usually guarded it were swiftly being deployed.

Here inside the park, Rashid watched from his place on the grasa as men and women from the Mosque, space blankets around their shoulders to help stave off the cold of shock that not even a hot day would hold back, stumbled past him. They looked like empty-eyed refugees in a news report from a war-torn region.

Having had reports of fires at the Mosque, some firefighters were checking out the boating lake for a natural water source for their hoses but Rashid knew from his first-hand experience that they were much too late for all that. Meanwhile, men and women in uniforms and white plastic suits were hastily and efficiently assembling the paraphernalia of a major crime scene, from marquees to Portakabins.

Soon the TV cameras and journalists would be here. The Mosque was just a few miles from their studios and offices: Sky at Isleworth, the BBC at Shepherd's Bush to the west, ITN closer still in Gray's Inn Road to the southeast. Easy to scramble studio cars, grab cabs.

'Sir,' the young policewoman repeated several times, to snap Rashid out of his trance of trauma. 'Did you see what happened?'

'What? Yes. Well, no. I was in the bookshop, working at the till,' he blurted out. 'He knew what he was doing. Bodies were burning. And the screams. The screams…'

'We're going to need a statement,' said PC Deena Campbell. 'We're setting up an incident room over there.' He turned to follow her finger pointing at the Boathouse Cafe.

'Can I take you there?'

'There was no explosion. It doesn't add up,' Rashid said.

'Perhaps you could come and tell me about that?' she replied.

Mumbling to himself, shaking his head with incredulity, Rashid walked slowly to the cafe and sat down at a table with two other stunned faces. He tried to force a smile, realising at once when it went unreturned how inappropriate it was. Smiling, at least this past year, was in his nature, though.

'Tea, coffee?' Deena asked him.

He saw the other two men clasping polystyrene cups and nodded. 'Coffee. White. Decaf,' he replied. 'No,' he quickly added. 'As much caffeine as you've got.'

'I'll get someone to you very soon,' she said and smiled.

'I was once one of you,' Rashid said. 'But I wasn't.'

'OK…' Deena replied, not knowing what the man meant, before setting off on her errand. The shock, she supposed.

Rashid buried his head in his hands then looked up to see her speaking to a man in a suit across the room. A detective he supposed. He had better work out exactly what it was he had seen.

He looked at the two men. Their own bewilderment had stilled them into silence. Rashid was still prone to bouts of jabbering incomprehension and streams of consciousness, punctuated by silences, but the young police officer's conversation, albeit minimal, had dragged him back from his own world.

'Did you see what I saw?' he asked them. They both nodded.

Rashid began to piece together his story in his head. He guessed they would probably also want to know why a white 23-year-old from Stanmore at the top of the Jubilee Line would revert to Islam, or convert as they would understand it, after being brought up a Jew. And change his given name of Richard while retaining his western family name of Johnson. Just now – he could not help himself, forgive him Allah – he too was wondering.

3

SAUL

BY the time he got back to Baker Street, Saul was aware of what had happened at the Mosque. All of London quickly knew. Speeding emergency vehicles were usually just part of the city's routine but the sight and sound of police cars, fire engines and ambulances all on the move at the same time had even the most self-absorbed of bystanders stopping to look and wonder.

He hadn't immediately put it all together when he arrived at South Kensington station and noticed on his walk to the Royal Marsden a couple of ambulances, sirens blaring, heading down the Fulham Road. They were not usual around a cancer hospital. They must be heading down to the Accident and Emergency at the Chelsea and Westminster.

Only when he reached the Marsden's outpatients department on the first floor, with its clean air and comfortable chairs, did he realise the severity of what was going on around him that day. Usually, the TV on the wall was tuned to something innocuous, calming, like a house makeover show, but every channel now was running the story. So much of modern news, even the trivial, was 'BREAKING' and ran across the bottom of screens. The letters for this, though, were double the usual point size and, in white on red and at the top of the screen, unmoving. It even had its own catchphrase reserved for the genuinely serious:

LONDON MOSQUE ATROCITY

Saul watched as he sipped the water demanded by his treatment: three plastic cups of 100 millilitres each some 30 minutes before the beams directed to both hips and his midriff. To be effective, the radiotherapy needed a full bladder, it seemed. He understood nothing more technical than that. He dreaded this part, his enlarged prostate making him increasingly desperate for an unpermitted piss as treatment time approached. It was worse if his regular time was pushed back unexpectedly when the machine was needed for more urgent cases. He worried about embarrassing himself by urinating involuntarily. Holding on could be agony, though the thing about this hospital, as he walked among people with more apparent tumours, on neck or head, for example, was that he could keep his own condition in perspective. Today, he acknowledged with some guilt, agony was not a word that he should be using about himself as the raw footage from Regent's Park confronted him. The death toll was five according to the bar beneath the newsreader, his lips silent as the volume in outpatients was always turned down. Eight more men who had been trying to help the dying had been taken to the specialist burns unit at the Chelsea and Westminster while more than 50 others, men and women, were being cared for at University College Hospital on the Euston Road, most suffering from shock, all being checked for it.

It all carried, the news report noted, eerie echoes of the 7 July 2005. The day of the suicide bombings in London on tubes and a bus the day after the city had been awarded the Olympic Games at a ceremony in Singapore. Just over seven years later, another wicked act had sullied the city's joy.

Saul walked down the two flights of stairs to check in at the radiotherapy department where the talk was of nothing else. Angela, the receptionist, wore a frown rather than her customary smile, her eyes red from tears. Even the man Saul had named Jolly Jack for his continual cheesy, risqué jokes that were subconsciously designed to deflect the anxiety about the growth that lay in wait behind his right eye had been shocked out of his denial and into the reality of death.

'How are you?' Sue enquired. Saul often sat next to her in the waiting area. Only in her 30s, her baldness actually enhanced her kind face. She had breast cancer and the radiotherapy was to mop up cancerous cells around the mastectomy she had undergone. Saul admired her refusal to wear a wig.

'Fine thanks, yes,' Saul replied. 'You?'

'Yes, fine.' she said. It struck him more than ever today how incongruous it was that two people with cancer, even in this seat of it, preserved the niceties of British culture by not sharing their anxieties. Fineness fitted all.

Today, fortunately, he was not delayed and breezed through his five-minute treatment. He was used to it now, today being the beginning of the last week, the 33rd of 37 daily treatments separated by weekends. The whirring and wheezing of the automatic arm moving across the three loions of his body no longer worried him as it did at first, like the noises to a nervous flyer as a plane took off then banked before levelling out. He concentrated just on staying still so that the beams hit their cankered targets. And not wetting himself with all this electricity about. The relieving piss afterwards, long and loud, was always bliss, until the frustration at the slow flow assailed him again.

He would not stay today for one of those delicious currant buns and tea served so cheaply in outpatients at the Friends coffee bar. He wanted to hurry back to Baker Street. He was no rubbernecker, but this was his territory and he was now concerned. The park he loved, knew so well, had been violated. He felt connected to it and concerned for its wellbeing after all these years.

On his way back home from Baker Street, Saul would usually cut off half a mile by taking a left from Clarence Gate up towards Hanover Island and crossing the bridges over the boating lake to the sports fields and Primrose Hill Bridge again. It was not as picturesque but by late afternoon, he would be growing tired, especially in this heat and after almost seven weeks of these walks. He needed some spare capacity for the final ascent of Primrose Hill.

Today, that route was not going to be possible, as the police officer informed him when he reached Outer Circle. He knew something was different the moment he emerged from the Underground on to Baker Street itself. There was no traffic now heading down towards the Marylebone Road and south towards Oxford Street.

Where Baker Street met Outer Circle, Saul could see that everything to the north, towards the Mosque, was blocked off now. When he crossed the road and got to Clarence Gate, he could see it was the same inside the park. Police officers stood on duty, fielding questions from pedestrians, tourists mostly wondering how now to get to London Zoo. They were being told that the whole of the western side of the park was off limits.

Some cursed, but Saul was not too put out, even if it meant 20 more minutes walking. He was feeling well today and could cross Clarence Bridge at the back of Regent's University, the business college that once had been Bedford College, part of London University, then cross Inner Circle and walk through the rose gardens to the Broad Walk at Chester Road, before retracing his steps of earlier today.

Vulgar curiosity did not beset him like it did others. The best thing he could do, he reckoned, was go about his business with respectful insouciance. Having missed his bun at the Marsden, he decided on tea and cake at the Honest Sausage on the Broad Walk, which would be about halfway home, when he was ripe for a rest. It would also fuel him for a bit of shopping at the mini mart before settling in for the evening with a simple meal and the page proofs that he had neglected during nights of watching sporting competition on the television. It would not be easy, though, when he thought about it. A deflation began to assail him after the uplift of last night's closing ceremony. The savage enormity of today's event was also beginning to sink in.

Saul hated that death had come to this special place, which was like a cosy village to him, and disturbed his, its, peace and equilibrium. Its neatness appealed to his sense of tidiness and need for organisation in his life. Outside the park was the structured chaos of central London, which had been built randomly, messily sometimes, over centuries; inside was a series of thoroughfares in straight lines and circles enveloped by a necklace of ten glittering jewels in the form of elegant cream terraces of high-ceilinged villas, designed by John Nash.

Outer Circle was linked to the Inner by just two short roads – one south, one east – and on either side of them stood the beautifully manicured gardens and playing fields. As well as the college and the zoo and the boating lake, it contained wetlands for wildlife and a heronry, tennis courts and an outdoor theatre that thrived in the summer. Hyde Park was the tourists' favourite, with its proximity to the hotels and the museums, but Saul preferred the variety here and enjoyed its location to the north of the congestion zone so that fewer ventured here. It was an oasis in which Saul could thrive, a controlled environment where he could enjoy the company of people without having to interact with them at all – something that was about to change.

At the Honest Sausage, he ordered his tea and a slice of a carrot cake and as he sat at a table outside, a group of half a dozen joggers ran by, led by a bronzed hunk in running vest, lycra shorts and expensive-looking trainers. Saul had barely taken a mouthful of cake when he noticed a hooded figure rummaging in a bin at the side of the cafe. It was the same kid he had seen a few hours earlier.

'Are you OK?' he found himself asking.

Startled, the lad turned to look at him and Saul discerned a fear in his eyes. His gaze turned above Saul's eyeline and down the Broad Walk. Fear became panic and the kid bolted, off between the trees somewhere to the interior of the park.

Saul turned to find out what had spooked him and saw two police officers running, breathing heavily. They came to a stop next to his table, a pair of middle-aged men sweating and spluttering out words.

'Bloody people,' one said.

'Who?' Saul asked.

'Those personal trainers,' said the other, pointing up the Broad Walk to the group of joggers who had just passed through, led by the hunk. 'They work in this park without licences and make bloody fortunes without giving anything back to the community.'

'Ah,' Saul said and smiled. 'I thought what with this thing over at the Mosque, you might be on that.'

'Disgraceful. Shocking.' said one. 'No, not us. We're parks police. The Met are all over that stuff. Life goes on, eh?'

Saul nodded. 'Maybe you'll get him tomorrow?'

'Bloody right. Or when we're a bit better, Pete, eh?'

His colleague laughed. 'Or when they fork out for bikes for us, Geoff. Maybe we could get one of those Boris bikes down by the tennis courts?'

'They wouldn't pay the expenses,' said Geoff and they both laughed.

Saul smiled at them and sipped his tea as he watched them head off. He got back to his cake, looking for signs in the tress of that kid who could probably get a job as a personal trainer himself given the speed with which he had disappeared. He was by now, however, nowhere to be seen, though that didn't stop Saul wondering about him.

4

DEENA

DEENA had been told to stand down. She was certainly ready to. It was not so much that the day had been long. She was used to that. It was more its intensity as brutal contrast to the reassuring, routine start involving the usual drinking of tea and fending off the flirting of the male PCs, who were anything but PC. Then came that call, the one that not only changed the day and the psyche of a city but the lives of so many. She knew even then, given what she had seen, that she would be one of them.

At first, none at Paddington Green had anticipated the severity of the emergency. An incident in Regent's Park was all they were told initially. But urgent. Highly urgent. There were not many left now who remembered the 1982 bombing at the bandstand in the park, but the stories had passed down into the folklore of the Green, with its role at the centre of the IRA terror campaign in London. This, though only five had died compared to the seven soldiers then, was shocking enough, as Bill on the desk, who had seen it all, kept saying throughout the afternoon as he shook his head.

Deena had been one of the last intake of recruits the previous year to have undergone the 26-week Initial Police Learning and Development Programme at Hendon Police College, with its courses on crime scenes and forensics, radio ops and driving – and serious crimes, including murder. That was before budget cuts meant just a 16-day induction. No training or course, though, long or short, could have prepared her for this most devastating sight of her 19-year-old life. She had already encountered dead bodies, but singly. Or two at a time, when that drunken motorcyclist ploughed into the night bus queue in Edgware Road. But then again, no one at the station, no matter their age, could have been prepared for the carnage at the Mosque today.

Having rounded up survivors for the detectives to interview in detail – and how she envied them and their jobs – she was seconded to crime scene duties, fetching and carrying, taping off areas. The vision of the dead bodies was a scene from a horror film, made worse by the knowledge there was no leaving the cinema.

Because they weren't just dead bodies. They were charred dead bodies. Some were burned to their skulls, others retained bubbled, blistered skin and sinew. It just depended at which stage of agony the flames on them had been doused. Incongruously, the water from the sprinklers ran off their remains onto the puddled carpet. The five dotted around the prayer hall resembled fallen black chess pieces on some grotesque board, as if someone was losing and had upturned it in a fit of pique.

She knew, even at such a young age, that the sight would remain with her for the rest of her life. And the smell. Hours later, as she sat watching the news footage in her bedroom at her parents' terraced house in Stockwell, she still had that stench of burning flesh in her nostrils. She recalled singeing her hair over a stove once but this was so far beyond that. She thought the aroma of curried chicken might help but its plated remains on her bedside table were doing nothing to shift it.

The search was on now for the perpetrator. Forensics would be going over the scene for the next day or two but that was about gathering evidence, joining the dots. Word around the station was that they knew who had done it. Or at least they knew from the CCTV cameras positioned at regular intervals around the Mosque complex that it was the act of one man, a young man, by the way he moved and the descriptions of his physique from eye witnesses. The problem was that neither they nor the footage described or revealed a face. The balaclava atop the blue overalls showed only eyes and mouth.

Then there was the plain black backpack – though not a bomber's backpack. Bill on the desk told her that the detectives had been stunned to hear from survivors that some kind of flamethrower had been drawn from the bag, before having it confirmed by their own eyes from the CCTV.

More might be known about his identity once they had accounted for all the cars in the vicinity. About 50 were parked in the Mosque's car park, another 20 at the back, on Outer Circle, on machine parking. He must have got here somehow and he would not have taken public transport, not in that garb, not with all the walking that would have been required. The Mosque was halfway between Baker Street and St John's Wood tube stations, about half a mile north up the Park Road section of the A41, the same south down Wellington Road. And he wasn't going to be carrying that heavy backpack on to buses.

The statements might reveal something too; her job was just to get some basic information from people and pass it on for the detectives to follow up and discover more. Apart from to her working partner Darren, she couldn't be honest enough with anyone to admit that she struggled to understand some of them, such had been the confluence of London and ethnic accents, but she had done her best, and at least got names and addresses.

She had been intrigued by Rashid. She would like to have spent more time with him, to find out what had prompted him to convert to Islam, but that would have been personal curiosity when she knew she had to be professional. A white 23-year-old from Stanmore, like her still living with parents, working in the London Islamic Centre bookshop? What was that all about?

She would also like to have known if he was living at home for the same reasons as she, the curse of modern youth: too small a salary to save a deposit for a flat of her own, let alone get a mortgage. It was one of the iniquities and inequities of modern London, with property prices fuelled now by the wealthy of the world buying for themselves and their offspring. Many, notably those in oil, were surviving the recession, and things would only worsen for those such as her following these blue-sky, picture-postcard Olympics that would attract more moths to her city's flame. Meanwhile, one day, she hoped she would get to find out the backgrounds to people like Rashid. It was frustrating being in on the start of a story but never the end, as the detectives were.

What, for example, would they make of Rashid's statement? He had gabbled to her about having seen the man, watched him walk through the reception area, but had then frozen as the man methodically inflicted his evil. By his own admission, Rashid had neither stayed to help nor rushed to chase the man who had wielded the flamethrower to devastating effect. And what was that about him having been one of us?

Mum and Dad had been inquisitive when she got home, though more interested in her welfare. She was fine, she said, and wanted to be in her room alone with her thoughts and they understood that. They were just grateful she was home safe.

Now she looked up at the 18-inch screen sitting on her chest of drawers and caught a glimpse of herself in a news report as, behind the reporter, she was escorting a survivor to the Boathouse Cafe. She was unaware that downstairs, Mum and Dad were bursting with pride at their daughter's role in events. 'See,' they would tell guests next Sunday, 'she is at the centre of big inquiries now.'

At least, Deena thought meanwhile, her boss might be happy with her but she quickly realised he would barely notice given the heaviness of other matters on his mind. She had looked busy, efficient and was pleased with her professional self. She then felt a pang of guilt that amid the personal sadness of it all, her professional self had also almost enjoyed it. She had been energised, in on something significant, vital, and which held the nation in its grisly thrall.

And, she knew, there could well be more intriguing work to be done in the aftermath. Paddington Green was in fact a tower block and its bucolic name concealed its urban realities. The Green's cells, for example, would be home to any terrorists involved in the plot for their interrogation. They had held IRA bombers and the failed suicide bombers of 2010. Actually, they were no longer just cells. 'A central London location' to which suspects were taken in the news reports, was in reality the station's custody suite, a modern euphemism.

Not that some of the papers thought so. They cited the ceiling windows, yellow walls, painted so to give an air of space, and blue chairs and comfy mattresses as signs of softness on the part of the police. Then there was the desk and access to books and music, all a far cry from the brown linoleum floors and grey wall tiles that would have greeted IRA suspects. It was out of police control, however, and many inside the Green agreed with the papers. A few years back, they had been ordered by some European diktat to make them more humane at a cost of half a million quid.

Deena's mobile rang. A picture of Dave appeared on the screen.

'You all right, babe? Just caught up with all this shit on the news. Seen you in the background of some pictures. Why didn't you call me?'

'Only just got in. Was about to,' Deena lied.

'Shocking. Fucking shocking,' Dave said. 'What sort of scum did this?'

'That's what we're trying to work out.'

'They're saying it's a block with a flamethrower…'

'Yes, looks like it.'

'Unbefuckinglievable. It's almost like every sick bastard has got to find a new way of doing these things. Fucking attention seekers.'

Deena didn't want this right now. She knew she should have done, should have craved the comfort of a boyfriend, but she was glad he was a third of a world away in Dubai, thriving as a personal trainer. She would have to tell him any day now.

'I can get a plane home tomorrow. Be there this time tomorrow night.'

'No.' she replied a little bit too quickly. 'I'll be fine. I can handle all this. It's just professional, you know.'

'Wanna Skype, maybe?'

'No, honestly. I'm going to have an early night.'

The last thing she wanted was eye contact. She knew it would betray her lack of need for him. Her relief, in fact, that he was not around with his centre-of-attention neediness to drain her energy. She knew too that he would inevitably steer the conversation around to questioning whether police work really was the right life for her, especially when he was making such good money. Dubai was fabulous, he said. Hot and wealthy. 'Like me,' he said with a laugh. She should come out there and live with him. Vacuous and restrictive for a woman like her, she thought. Dave never talked about what she might do out there.

'OK if you're sure,' he said. 'Sure, I'm sure.'

'See you soon, yeah? Skype tomorrow maybe?'

'Yeah, hope so,' she lied again. 'But not sure yet if we'll have our shifts messed about because of this thing. Let's see OK?'

'OK. Bye.'

'Bye,' she echoed and shut off her mobile.

She hated not telling the truth about anything, especially her feelings. At least the bit about her wanting an early night was not a lie. She was exhausted. She just hoped she would sleep, given what she had seen, given that her mind was still racing, even if her body was shutting down.

She showered and changed into a nightdress, hanging up her uniform, before carefully drawing her Afro comb through her thick hair and applying moisturiser to her face. Then she lay on her bed wondering whether Rashid would also struggle to sleep. She had seen the aftermath of death, which was distressingly memorable enough. He had seen the event's grim detail of dying.

5

RASHID

RASHID should have been traumatised, like many who had been there, or noisily outraged, like many who hadn't, according to the conventional standard reactions, which were often dictated by television's need for soundbites. He felt neither, however. In real life, feelings were not so neat, not so polarised. He was still discovering how he felt, though there was a numbness to him as he continued to process and ponder what had happened. As his mother had told him: there was no 'should' about it. Feelings just were. They were neither right nor wrong. Tell that to those expecting a reaction, he said.

Such was modern health and safety (and compassion, 'Don't forget that,' his mother had added) that all who had been uninjured – at least physically – had been taken anyway to UCH. He supposed that seeing writhing, screaming, burning bodies could leave something of a scar.

He did not feel scarred or wounded, though, even several hours on. He had made a call to his worried parents earlier when they heard about the monstrous event on the news, so they were calm when they greeted the ambulance at the door but were still garrulously curious about his experience and what the nurses and one of the host of trauma counsellors who had volunteered their services at the hospital had to say. He was in no mood to talk, however, and so, despite the fearing and fretting about their nice Jewish boy who had turned to Islam, they left him resting alone on his bed, gazing at the ceiling with his tortured thoughts and feelings.

Looking back, Rashid – then Richard – Johnson had been surprised himself by how simple it had been walking into the Mosque for the first time a year ago. He expected to be challenged at the entrance on Park Road, having walked down from St John's Wood tube station, but the only barrier was for those wanting the car park. In fact, he felt he should ask the man at the gatehouse if it was OK for him to come through. Of course, the man had said – looking at him for a few seconds more than he might have done a man of Asian or African extraction, though it was nothing really sinister – but he must remember to take off his shoes if he wanted to enter the prayer hall.

Made worse by his tallness, he had felt self-conscious walking through the concrete courtyard to the Mosque itself and was intimidated by the signs notifying of the existence of CCTV. The reception area was a wonderland to him. Clocks showed the time in great Muslim cities around the world and digital displays told of today's five prayer times. Pairs of shoes stood empty in rows. He expected something more, well, spiritual, than the many sets of trainers on view.

In fact, there was much unexpectedly banal and ordinary about the place. There was a sign pointing down some stairs to a basement restaurant named The Regent's Park Grill and pictures of meals were printed on a poster, as if it was a cheap kebab shop on the Kilburn High Road. He was surprised to see fish and chips on the menu. He had thought the dishes would be more, well, exotic.

He had seen then, too, through one of the four doors at the sides of the hall, the southeast exit through which the flame-thrower had escaped today, young men sitting in the open air as they waited for midday prayers. One was on a mobile. Another was smoking a cigarette. He noticed men in Ralph Lauren polo shirts, one even wearing Hackett, whose brand featuring the flag of St George had an appeal for some right-wing youth.

The flag of St George. He hoped that detail he had provided to the police in his statement about one being stitched into the back of the killer's balaclava would prove useful. The month spent at Hendon before he realised it was not for him had left a mark. Or several. That call earlier this year, that meeting afterwards with one of them from some department whose name he could not remember, had confirmed his view of working for the police.

On that initial visit to the Mosque, he had also noticed packets of sweets on sale outside the bookshop, just near the entrance to the Ladies' Prayer Room, and it occurred to him, watching kids running about the place, that every religion must have the same dilemma with their children: give them sweets to stop them from pestering, but the e-numbered sweets themselves can cause the hyperactivity. He had smiled.

(That was some small mercy, he thought to himself: the flamethrower had ignored the children, and there were quite a few around with it being school holidays.)

Amid such incongruity, though, were the signs of reverence, respect and sheer seriousness he had expected. He had followed a sign upstairs to the library, where, he would later find out, there were more than 24,000 books, including the *Qur'an* in 24 languages. No bags were allowed but no one seemed to be checking. Perhaps it was fear that somebody might secrete some stolen volumes but surely Muslims, any religious people around such an esteemed place, would not steal books? It could only, surely, be for security purposes. It was the only real hint of anxiety around the place he encountered.

Once inside, Richard was attracted to the General Reference in English. This was all too worthy, though, and he felt unworthy. Though no one stopped or challenged him, and someone even smiled at him as he browsed, he felt too self-conscious to linger and headed back down the stairs where it was less quiet and easier to blend in.

He dared not enter the prayer hall, even though it was allowed if he just took off his shoes. He simply didn't feel qualified. Or ready. This was just a look, he was ready to tell anyone if they spoke to him, just an exploratory visit to see if he might fit in here. A fact-finding mission. Actually more of a feeling-finding mission. He felt drawn here but didn't yet want to get drawn into discussions about his disillusionment with Judaism. He wanted to see how his heart felt in such a place as a response to the questions his head was posing.

The signs outside the hall amused him, not least the list of Common Mistakes and the instructions: women were allowed in, but not to pray, and should not wear perfume that might sexually arouse; no bad breath; no quarrelling; no mobile phones. He supposed the guy on his mobile in that doorway was technically just outside the hall. He was also surprised to see men lying down in the prayer hall. Meditation took many forms, he guessed.

Suddenly feeling conspicuous, he moved towards the bookshop some 10 yards to the right of the hall and began to browse the books. *The Qur'an Explanation* attracted him, along with *The Man Who Killed 99 People*. He wanted to peek inside the book to find out more, intrigued by a title that surely couldn't refer to a glorification of violence or an introduction to Islamic extremism. He feared that if he was caught reading it, he might be noticed, seen as a potential terrorist and be thrown out or, worse still, be reported to the police. (Later, when he got home, he Googled the title. It turned out to be a story, what Christians would call a parable, about repentance and forgiveness.)

Instead, once the man at the counter was free and the room was almost empty, Richard quietly approached him.

'I am interested in Islam,' he found himself whispering.

'Oh yes?' asked the man, not whispering, and Richard couldn't quite discern from his tone whether he was being inquisitively helpful or suspicious.

'Would you have a basic guide that might tell me more?'

The man looked at him for a moment perhaps to gauge if what he was seeing was authentic. Richard's heartbeat rose as he suddenly considered how sore a thumb he must look. He certainly felt vulnerable.

'Hmm,' said the man, stroking the beard that gave him a studious air, as did the black *kufi* hat he was wearing. Some months later as Rashid, after having taken a Muslim name, he would joke about this moment with Omar, who was a benevolent man in his late 30s, but for now he felt intimidated by this figure coming out from behind the counter wearing a full-length *galabiya* gown. Richard was tempted to make a run for it, fearing he was about to be confronted and others summoned to interrogate him about why he was here. Instead of going for Richard, however, the man went to a shelf in the corner and returned with a slim paperback.

A Brief Illustrated Guide to Understanding Islam, the cover read. You couldn't get more appropriate than that, Richard thought.

'Perhaps this will help,' said the man and smiled. 'By the way, my name is Omar.'

Richard thanked him, said he would take the book and paid the £3 price. It was the least he could do; it almost felt like a donation given the time he had spent around the Mosque, had been allowed to spend, without being challenged.

Not wishing to outstay his welcome, and feeling sensitive to every glance, he decided it was time to go. It had been a long way to come, 45 minutes each way from Stanmore for a 15-minute visit, but it would prove to be probably the most important quarter of an hour of his young life. And that book would become the basis for a life-changing event. Its answering of questions – What does Islam say about terrorism? ('Islam, a religion of mercy, does not permit terrorism.') – and comforting illustrations that evoked scientific books of his youth, were just what he needed.

He had been searching for something. His brief spell as a police cadet had exposed him to a racism that may have been far short of the blatant 1970s version he had heard about but it still simmered among police ranks, along with a prejudice against Muslims in London that was growing with the profile of the religion. He wanted to find out for himself what Islam was truly about but had never expected to be drawn into it himself.

His doubts about being a Jew had also grown. The complied rituals and observations rankled, as he saw it almost presenting a barrier to God rather than facilitating a closeness that he would come to find in the simplicity he saw in Islam's fewer priests and the simplicity of its prayer.

He had also been drained by the endless justifications for what in his idealism he saw as Israel's intransigent attitude in the Palestinian question, and its over-reaction in bombing the Gaza strip every few years just as the occupants there had established supply lines – of life's essentials as well as arms – through the network of tunnels. He was not naive enough to believe that the Palestinians were blameless but this, he believed, was unleashing a pride of lions on a few wolves. There would be blood and the wolves would inflict damage, but they would ultimately be overwhelmed.

Yes, Israel needed to defend itself, and the history of the Jews demonstrated just how fiercely, but it had been tedious trying to explain to people the difference between Judaism and the Israeli state, that you could embrace one without the other, believe in the principles of one but not the actions of the other. In the end, however, he himself had not believed – not *felt* – his own arguments.

Having previously felt restricted in religion, he had been empowered by that visit to Regent's Park, uplifted by the openness with which Omar had greeted him and eased his embarrassment. Thus had he felt safe in booking himself on an induction day at the Mosque. He had been amazed that more than 80 people from all over the country, and even other nations, had turned up on a Sunday, half of them women, and had been surprised at the friendliness of it all. He had not felt at all conspicuous, as he had feared he might. Indeed, he had been surprised to discover a belonging that he couldn't ignore, with his previous doubts replaced by a calm acceptance.

The time came for Richard, with a mixture of nerves and certainty, to tell his parents that he would be converting – or reverting as Muslims called it, since they believed all were born Muslims and were then given a religion by their parents – and taking the name Rashid. He sort of felt, he said, that as well as him needing Islam, they needed him, as a defender in his white world. Naturally, they were shocked. Dad shouted that he had thought his son was about to tell him that he was gay, such was the portentous tone. And now he wished his son *was* gay, he shouted even more loudly. Mum just cried. The shame in the district, the disgrace of it all.

In the weeks leading up to his *Shahadah*, his conversion through a declaration of faith, the arguments with his father grew more intense. Yes, he would agree, Islamic fundamentalists have committed terrible atrocities but these are militants, extremists, who have misinterpreted the *Qur'an* and the teachings of the prophet Muhammad, the *Hadith,* one of whose instructions to followers of Allah was not to harm those who do not associate with him.

Anyway, Richard would add, terrorists simply do not represent the vast majority of Muslims who live their lives in peace and harmony according to Islam. By contrast, the Israeli government are mainstream. What about their periodic bombing of

Gaza, which the West condemns only with words, but permits through its lack of action?

Ah, said his father, turning and deflecting the accusations, but the Gaza government is little more than a cowardly, terrorist organisation that uses its citizens as human shields by siting the weapons that fire missiles at Israel in residential quarters. They strike first, Israel retaliates. But it is an unfair fight, Richard responded. Israel has a defensive shield that picks up the missiles and neutralises 99 out of 100, and the whole military system is financed by the West.

'You're now defending terrorists?' said his father, shaking his head. 'He's now defending terrorists, Mother.' She would carry on preparing dinner, torn between the two men she loved in her life and whose own love for each other was so often submerged in the conflict of age and youth, realism and idealism, in which both were absorbed.

In the end, love had prevailed, a love bonded at birth and which no rift in religion could break.

His parents, and indeed Rashid, had been surprised at how well family and friends had taken it, even if a few were soured into severing contact. This was the 21st century, they said. He should be applauded for his bravery and they should be proud of a boy building bridges. Thus they could only embrace it themselves. And he was their son. Their only son. Even if they would have to endure being talked about at the Synagogue, they preferred him in the fold. They could not have borne the thought of him leaving, of living in some Muslim enclave and losing him. Did not the family show mercy to the prodigal son? And Richard would surely come back to them once this phase of his life was over.

Tonight, when he arrived home from UCH, Rashid could see that their love was genuine. They had been disgusted by the murders of five Muslims. Humanity overcomes religious division, if only people would allow themselves that compassion,

Rashid thought as he lay on his bed, having just performed the *Isha,* the fifth and final prayer of the day. There was a knock at his door and he told his mother that she could come in.

'Chicken soup,' she said, carrying a tray.

Rashid smiled. He no longer needed to ask if it was Halal. Mum bought it specially for him now. And chicken soup tasted good in any religion.

6

TOM

TOM checked his Swatch, the prized, proud claret and blue one that Rachel had bought him in Ibiza last year. It was her way of saying sorry for dragging him on holiday for the first week of the football season, meaning that he would be missing Villa's opening home game. He didn't let on that he didn't mind too much as it was only Blackburn Rovers and he knew there would be a bar showing an illegal TV feed. The time showed 8.45pm and the sun was sinking to bring him the safety of darkness he had been hurrying along.

He could scarcely comprehend the difference from the start to the end of the year that had marked his passage from 20 to 21. This time a year ago, he was necking the first beer of the evening ahead of a night of drink, the drugs that were cheaper, some dancing and a finale of sex on the beach; the act not the cocktail. Now, with the occasional chill of the breeze that hinted of autumn punctuating the mildness, he was contemplating a night trying to stay warm and hidden behind a concrete rain shelter in a London park.

He couldn't even get into the shelter and lie on the slatted benches inside, though he thought about it. There would surely be night patrols by police or park employees, he reckoned. He had to stay concealed, as uncomfortable as that might be amid the soil and the bushes. At least he had some sandwiches and half a bottle of water, discarded round the back of that cafe when everyone had gone home, though he had to fight off an old drunk for the cheese-and-red onion-relish sarnie that had the barely believable price of £3.95 on it.

What the fuck was he thinking about getting himself involved in this, he wondered now as he looked back on the day, the last couple of months in fact. And what the fuck exactly had he got himself involved in? Jason had just asked for a lift to London and he was at a loose end after graduating so he obliged his brother. He always did. Jase was persuasive and charismatic and Tom had always looked up to him. After what Jase had done for him all those years ago, he would always be grateful to him, always owe him. Besides, he needed the £50 he was offered.

Tom admired Jason's courage in joining the army, envied his life of action which he could never emulate, and was grateful he came home safe from Afghanistan. They were different in so many ways, not only in their lives – one that of the intellectual, one of the physical – but also in appearance. Jason must have taken after the father Tom had never known: squat, powerful, his preference for close-cropped hair. And he had taken over a dad's role towards Tom.

As Tom thought about it, though, his mind running in all directions in search of theories and explanations, there had been lately a tougher edge to the figure who had spoken so warmly at his 21st back in May at the restaurant.

Jase had been pissed off, he told the gathering of some 25 friends and family paid for by Mum, at having to look after a brother five years his junior, cramping his style with girls he brought to the house. With a feigned annoyance in his voice (or at least Tom thought it was feigned), he told of how Tom had always found a reason to come into the living room just when things were getting interesting with any teenage girlfriend. And then – cue the laughter that regularly came when he told the tale – Tom would tell the poor, embarrassed girl that Jase was fond of picking his nose. Jase could laugh now himself at the memory, judging by May's speech.

Spring turned into summer, though, and rage replaced laughter one sad night, a vicious reality ending the age of innocence. Tom's life would be forever changed.

It had been a warm June evening of the sort that prompts joy at the prospect of three more months of balm after the cold and darkness of winter and the capriciousness of spring. University was over for Tom, he would get that 2:1 in French, and could look forward to a month camping in the Dordogne with Rachel before seeing if a language degree was any kind of qualification for a career writing music. Drinking outside the pub in Edgbaston, Jase told him he could always pen a couple of new songs for Johnny Hallyday. The old frog needed some new material, he reckoned. The laughter was interrupted by the text message from Rachel. Tom's face dropped.

'Bet that's Rachel. What's she want?' Jase inquired. 'Can't even let you have a night out with your brother?'

'She's at the police station. Wants me down there,' Tom replied.

'Bloody hell, what for?'

'She doesn't say. Just says she needs me.'

'OK, so let's go,' said Jason, taking control. 'We'll take my car.'

Tom was worried and baffled, Jason calm enough as they got into the old VW Golf that was Jase's pride and joy. Perhaps his military training was taking over. That all changed once at the police station, however, and Tom thought again of the differences that brothers could embody. He was sickened and saddened by Rachel's sobbing as she told him that she had been raped. Jason reacted with fury.

'What? Who? Where?' Jason blurted out and Rachel wept, lacking the energy to repeat the detail she had just given to the police. 'I'll fucking kill him.'

'Them,' she mouthed quietly amid the tears. They hung on a pause that seemed to last minutes rather than seconds. 'Five of them. Asian.'

Jason strode around the police station banging walls, bellowing obscenities and being pacified by police officers. Tom just sat there numb, staring into space, shaking his head. It was too big an event, too gross an act, to contemplate. He could barely bring himself to look at Rachel's face. Usually, it was a beautiful portrait painting to him, now it was a daubing of matted black hair, mascara smudged by tears that moistened blotches and bruises. 'Tom,' she whispered. 'Please say something.'

He could not. Revulsion overcame him. The words for what he was feeling were so shameful and selfish. He knew he could not be of help to her, much as he knew she so badly needed it. He knew he could not touch her again. Certainly not now.

He rose slowly to his feet and took in the scene. Jase was crying, his tears telling of rage as he shouted about Taliban bastards he had seen before 'out there'. A policewoman was trying to calm him with a soothing voice but was clearly afraid to get too near. Poor, battered Rachel's eyes were pleading with Tom to offer soft words and a reassuring hug. Tom's response was to run through the doors and into the night, pushing out of the way Rachel's parents, who shouted plaintively and vainly after him.

Tom had not seen Rachel since, had ignored the texts and voicemails, as he tried to work out whether his disgust was for her or himself. His self-loathing at his inability to support her, his lack of loyalty, overwhelmed him at times. He hadn't seen or heard much of Jase either, his brother having gone back to work on the oil rigs for the last couple of months.

Until he phoned a couple of days ago, wanting Tom to drive him down to London.

'Why?' Tom asked.

'Cos I'm staying down with an old army mate in London for a couple of weeks,' Jase had said.

'Why can't you get the train?'

'Too much luggage. And I've just got an errand to run in Regent's Park. Then I need you to take me on to Balham.'

'Where's that?'

'South London. After that, you can drive the car back to Brum for me. Fifty quid in it for you.'

It was easy money, Tom thought and agreed. He had thought it strange this morning that Jase, normally a neat dresser with the good money he made, turned up in jeans, a polo shirt and black trainers driving an equally scruffy old 52 reg dark blue Honda Accord with worn cloth seats. 'Borrowed it off a mate,' said Jase when Tom inquired. 'Don't want to put mileage on the Golf. It'll do for the day.'

Tom, in his usual garb of skinny jeans, brown ones today, white trainers and his old university hoodie, joked that he was dragging Jase down to his level but his brother seemed in no mood for breaking the ice of the tension that had existed between them since June.

The journey down was strained, Rachel the great unspoken subject. There was something about Jase's scratchy, edgy manner and mood that deepened Tom's unease with himself. It was as if his big brother had lost all respect for him after he had not responded with compassion but had walked away from her in her time of need. Tom wanted to explain, to talk to Jase about this horrible feeling inside of him – of what? Guilt? Shame? But he knew it would be to light blue touch paper and Jase would explode. Two-and-a-half hours in a car represented a long time to be shouted at.

Instead he stuck to trivia, to sport, which was so often the bond between men. In fact, it seemed to exist sometimes just so they could communicate when there was material too painful to broach. No wonder that supporters' band that drove everybody nuts at England games continually played *The Great Escape*. Tom and Jason discussed instead the Olympics, Usain Bolt and Mo Farah, and last night's closing ceremony and agreed it had been great. Great to be British. And Jase took the piss out of Aston Villa, gave them no chance against West Ham in London this coming Saturday.

The M40 turned into the A40 just after they had crossed the M25 on the outskirts of London and Tom, under instruction from Jason, was careful not to break the varying speed limits on the way in through Hillingdon and Greenford, Hammersmith and the Westway at North Kensington, passing Queens Park Rangers on the right, next to the Westfield Shopping Centre and the BBC.

'Too much money in this place,' Jase observed, though Tom looked down on some of the houses and flats with their peeling paintwork, and up at tower blocks blighting the cityscape like rotting teeth, all in unhealthy proximity to the noisy elevated road, and felt fortunate. He had grown up in a three-bedroomed semi in leafy Edgbaston, which Mum had bought outright with the divorce settlement after Dad had left them just after Tom was born, never to be seen again.

The shabbiness changed when the Westway dropped them – eventually – at the start of the Marylebone Road and the genuine wealth of Central London. Jason, insistent they should not go into the congestion zone, barked at Tom to turn left up Gloucester Place. Tom tensed momentarily at the order.

They passed through Dorset Square, where Jason pointed out a terraced street at the back. 'There's where the IRA staged the Balcombe Street siege back in the 1970s,' said Jason, who had always seemed to have had an interest in the more notorious, even morbid, events in modern British history, especially any involving the military. And the paramilitary.

A couple of hundred yards up Park Road, Tom could see the dome of the Mosque when Jase instructed him to stop just beyond some traffic lights opposite. His brother got out onto the pavement, took some things from the boot, then told Tom to drive up to the roundabout ahead and come back down Park Road, turn left into Regent's Park at the first lights, through Hanover Gate, park up in the metered bays at the back of the Mosque and wait there for him. He would be 10 minutes, 15 tops. There were coins for the parking in the glove compartment, he said.

'Why are we here?' Tom asked. Now the misgivings were setting in. There's nothing round here, so what kind of job has Jase got on?

'Never mind,' came the brusque reply. 'Just do as I fucking ask, all right?'

Any idea of a conversation was quickly dispelled, though, as Jason got out of the passenger door and a car honked at Tom blocking an inside lane. The traffic was light, being late morning now, and it was just a driver who was enjoying making a righteous point. In his mirror, Tom saw a red double decker bus some 100 yards away and so drove off, Jason having slammed the boot. Looking again, he now saw Jason, wearing black gloves, donning some blue overalls over his blue jeans and black polo shirt and strapping on a black backpack, though it looked larger than a normal bag. This was beginning to smell funny...

By the time he had been up to the roundabout and driven back down Park Road, Jason had disappeared into the Mosque. Tom turned left at the lights and parked just down the road from the back of it. There was plenty of space in the bays. He was halfway between the zoo and the shops and transport of Baker Street so fewer cars parked up here. Not that he knew it, nor this area. Only later would he realise that Jase must have.

Agitated now, he noticed a traffic warden coming up the road so dashed out and fed the meter. Tom was astonished at the price per hour but Jase was paying. Ticket displayed on the window, and the warden having passed by appeased by the sight, he got out of the car and rolled himself a cigarette. It had been nearly three hours down from Birmingham, would probably be another hour to Balham in London traffic – whenever he came here, all journeys within the city seemed to take an hour – and he needed to nicotine himself up. Anxiety, too, was increasing his craving.

He was interrupted by what he thought was screaming in the distance but it was muffled and, looking around and seeing nobody, he went back to finishing making his roll-up with a lick of the paper. He was just imagining things, he told himself. He was out of his comfort zone. Relax. He flicked his Zippo and lit the cigarette, drawing the smoke deep into his lungs in satisfaction.

As he stubbed out the cigarette a few minutes later, he saw young men emerging from a door across the road at the back of the Mosque, running and shouting in panic. Seeing the set of black wrought iron gates padlocked, they disappeared into the trees and ran round the side of the building, next to tall railings, to get back round to the front.

'What the...' Tom wondered and suddenly he saw a flame across the road, at the back of the Mosque. Then, through the open door, came a figure in blue overalls, black trainers and wearing a black balaclava, just eyes and mouth visible. He was carrying a tube, like a vacuum cleaner's extension. Was that Jase? What's that he's got? What was he doing?

It was Jason all right. From a big pocket on the trouser of the overalls, he took some wire cutters and severed the chain to which the padlock was attached. He pushed the gate open and ran across to Tom and the car, peeling off the balaclava. He opened the boot of the car, throwing it in, along with the backpack and the tube.

'Get in the car and drive,' Jason yelled.

Out of instinct with Jason, Tom obeyed the first part of the instruction but then sat in the driver's seat as if paralysed. He was looking across the road at the back exit to the Mosque.

'What the fuck have you done?' Tom asked.

'Just fucking drive,' said Jason.

'No way, Jase. What have you done?'

Jason leant across and opened the driver's door before pushing Tom out into the road. A speeding cyclist almost hit him but just managed to swerve and avoid him.

'You twat,' the cyclist turned to shout as he continued pedalling.

Jason got out of the car and dashed round to the driver's side. Tom was now on his feet and stumbled back to the pavement. There was no way he was going to get in the way of his raging, wide-eyed brother.

'Fuck off, Tom,' he shouted through the open window as he turned on the engine. 'If you of all people don't understand then there's no fucking hope.'

With that, Jason revved the car and sped away, the old engine of the Honda struggling to agree to the driver's demands on the accelerator.

Tom stood watching for a moment as the car disappeared south. He staggered into the park, where he sat on the grass getting his bearings, assessing his situation, watching mothers and toddlers at the paddling pool, themselves trying to find the source of the screams in the distance and the shouted voices before hurrying their kids away.

'What's happening?' one of the women asked Tom.

He knew but he didn't know. He knew that Jase must have done something terrible but could not yet imagine what, even if terrible thoughts were insinuating themselves into his mind. He knew that he couldn't stay here. His head was clearing enough to realise that he was implied in something shocking and he had better not hang about.

He knew only football grounds in London and the directions to them. From Euston, it was the Victoria Line to Tottenham and Arsenal, to Seven Sisters and Finsbury Park respectively. Chelsea and West Ham were at opposite ends of the District Line, at Fulham Broadway and Upton Park.

He didn't know where the nearest tube station to here was. Where Euston with its lifeline to Birmingham was. His buzzing brain considered checking the map on his phone but suddenly sirens were renting the air and he was distracted. He guessed the police would be on the look-out for a kid like him, maybe spotted by a traffic warden, a cyclist and a woman with a toddler. As survival instinct took over, he guessed hopefully too that they might not be looking close to the scene of the crime, figuring that the Honda had been seen and was no longer there, so they would be trying to find that and its driver. Or drivers.

And so he walked further into the park, away from the Mosque, past the Boathouse Cafe and across the bridge over the boating lake. This was a pretty big park. You could lose yourself in here. He would mingle. If it meant spending a night sleeping rough until the focus switched from the park, so be it. He turned right down a path through some trees and kept walking, kept to the trees rather than head for the conspicuous open spaces where those sports pitches were. He went through some gardens. Roses. Smelt nice. In other circumstances it would have all looked very pleasant to him.

He came to a little tea hut, The Cow and Coffee Bean it was called, and reckoned there might be food around here to be scavenged later, as the sandwich and water proved. He couldn't pay. He had only a few quid in coins in his pocket. Jase had bolted without paying him the 50 quid.

Then there was that bloke staring at him around lunchtime, and smiling at him later in the afternoon when he encountered him again. That was a bit weird. Surely he couldn't have suspected anything?

Sitting here now tonight with his back up against the rear wall of the shelter, Tom told himself that if he could endure Glastonbury, he could survive this. It brought a half-smile to his face but it was fleeting. Very quickly the reality of his situation returned. Rachel's ordeal and his callousness towards her wormed its way back into his brain. The visions of what Jase might have done assaulted his mind's eye. The night was growing chilly, though he was not to know just how heated it was becoming elsewhere in this city and indeed the country. He huddled into his hoodie and started to shake.

PART II

TUESDAY
AUGUST 14TH
2012

7

SAUL

SAUL had organised his radiotherapy for lunchtimes because it gave him the morning to edit manuscripts or correct page proofs. He could also pursue his favourite activities of pottering around his Primrose Hill flat drinking tea and dunking biscuits while listening to the radio's comfortable and comforting pre-noon programming before meandering peacefully through the park down to Baker Street. Today was not a day for easy listening or peaceful walking, however.

Yesterday's event had provoked some violence and looting on the streets last night, though thankfully nothing nearly as serious as last summer's riots when Britain's suitability to host the Olympic Games had been called into question, if hardly in the host country then certainly abroad in the way it would have done at home had the venue been overseas.

These were more demonstrations than riots, however. Muslim youth was outraged, as the young black people had been after the shooting dead in Tottenham of one of their number in 2011, but this time there were not disaffected white youths angry at the shortage of employment and opportunities in the same numbers, though some still used the opportunity to secure new televisions and trainers.

The main problem for the police was keeping white right wing elements away from those in the Asian communities venting their anger, such as in Tower Hamlets, Sparkhill in Birmingham and Heaton in Bradford. The English Defence League and other hangers-on knew they were outnumbered, however, and discretion largely overcame their valour. They knew, too, of the theory that the Regent's Park Mosque atrocity was a racist or anti-Islamic terrorist act and that it would make them vulnerable if they ventured into the spotlight.

In addition, Muslim leaders and parents had more control over their sons – few of whom would be out in the streets disobeying the no alcohol or drugs demands of their religion – than many in the black and white communities. Their appeals, both through media and on the streets with megaphones, gradually eased the unrest. Whereas social media, via especially Facebook and Twitter, had been the preserve of the rioters the previous summer, along with some using secure Blackberry networks, this time the Mosques and community groups had their own feeds that could attract thousands of retweets to prompt second thoughts among those on the streets once their passion dissipated. The worst was over by midnight, any fires doused by the early hours.

It did not stop the first editions of the newspapers shown on TV late last night, Saul noted as he listened to Radio 4, from describing the nation as **POWDER KEG BRITAIN** or **TINDER BOX UK** on their front pages. The overnight peace was indeed fragile. Today would be largely about Muslims accepting this as the work of a lone wolf rather than a widespread attitude towards them. And trying to suppress retaliation.

This morning, the three digital Pure sets that Saul kept in the flat debouched the follow-ups to the Mosque murders. Radio 4 in the bedroom rowed back on the events themselves and the night's response, before analysing whether this was the true and terrible reality of modern Britain, while the bonhomie and camaraderie of the Olympic Games had been simply a fantasy world.

In the kitchen, on Radio 5 Live came the inevitable babbling of the cheap phone-ins with their rantings at what this Bastard in the Balaclava, as one put it, had done and why he might have done it. Radio 2 on the hour reported that Muslim leaders were appealing for calm after yesterday and last night. Saul was grateful to the station for continuing with PopMaster at 10.30am as a soothing reminder that life was going on.

After Kevin from Redditch had failed to name three top 10 hits for David Bowie in 10 seconds, to Saul's frustration, it was time to venture out for his treatment again. Today, the late morning walk down the Broad Walk and across Inner Circle was as sombre as yesterday's had been buoyant following that Olympic closing ceremony of the night before. The west side of the park remained closed as police continued to keep the public at a distance from the crime scene, needing as much space as possible for the convoy of vehicles and forensic paraphernalia surrounding such a major incident.

Like many others, Saul was lost in his own thoughts, prompted by the front page of *The Daily Telegraph* that had Frank the newsagent shaking his head and mumbling: 'They should bring back the death penalty' as he took the money. It revealed the dichotomy of modern Britain – a liberal sympathy for the Muslim community and a rightwing desire for draconian punishment.

MURDER AT THE MOSQUE said the *Telegraph*'s headline across all six columns. As if departing from their tedious three decks of headline about interest rates across three columns didn't tell you how serious this was, their lack of photos atop the masthead of comely columnist or latest sports pundit paid fortunes, but who didn't write his own material, certainly did.

The weather had turned from the sunshine of yesterday to overcast and gloomy. It was a reminder that in a month or so, the leaves would begin to fall from the trees, the process probably a week or two later these days due to climate change, or so went the assumption. Not that Saul minded the promise of autumn. In the past, before this summer had cheered him so, he would have hated the imposed pressure of being happy in warm weather, as if it were a duty or requirement of life if one wanted to be mainstream.

In fact, he loved the seasons, particularly the changing of them. In summer, the park was enveloped by its foliage, just the hum of traffic to disturb, depending on wind direction. Except when sirens filled the air. By winter, though, with its tea-time darkness, the lights and sights of Central London could be glimpsed through the bare branches. The BT Tower would become the unmasked city skyline's beacon. It was curious how Saul feared change in his own life, how he always ranted before grudgingly adapting, but was reassured by nature's cycles. It was because, he supposed, he knew things would get back eventually to how they were. He liked to know outcomes.

He approached Chester Road, which linked Inner and Outer Circles and where the cherry blossom was always so spectacular in spring, with his customary caution. A zebra crossing ran across the road but too often cars drove too quickly and did not see pedestrians emerge from behind hedges. Joggers often saw it as their right to run without having to stop and unknowing drivers often had to brake sharply. Crossing into the southern section of the park, he turned right towards the shelter where he often stopped for a rest. It was there that he saw him again.

The kid was sitting, bending forward and examining his bare feet. On the bench to the left of him wet socks, to the right his trainers, no longer pristine white but sullied by dirt and soil. Saul's appearance and voice clearly stunned him.

'You here again?' he inquired. Tom sat bolt upright.

'What?'

'I saw you here yesterday, didn't I?' Saul asked.

'Me? Might have done. Why? Something wrong with that?' Saul was taken aback by the boy's defensiveness but pressed on. Despite the horrendous events of the previous day, some Olympic spirit remained.

'No. Nothing,' said Saul. 'You have problems with your feet? I've got some clean socks if you want.' He moved to retrieve a pair from his shoulder bag and held them out.

'What? No thanks, mate. Weird or what?'

With that, the boy scooped up his shoes and socks, pulled up his hood, Saul now registering the hoodie as purple and bearing a small logo and letters on its chest, and was quickly walking away barefoot, heading back out on to Chester Road. Saul followed him briefly, thought he was probably heading for the toilets just through the huge ornate gates to Queen Mary's Gardens, but left him to it. He had his own concerns.

He was hurt by the refusal of the socks, when it was simply a kindly gesture, even more hurt by being thought of as weird. The socks were for the homeless. He had grown tired of giving money, often for beggars just to get drunk, and he knew enough to know that he didn't want to just help them get drunk. Enabling, wasn't it called? They themselves were fed up at being offered sandwiches, which they could get easily enough anyway in London at closing time for the chain sandwich shops. The twin enemies of the rough sleeper were the cold and wet. Dry socks were a weapon in the fight. And the kid was sleeping rough.

Saul looked at his watch and headed back down the Broad Walk. With the closures, it was going to take him more time to get to Clarence Gate and Baker Street so he had better get a move on. He was also growing edgy at the thought of the rigmarole of filling his bladder, of enduring the daily angst of not pissing before the treatment. He didn't want this to be the day, so near to the end, when he wet himself. He wanted to go the whole stretch not having to use the clean boxer shorts he kept in his shoulder bag in case of emergency and embarrassment.

As he reached Clarence Gate, Saul saw a clutch of yellow-jacketed police with clipboards. One approached him.

'Do you have a few minutes please, sir?' PC Deena Campbell asked him.

'Well, I'm in a bit of a hurry to be honest,' he said. He didn't really want to have to explain to a young woman that he needed very soon to start drinking enough water to fill his bladder for a radiotherapy session.

'It is important,' she added quickly.

He agreed, just crabbily enough to hurry her along, and she wondered initially if he came here often. He made a feeble joke about chat-up lines, quickly realised that it was about yesterday and went back to his old self. He told her of his regular journey. Had he seen anything or anyone unusual yesterday, she asked? Not really, he replied. He had only found out about it all an hour or two later.

'It wasn't like a bomb that you could hear, was it?' he said. 'Look, sorry…'

She thanked him and Saul hurried down to Baker Street and dashed to take the Jubilee Line to Green Park before the Piccadilly to South Kensington and a sprint to the Marsden. He liked to be there an hour before his appointment but by the time he arrived it was just 35 minutes till T (for treatment) time. He had to gulp down the water in the next five minutes.

Luckily, having checked in, his wait did not stretch beyond the half hour, meaning that he had survived another day without wetting his chinos. He had invested in a black pair after his worries of the first couple of weeks. He also had less of Jolly Jack to endure, but less of the kindly Sue to enjoy.

It was only as he lay on the treatment table, lined up carefully, listening to the whirring of the machine and watching it move through those three phases of left hip, abdomen, right hip – with the beam hitting the tiny dots that had been tattooed on him by a radiographer ahead of his treatment – that he began to think about his two encounters in the park.

That young lad who was there yesterday afternoon and this morning might well come under the category of something or someone unusual in the policewoman's question.

8

JAN

THE day after used to be follow-up day for newspapers. Having reported the event and what everyone said about the event, and publishing pictures of the carnage – and rejecting plenty on the grounds of public taste and decency – this was the day for filling in the gaps, for giving context and background, drawing it all together.

Newspapers had changed, though, in the Internet age. Print journalism's follow-ups were happening even as it was all unfolding on TV, radio and now the web, where conspiracy theorists, crackpots and trolls shouted loudly on Facebook, Twitter and YouTube and vied to be heard with those directly involved or who had witnessed events, making it ever more difficult to find the truth amid the clamour, the light amid the heat. This was supposed to be where the papers came into their own.

There would also be an act today to fan the flames and force the media to change direction in pursuit of the fire engines.

In previous times, Jan would have been cursing that yesterday had been a day off and she had missed all the action. Actually, she wouldn't have missed it. She would have rung in to tell them she was on her way, then spent 12 unpaid hours on the story. Once upon a time, in fact for a good 20 years after leaving school to join her local paper in Yorkshire, she loved newsrooms on such days and nights; chasing the story, selling angles on it to a news editor, watching it roll off the presses near midnight.

Seeing it in the paper under the byline: Janet Mason. The combination of adrenaline and coffee, with lunch and dinner at your desk and a late night lock-in at the local at the back of the office by a landlord whom they rewarded with tickets to film premiers and football matches, was her very lifeblood.

These days, though, she felt emptily disengaged with the paper. She came in and did her job, to the best of her ability, but at the age of 41 it was more about still earning to pay off as much of the mortgage on the two-bedroom flat in Maida Vale as she could before the inevitable redundancy as the industry contracted – in terms of numbers of people, that was, though not in its ambition. Fewer were just spread more thinly. She was a high earner, too, having been hired in the halcyon days, and thus vulnerable.

On top of all that, she was treading thin ice. The verbal warning had come when she had refused to accept the positive spin on a government press release that said fewer hospitals would need to be built as we were all getting healthier, and then write the subsequent puff piece.

'Just fucking do it,' Vickers had said. 'Editor's a mate of the health minister, OK.'

'But it's bollocks, Ivan,' she had replied to her News Editor. 'It's just an excuse for lack of investment in the NHS. Go and sit in an A&E one night and see what's happening.'

Then came the first written warning. Word had got back to Vickers that she had left a job up in Great Yarmouth early. This was in the days when she was still sent out on stories. It concerned a paedophile ring in which a government minister was implicated and she was supposed to be door-stepping a recently released nonce who had taken a house overlooking a primary school, though she knew the bloke had disappeared. She had had theatre tickets in London with her brother and bunged a local reporter 50 quid to cover and keep her in touch. But somebody had snitched and she had broken the paper's golden rule on any job: you are always the last reporter to leave.

It meant that one more written warning and she was but a Vickers whim away from the sack. She did think that might be desirable some days. But that mortgage… God knew there were plenty of unpredictable moods involving a man who delighted in the title of Nastiest News Editor in Fleet Street. Jan always referred to him as TGV. It was not just because he could come at you like a French train. It stood for That Gobshite Vickers.

And so, with how she was treated and the office-bound hours she was forced to keep, she had watched the TV coverage of the unfolding Mosque story on her day off from her sofa with a glass of wine and a growing sense of being marginalised. With that dilemma of the disaffected, she had no desire to force what had been described by grudgingly admiring rivals as the sharpest elbows in journalism into the middle of the fray but she still resented that no one rang her to ask her to get in the middle of it.

Now it was all about satisfying websites and being forced to tweet updates. Relentlessly, hour after hour. The paper felt like an afterthought some days. Churnalism, they called it; clickbait the result – web-angled stories, often spicier than the paper would submit to Middle England but titillating to the world beyond – to show to advertisers how many people they were reaching and so increase prices to try somehow to make the Internet pay for beleaguered news organisations.

Reality show 'stars' in various states of undress vied with dysfunctional showbiz families for attention. Alongside, readers would be invited to discover five things they might learn about fast food or find out why the middle classes had been driven to drink by the recession. The Internet had spawned Wikileaks, which was, astonishingly, telling us that the US Government had been spying on other governments, and this was the best we could do? It smacked of that time when that *Big Brother* reality show had gone out online when off air and a couple had had sex. 'The day the Internet came of age,' was the headline on a leader by one of the red tops.

Jan watched people on the tube this morning on her journey round to the paper's latest offices in a cheap new block in the City of London, lamenting that she had no reason today to feel that old frisson of seeing someone reading your story, under your name, and watching their reaction. The curious thing was that the younger reporters on about £25k a year in the modern national newspaper sweatshops loved seeing their name in the paper too, even if so many more readers would see it online. It was to do with ego and anonymity, she guessed. With print you had visible proof that you were involved. Online, you relied on your imagination of somebody in their back bedroom logging on. To what else besides she stopped at contemplating.

The paper still sold well, though at 1.5 million it was around half of what it did 20 years ago, and some were reading it, with room to do so now that the rush hour was over. She noted the headline **POWDER KEG BRITAIN** and sighed that again it was follow-up stuff, or actually more like speculation, rather than just telling the real story from yesterday before and above anything else. At least the front page of one of the few copies of *The Telegraph* had it right, if you asked her: **MURDER AT THE MOSQUE**. The problem was that nobody did ask her these days.

She bought a double espresso in the ground floor cafe and wandered through the atrium that was the paper's copious reception area, not stopping to speak to anyone, nobody speaking to her. People were too busy in their own worlds or gazing at the news channels on the TVs to notice or care about each other. She took the lift to the third floor and walked to her desk, neither saying nor receiving a hello, and had taken but one sip of her coffee, not even sat down, when TGV arrived at her side.

'Conference room now,' said Vickers. She picked up her coffee and traipsed dutifully from what was now called the news hub to a glass corner 'think tank' office with a view of a concrete city square. Around a dozen reporters were gathering around a long, rectangular black table.

'Nice front page this morning,' said Natalie Bridges, a 25-year-old who had come through the training scheme and the website and whose name was on the front-page piece, turning inside. Jan would have hesitated to say she wrote it. More probably it was pulled together from other reporters' work and news agencies and assembled by a talented sub-editor. She was just young flavour of the moment and her picture byline, with its long blonde hair, looked good. Vickers nodded and all agreed with her analysis of the front page. Actually, Jan wanted to say, it was fucking terrible and this paper has lost its way and its identity in the rush for rubbish, knee-jerk material to fill the website. Of course she didn't.

Vickers ran through what they had from the police at that morning's 9am briefing, first what everyone knew: some nutter in blue overalls and a balaclava had walked unhindered into the Regent's Park Mosque yesterday at 11.45am and torched to death five people from a flamethrower taken from a back pack. The events were picked up on CCTV but the bloke's identity was not. Soon after, a blue or black Japanese car, a witness couldn't be sure which make, sped off down Outer Circle. The witness did say he was white. There are no cameras on that road, so the car had not been immediately identified.

Vickers then added new material that was emerging from the Met press office. A traffic warden working the park remembered someone, also white, sitting in a dark blue or black Honda around that time but he didn't pay too much attention as the car had a valid parking ticket. A cyclist also recalled almost being knocked out of his saddle when someone opened a car door on him there but there were two men in the car.

'So the Met's theory,' said Vickers, 'is that the nutter had an accomplice who probably dropped him at the front of the Mosque then drove round the back and waited for him. One woman with a child also remembered a short conversation with a young bloke in a hoodie nearby in the park. He looked spaced out, apparently. Whether he's involved or not, they don't yet know.'

And that, Vickers said finally, was pretty much all the police had, apart from the obvious theory that the motive must be religious, racist or both. They were now trawling congestion charge and traffic cameras on roads surrounding Regent's Park to see if they could get a sighting of the car and thus the number. Oh, and they needed press help.

The police always did need press help, Jan mused. It was something people forgot, as she always argued with friends and often of an evening on her third glass of wine with ignoramuses on Twitter who accepted simplistic arguments against phone hacking. They also forgot that journalists on the Millie Dowler story, in the wake of which episode newspapers were dying, were actually trying to help, trying to find a young girl's murderer. Often in the past they had done so for a police force, stretched and in need of fresh eyes, who used reporters as supplementary detectives. And the reporters were from newspapers; rarely, if ever, from TV or radio.

Her industry had always been under siege, always been seen as not fully trustworthy. There had always been some respect, however for holding government and institutions to account, for exposing, and for – at its best – helping those who could not help themselves. For entertaining and informing, for stories well told.

Now, since phone hacking had been uncovered, they, she, were largely scum. The Leveson Inquiry into newspaper practice, set up after revelations about hacked mobiles by red-top journos, was being televised. It was in part revenge for the exposure of MPs' bloated expenses some three years earlier and it was showing up the industry and reporters she had known and worked with in a shockingly poor light. Celebrities were queuing up to get their own back, lawyers were milking their moments, playing up their costly parts. The Inquiry would be reporting soon and newspapers could not expect to carry on the way they used to. That, she had thought, was a case of being careful what you wished for. To emasculate the press would be to play into the establishment's hands.

Vickers assigned people to the various parts of the Mosque story, starting with Natalie. He wanted more on this car – someone must know who owns it and where it is. It would lead to the killer. Jan was the last taxi off the rank. Vickers told her to help and guide the kids, use her experience. Be their bloody leg worker in other words. She hated being at the beck and call of someone like Natalie bloody Bridges, someone who had found herself in the right place at the right time, like yesterday. Jan used to have that knack. Yes, she had been ambitious and keen like her once but at least she had some respect, even reverence, for more experienced and senior reporters while she was learning the trade. These kids reckoned they knew it all and held in contempt the likes of her, whom they believed to have had their day and now it was time for the new, entitled breed.

'Jan,' said Natalie as the meeting broke up, 'I was just wondering if you might give one of your contacts at New Scotland Yard a ring about this car…' Jan smiled at her and said OK, of course she would. She would do no such thing, though. Natalie could get her own fucking contacts and do her own job. And hopefully get found out because she couldn't.

Jan heard a raised voice behind her as she made her way back to her desk, uttering its trademark phrase. 'Just fucking do it,' Vickers was shouting at some fresh-faced kid questioning his assignment. Jan reckoned the paper had a factory somewhere in the Home Counties where they produced a job lot of these kids every year. The kid scuttled off, terrified.

Vickers saw her watching. 'They don't make them like you any more, Jan,' he called across. 'You've long since learned to do what you're told.' He laughed.

'I', she thought to herself, 'have long since learned the art of making it look like I'm doing what I've been told.' She walked over to Vickers.

'This kid in the hoodie the woman mentioned…' she said.

'Some junkie by the sound of it,' Vickers replied.

'Was wondering if he could be the driver, perhaps? The Met's accomplice.'

'Well, ring them then. See what they say.'

'I was thinking that if maybe I went over to Regent's Park, I could sniff around a bit. Maybe talk to regulars. Dog walkers, joggers. Find out something the police may have missed. You never know.'

'Look just get on the phone will you. The days of spending all day walking round London on the off chance of a story are long gone. I know how it works, disappearing into pubs for lunch with your other hack mates, divvying up info. We need you in the office, filing updates for the website. Tweeting. OK?'

Jan shrugged her shoulders and nodded. But you did never know. And as Vickers summoned over some other terrified young reporter to go and get him coffee, she took advantage of his distraction to pick up her bag, grab her Mac, slip to the lift and out of this impersonal, glass prison towards the tube station for a train to Baker Street.

She was sick of watching these kids take all the glory. This, the biggest story since 7/7, was a chance to get herself back in the game. And she wanted, needed, to be back in it. It was shit or bust time, she reckoned. May not get another tale like this, not before the next round of redundancies. Anyway, what was a second warning between enemies? She would still have one more strike.

9

SAUL AND TOM

THE sound of gunshots stopped Saul in his tracks as he made his way home from his treatment through the park, through the rose gardens. They came from the direction of the Open Air Theatre. He thought it might be something to do with rehearsals but since this month's offering was Julian Slade's *Salad Days*, and unless it was Sam Peckinpah's version as once imagined by Monty Python, he thought it unlikely. Then he heard the screams as people fled and felt guilty at his flippant thought. Adults were scurrying and scooping up children who were anticipating a day at the zoo. Some headed for the bushes surrounding the rose beds. A few had been too slow, though. Saul suddenly noticed a few bodies, some 50 yards away, strewn on the path near the public toilets. They lay in pools of blood.

It was then that he saw the man, striding towards him. He could also make out the outline of a rifle. Saul's thoughts came in a rush and he decided that his best escape was through the giant gates by the rose gardens, across Inner Circle and down Chester Road. Often taxi drivers would take their breaks there, reading the paper, drinking tea from their flasks. Perhaps he could jump in one of them and the driver would speed and spirit him to safety.

The cabbies were swiftly out of there, though, bundling panicking people in the back of their cabs in the chaos, families first. So Saul ran down Chester Road until his ageing lungs betrayed him and the weight he had put on with the anti-testosterone drug, despite all his walking, took its toll. The gunman was still some 50 yards behind, strolling now, arrogantly knowing there would be plenty of victims within range and he had no need to run.

Now Saul heard the sirens and saw ahead of him a police car turn from Outer Circle into Chester Road. If he could just get out of the man's line of fire, he would be safe, he was sure. Out of sight, out of mind. It was clear this was indiscriminate and the gunman was not chasing particular people – though Saul would later find out that all the victims were white – but shooting rather at those he just stumbled upon.

With one more effort as he ran out of breath, Saul veered right at the zebra crossing, back into the park at the Broad Walk, at the top of the Italian Garden. To his right, he saw again the kid in the hoodie standing next to the concrete shelter. The kid ran towards him and Saul was suddenly rooted to the spot, astonished and with little left in his legs. The boy grabbed him and bundled him behind the shelter, dragging him to the ground, amid the soil and bushes.

'What the…' had just come from Saul's mouth when the kid put his left hand over Saul's mouth and his right index finger to his own lips with a firmness that demanded Saul be quiet. He sought to quell the wheezing of his shortness of breath and could hear the gunshots, now just odd ones, getting closer. He also heard a couple of chilling screams, whether indicating pain or death, Saul could not tell. The gunman had picked off a pair of stragglers.

'Jesus,' said Saul.

'Shh,' said Tom and they heard the footsteps, maybe 10 yards away, in front of the shelter. Then, a shot that sounded as if it had been fired south down the Broad Walk. A menacing, oppressive silence descended. Saul guessed that the gunman was wondering now where to go, whom next to target. Then the sound of a megaphone gave Saul a start and he sensed a shake in the boy crouching a yard away from him.

'Stop. Drop your weapon,' came a loud instruction but it was not immediately obeyed. Saul and Tom could hear instead the metallic sound of a rifle being primed to be fired. The sound of the next shot, though, came not from a few yards away, but at least 50. It was followed by a thud, of body on pathway, a sickening sound of a head hitting asphalt first. For a moment, the shot's echo hung in the clammy, overcast air of early afternoon and a new silence fell.

Tom and Saul both craned their necks around the side of the shelter to see what was going on. They could see a policeman in thick, visored helmet and body armour, short-barrelled automatic rifle in hand, standing over a body, face down. A face of Asian heritage. Blood oozed out of the still, prone figure, from the vicinity of his heart and snaked its way out from his T-shirt towards his blue jeans. A few splashes sullied his white trainers. It was the gunman and he was clearly dead. Other police arrived quickly at the scene.

Saul could hear some muttered conversation, the odd 'Fucking hell.' 'Top shot Jed,' somebody said, and 'Make sure we all agree he shot first, yeah?'

Exhausted by his experience, Saul was also numbed but thought after a few moments that he should get up, that he might be needed. He had witnessed it all, after all. Tom stopped him by placing a hand on his arm and shook his head. Saul was about to protest but Tom whispered:

'I helped you didn't I? Now you help me.'

Saul sat motionless, looking into the boy's eyes. They contained a mixture of terror and determination. Saul's feelings were mixed too; he was touched by the plea in the expression, fearful of the consequences of not agreeing. Saul had become increasingly suspicious that the kid was somehow involved in yesterday's events and could perhaps be dangerous, even if he did see a wounded vulnerability in him that had attracted his interest. Anyway, his youth and strength would be too much for Saul. If this kid had been complicit in a crime yesterday, complying with him today was probably the best option.

Saul looked him in the eyes, the boy's ice blue, and nodded. Tom let out a short sigh of relief and beckoned for him to follow. They both knew that a crime scene would quickly rise around where the dead gunman lay and that the area would soon be closed off. They climbed over a small wire fence at the back of the shelter and headed south through the park down towards the Marylebone Road, keeping to a covering of trees. To have gone north would have meant going back on to Chester Road, which was now awash with police and ambulance crew poring over and removing dead and wounded bodies.

They slipped out on to the south side of Outer Circle near Park Square West, now eerily empty of traffic and people. Saul reckoned that by getting out on to the Marylebone Road, and walking west to Baker Street they could mingle, not attract any attention. Between the grand terrace of white Nash buildings on Park Square and the gardens at its centre, Saul began demanding some answers.

'OK. What the hell is going on here?' he asked to a soundtrack of sirens coming from the east, probably the A&E at UCH, and heading into the park at the lights on Park Square East.

'Not here, not now mate. Please.' Tom replied. 'Can we find somewhere safe? I don't know where I am.'

There was something about the last statement that moved Saul to sympathy. The boy sounded helpless, pathetic. It was the plea for help of someone who had asked him directly for help once and didn't want to again. Somewhere, sometime, rejection had damaged him.

'Do you know somewhere round here I could get a wash?' he asked. 'I promise I've done nothing wrong,' he added, desperation in his voice, when Saul didn't reply.

Saul stood staring at the boy – who was actually more of a young man, he realised, even if the facial hair was thin – for some more moments and wondered why he should help him now. With his knowledge of the park, he had led him away from the immediate scene of the crime in return for the kid dragging him away from the gunman's path to a hiding place. Now they were quits.

He couldn't deny he was drawn to the boy's story somehow though. If he was involved in yesterday's events, if he was the madman, why hadn't he just fled the scene? Why was he hanging about Regent's Park? He could have been long since gone by now. And that 'I don't know where I am,' did not suggest a murderer who had planned something. Saul was beginning to believe that he had done nothing wrong but instead that he might have been caught up in something way beyond his ability to deal with it. He knew that he might bitterly regret further associating with the boy but at the same time found his gut telling him he couldn't walk away.

'OK,' said Saul. 'But I'm going to need a name.'

'Tom. Tom Judd.'

'I'm Saul Bradstock.'

And he held out his right hand, which the boy shook limply. 'Right, Tom Judd. Follow me.'

Saul was now the one issuing orders, the boy in no position to argue. He followed Saul out on to the main road and they turned right towards Baker Street station, passing Madame Tussaud's.

'Blimey. I came here once with my mum,' said Tom. 'I'm always amazed by London and how it all links up, though I wouldn't have a clue where things are.'

Saul detected in his voice a slight Midlands accent, though Tom was quite well-spoken, he thought. Saul steered him right past the Planetarium down a side street, Allsop Place, which would cut a corner and bring them out at the top of Baker Street where it turned into Park Road.

Saul's plan, with the park closed and police all over it, was to walk up past the front of the Regent's Park Mosque, turn right into Prince Albert Road on the north side of the park, but outside it, then up Primrose Hill to his flat. He thought the walk might reveal something to him, too. As they neared the Mosque, and Tom suddenly stopped, Saul was proved right.

'I recognise this place,' Tom said, anxiety in his voice. 'I was here yesterday. Where are we going?'

'To my flat,' said Saul. 'I may be nuts but I'm going to take a chance on you because I think you might just deserve it.'

Tom looked at him with a mixture of relief and gratitude.

'It's not too far,' Saul continued. 'Just keep your head down. If you tell me you've done nothing wrong, then you're all right, aren't you?'

'But I know somebody who has done something wrong...' said Tom.

'Let's get home and think about where you, where we, go next, OK?' said Saul.

Tom nodded. 'I definitely need to get away from here,' he said, peeling off his hoodie. Standing opposite the road that led to where he had parked the car yesterday, it suddenly occurred to him that he needed to ditch it.

10

JAN, DEENA

COURTESY of the BBC Breaking News app on her phone, Jan had the information that a rampaging gunman had been shot by the time she emerged into Baker Street from the tube station. The scenes around her told her the background to the headline, too. People were milling, discussing it, hands over mouths in disbelief. This, coming on top of yesterday. What was happening to this city? Tourists disembarking from a cramped orange easyBus delivering them to Central London from Luton Airport were about to discover that they had not landed in the sunny country of shiny happy people enjoying those exciting sporting events on their TVs in the last few weeks, but an overcast, downcast nation stunned by not one shocking event but two.

She also had a text message from Vickers: 'Where the fuck are you?' it read. 'Breaking story. Need you for live blog.' She made a quick call to an old contact at New Scotland Yard.

'Hello. Long time no hear,' said Frank Phillips. 'What's happening?' So he's kept my number in his phone then, Jan thought.

'Rather thought you'd know that,' she replied.

'Nightmare,' said Frank. 'We prepared for this kind of thing during the Games but now? Caught us out. People had booked holidays. Bloody nightmare. And that's off the record.'

'Just a quick question for now,' she said. 'Where in the park did this all happen? And what's the state of the gunman?'

'What? Why?'

'Just do me a favour Frank and I might be able to do you one soon.'

There was a pause. And then he spilled, giving her the details of where the dead and injured had been concentrated, and where the gunman had himself been shot – and killed. It would be all over every media outlet soon anyway, he added.

'Coppers on the gate will let you through.' She thanked him.

'Meet soon maybe?' he said. Good. He had bitten. She hadn't asked anything too demanding, hadn't scared him off.

'Maybe,' she replied and ended the call.

She called up a map of Regent's Park on her phone. Outer Circle would be taped off by now, she reckoned. She walked along the Marylebone Road, past Madame Tussaud's, past the comparatively little-used Regent's Park station, to which tourists came believing themselves to be near to the zoo only to find it was a bus ride away or a mile-and-a-quarter walk through the park.

There would be none of that today, though. The zoo was closed and had been evacuated of people. Indeed, the whole park was sealed off at every entrance and opening, police guarding each one. At Park Square East – the closest entrance to where the gunman's body lay – the gates that only came down late at night to stop cars and bicycles entering the park were already in place. Motorcycle police patrolled them ready to open for media and emergency vehicles and escort the former to a holding area, the latter to the scenes of the crimes.

At the gates adjacent to the pedestrian entrance, police were blocking the way. Jan pushed through a small crowd that was peering up towards the park, though there was nothing to see, and showed her National Union of Journalists press card, which asked police officers to offer the bearer their assistance, to a PC. He nodded, as Frank had told her he would, and she walked up towards Outer Circle. There, she could see to her left, by the parking bays opposite the Royal College of Physicians, that a few TV vans were already parked up and reporters were hastily preparing themselves for quick, sketchy pieces to camera. Rolling news was as voracious a beast for broadcast journalists as the Internet was for the written press.

A couple of reporters Jan recognised from other papers – their offices nearer to here – were loitering, talking to some radio reporters. She walked over, said hello and inquired casually, without wanting to appear too keen, about what the police were saying so far. Not much, it seemed. There were deaths, and more wounded. Victims had been taken to UCH. They had taken out the gunman, though it wasn't clear yet whether he was dead or wounded. No name yet and no motive offered, but there had to be a link with the Mosque episode, everyone reckoned, especially with it being so close, both in time and geography. Not known if the victims were white or Asian or whatever, though.

A reporter began to go live to camera nearby and the other newspaper journalists watched to see if they might pick up anything new. With them occupied, Jan decided to slip away to a gate at the corner of Outer Circle where three PCs, one a young woman, were keeping watch. The woman stood on her own while the two men chatted, some 10 yards away. These were still the early moments after a major incident and the arrangements were still being made on the hoof.

Jan had been dealing with the Metropolitan Police for years, since the days when buying them a pint was deemed sound practice and not corruption. You could sit down with a copper, share information, put in an expenses bill. It was good journalism and good coppering. Both knew their roles and the rules of the game. You needed each other and it usually helped with quicker arrests. Sometimes relationships did get blurred, she recalled. Frank sprang to mind.

Nowadays, under public scrutiny and surprise at methods that had been revealed, both parties were wary of each other, though retained their instincts. Both wanted help, and wanted to offer it, even if the procedure could be risky. Jan also knew how police officers thought: simply, honestly, despite the erosion of respect for them. She walked over to the woman PC and brandished her press card. The NUJ was old-fashioned, in many ways impotent in these days of non-unionised offices since Rupert Murdoch had broken them in the 1980s, but there was a leftover respect simply in its title.

'Two in two days. Bloody nightmare, eh?' said Jan. It was a technique. Make a statement but with a question at the end that required a response.

It put the PC off guard. The press card had made her nervous.

'Yes… But I think you need to speak to the press office.'

'I'm doing that, don't worry. They're giving us all the details about number of dead and everything. Just on the way back to my office with it all now. Don't worry, won't quote you. Sorry, I didn't get your name?'

The woman relaxed. 'Deena, PC Deena Campbell.'

'Shocking for all of you on the ground. Still, at least you've got the bastard this time, haven't you?'

'That's true,' said Deena. 'This one won't be going to court.'

'Revenge killing?'

'Looks like it. Asian guy apparently.'

'How many did he get?'

'Three dead so far, I heard. Another two wounded. Fired a lot of random shots but just hit five. But the press office…'

'Yeah,' said Jan. 'that's what they're telling us as well. Terrible. My heart goes out to them and their families.'

One of the two male PCs, her regular oppo Darren, suddenly noticed Deena talking to someone, broke off from his conversation and wandered over.

'Everything OK Deena?' he asked.

'No problems, Daz.' she said brusquely. Jan took the hint.

'Well, OK thanks for your help,' said Jan. She quickly turned on her heel and headed back down towards the Marylebone Road. Pushing her way through the crowd at Park Square East, she saw Great Portland Street tube station to her left and spotted the coffee shop next to it. There, she ordered a flat white, settled in and took her lightweight laptop from the copious bag in which she carried her life, including an old-fashioned Filofax containing hundreds of phone numbers accumulated during her career. She did not trust the vagaries of a mobile phone with them.

She began to type about a now-dead gunman who had inflicted a death toll of three with a further two casualties in what was clearly a revenge killing – given the number of people hit – for yesterday's Mosque atrocity. The gunman, she wrote, was a man of Asian heritage (the paper's new house style) gunned down by police in a shootout. Its 500 words represented a model of brevity, containing new information dramatic enough in the intro not to need what Vickers sometimes called 'a footpump putting under it' and background detail to put it all into context. It was done in 30 minutes.

The call from Vickers came within five minutes of filing it.

'Where the fuck are you and where did you get this from?' he asked. 'This is wrong and another fucking written warning is coming down on you like a shitstorm...'

She told him she was near the crime scene and that police sources – good ones, one high up, the other on the ground – had given her the information. Vickers, who knew that Jan's story would reflect well on him too, was beginning to calm down from his default red-faced anger at her disobeying him, but he was not going to let her off the hook quite that easily.

'None of this is what the Met press office is saying. They're saying wounded but giving no deaths and no number of casualties. And they're not confirming the fact he's Asian and this is some sort of revenge mission.'

Jan repeated, insisted, that her info was good but they could carry the official police line in the piece if they wanted. The numbers and the other detail were all solid.

'That's good work then, I suppose,' he replied. 'Did you ask about the gunman, who he was?'

'Give me a break, Ivan,' Jan said. 'I had two minutes. I got what I could.' Vickers had to acknowledge that what she had was pretty good. 'You want me back in the office?' she asked him.

'What's the lie of the land there?' he responded. Bloody hell, she thought, maybe he's getting back in touch with what constitutes proper newspaper work by proper journalists doing proper legwork, rather than googling and 'content harvesting'.

Jan reckoned she might sniff around here for a while, might even get over to the Mosque, see what was happening there. That, she reminded herself as much as her News Editor, was still a huge story despite this new development.

Amazingly, Vickers agreed and she tapped 'End call' on her phone. In a few more minutes she checked the paper's website. The story was up already. She tweeted the link to her 7,468 followers.

Her phone rang but she wouldn't be answering this call. The number belonged to the Met press officer, Dean Broadhurst. When she dialled 121 for the voicemail, she heard a rant wondering what the hell she was up to. She smiled. The only reason she hadn't answered was that she wanted now just to savour the moment. She would enjoy returning the call later when the accuracy of her story was confirmed. Delayed gratification, didn't they call it? For now, she could luxuriate in what was these days a rare bit of glory, a bit of the buzz of the old days, and celebrate with another flat white and a bar of chocolate. She checked her Twitter feed. Gone over 9,000 followers in the last 10 minutes. Not bad.

Caffeined up, she headed back to where that young officer had been so helpful, just to see if she could go to the well one more time. When she got back, through the now dwindling crowd with the ambulances having long since left through Park Square East, she found Deena with some bigwig with braids on his shoulders and wearing a peaked cap towering over her. Her two colleagues were standing 10 yards away again, clearly distancing themselves but wanting to hear what was being said.

For a while, Jan watched unobserved from across Outer Circle. She could hear the senior officer's raised voice but could not make out the full content. She felt for the girl, momentarily. One person's bollocking is another's herogram, she mused. Anyway, the police would have released the identity of the gunman soon enough and the fact they had shot him dead to discourage anyone else wanting revenge for the Mosque murders. They would also want to show the right-wing nationalists they had this situation under control.

Back in newspaper, TV and radio offices – along with the opportunistic websites poncing off proper news organisations and the few new decent ones set up by young people alienated by the mainstream media – the search for the human interest was in full swing. There would also be the questions and editorials about whether the police should be shooting people dead in one of London's Royal Parks but that was for commentators and leader writers.

She was more interested in heading back over to the Mosque and seeing if she could pick up anything from the aftermath there. After all, there was something being forgotten, overwhelmed in today's mayhem. There was still no trace of the flamethrowing madman who had triggered all this.

11

RASHID, JAN

NOT even staff were allowed back into the Mosque. It remained a crime scene. All Rashid could do was gaze at the place he had come to love, a way of life rather than a workplace, from across the four lanes of Park Road. Traffic passed slowly in both directions, sometimes not even passing at all, just standing still. It was partly due to the closure of Regent's Park in its entirety after the shootings. Those who knew what a smart route the park was from Central to North and North West London, cutting out a clogged chunk of the Marylebone Road, Baker Street and Gloucester Place, were thus forced out on to the busy A41 to join those who used it out of dull habit. The congestion was also due to the rubbernecking of drivers who were expecting to pick up a quick sight of something that wouldn't be on the news, something intimate with which they could regale their fellow drinkers or dinner party diners in the suburbs to make themselves and their lives sound more interesting.

Rashid's experience was that of all Londoners. For all its diversity and shades of opinion, the city seemed to adopt a singular mindset when it came to major events, whether they were to do with promoting good or reacting to bad. Road closures must be kept to a minimum, to allow as free passage as possible to buses, cars and the headlong dash to match Beijing for bicycles. Trains and tubes must run (if not always on time), planes must fly into Heathrow, Gatwick and London City. It was the capital's response to the world, to show that its spirit could not be daunted, that the legacy of the Olympic Games included indomitability.

Naturally, and above all, the city had to show, too, that it was open for business. The Prime Minister had told the nation as much as he emerged on to Whitehall from a crisis meeting with police and senior security figures in Conference Room A in the Cabinet Office Briefing Room – hence the acronym COBRA, a gift to the media – and insisted that the country could not be bullied by terrorists and racists.

Today, a few people stood around Rashid, also gazing across the road, including some fellow Muslims wearing *kurta* and *kufi*, but none so closely involved as he. He had spent the morning phoning friends and fellow staff from the Mosque to swap stories. He knew all of the five dead by sight, had served them in the bookshop at some time, along with some of those injured. Omar had suggested they attend the funerals and he agreed he wanted to go to his first Muslim burials whenever they took place. Usually they occurred on the same day as the death, or at most the day after, but it had not so far been possible, not while police completed their forensics. The families and community had had to accept this. For now, he was drawn back to the park. He had heard of the shootings on his way, from people at St John's Wood tube station. He thought about turning back to go home, but they had talked also of the gunman being shot down and the immediate danger having passed.

Despite the lack of traffic noise as the cars moved in first gear only occasionally towards the roundabout and the lights at Lord's, the place remained a hubbub of sounds. A helicopter hovered over the park and sirens wailed for the second day in a row. This time, literally and metaphorically, they were more distant to his ears.

His blank eyes gazed on the scene at the entrance to his workplace, which was taped off and patrolled by armed police.

They had always prided themselves on being a liberal Mosque, an attitude reflected in the easy access to the place. Sometimes, unless people came to see and sit with him, to drink tea, there would just be Jamal at the gatehouse, pointing strangers in the right direction, keeping his eye on the courtyard, making sure cars didn't clog up the place. Yesterday would change things forever. Suspicion would prompt increased security.

Now the police were there to stop access, just lifting blue and white tape for the coming and going of official cars containing crime scene investigators and forensic scientists. That could have been him in uniform, he thought. He was glad it wasn't. He had lost a lot of faith in them, and respect for them, having naively agreed – because he was an old-fashioned kid who felt he had a duty to help the police – to that meeting with some anti-terrorism spook or other a while back. No, of course he wouldn't report back to them on goings-on and people inside the Mosque, he said. How could I do that to my friends? How could I look people in the eye?

Beyond the police officers, Rashid could just make out figures in white hooded suits going about their business. It reminded him of those scary men who came for ET and who had so disturbed him when he had seen the film as a boy. He guessed, when you thought about it, these men were like the men in the film, trying to help in their way too. Appearances, although sinister, do not always denote evil, he tried to remind himself. People were not always bad. Today was just a hard day to cling on to that thought, not helped by his self-disgust at having been so trusting and off guard just over 24 hours ago.

His thoughts were interrupted by a voice, a woman's voice.

'Too shocking for words, isn't it?' said Jan.

Rashid, annoyed at the intrusion, turned slowly to look at her. She wore brown court shoes, fawn jeans, a white T-shirt and dark blue jacket. Her hair was black, short, tidy. A large bag was slung over her shoulder.

He thought of saying nothing. This was his private moment after all, but the question irked him.

'So why say anything?' he replied.

Jan was used to such curt responses and knew just to let people be, rather than take offence or take things personally. Unless interviewees were media-savvy public figures who had been trained, people filled silences themselves, usually uncomfortable with the vacuum.

Rashid was too good and too young to be smart in the ways of the media. And too well-mannered a young man to be comfortable with his sharp response. Appearances, although sinister, do not always denote evil. People were not always bad. Here was a chance to rediscover that truth.

'I'm sorry,' he said. 'I'm very upset. I knew a lot of people in there.'

Jan's ears pricked up and her heart leapt. Her instincts in engaging a young man wearing Muslim garb and staring intently at the Mosque had been right. She tried not to react, though, not wishing to spook him or give herself, her job and her motives away.

'Oh dear. I am sorry to hear that,' she said. 'Did you know them well?'

'I worked there. I met them all. Knew some better than others. But they were all my brothers.'

This one was ready to spill, Jan thought, the professional delight in her taking over from any personal sympathy that she might genuinely have felt had she been in touch with it just now. Since her training as a junior on local papers, she had seen it happening to some people in early grief. Far from resenting the knock at the door from the *Gazette*, they positively welcomed it. Often they wanted the community to take an interest in their loss, to share it, and for the life of their loved one to be recognised, their passing to be marked. People overlooked that, she had come to know, when they talked about press intrusion.

'It was just so… so ordinary to start with,' said Rashid. He stopped. He was unsure about opening up to a stranger. But then he hadn't been able to talk to anyone properly so far. Not Mum and Dad this morning. Being back here on the site brought it all to the forefront of his mind again.

And this was a harmless woman, not young but not old. She seemed sympathetic. Her next sentence clinched it.

'Sorry. I don't want to intrude…'

'No, no. It's OK,' Rashid began again. 'Sunday was a great day. Full of family joy and peace and fun. Yesterday was about clearing up. People came to the Mosque to pray as usual just before midday and I was working in the bookshop. I loved that job. Loved the people. Then he came in.'

Tears, one snaking from each eye, slithered down his cheeks and he turned to look at Jan. She raised her eyebrows and offered a half- smile. It said that she knew and understood how he must be feeling. It also said *Don't stop now*. She needed a name.

'Oh no. How horrible and painful it must have been for you, er…'

'Rashid,' he replied.

Gotcha, she thought. She didn't need a family name in this day or age. They were easily available on the Internet. She could Google the Mosque later and find its staff and their biographies. To have asked for a family name now would have taken her beyond the inquisitiveness of a stranger and provoked suspicion in the guy.

'All still very raw for you, I would imagine?'

Just how raw Rashid was would emerge over the next 10 minutes in his account of yesterday's events to this kindly woman, who periodically nodded her sympathy at him. As he walked back towards St John's Wood tube station, he felt a little better for unburdening himself, he realised. He had it more in order in his mind now. He recalled how the flamethrower had been so blasé about the whole thing, moved around as if he knew the place, had done his homework, and then disappeared so quickly out of a back door. The scene of black, charred bodies would stay with him forever, Rashid had told her. He was grateful to her for listening.

It was also kind of her to ask if he needed any counselling. She felt sure he could readily get some, she said. That was OK, he said, the police had said the same and he might take them up on the offer, but the Mosque had access to trained people too, and he would use the fellowship of his brothers in Islam to come to terms with it all. For now, he was just angry – full of rage in fact, he had to be honest – that this had been visited upon a place and people he loved so much.

The woman had been brusque in saying that she needed to get away when he started to talk about the beneficence of Allah and the prophet Muhammad ('Peace be upon him') and how this was a challenge to any faith, but then he also thought it about time he headed back home. Mum and Dad were worried about him, he knew that, and he was sensitive to their needs.

'As-salamu alaikum' were his parting words to the woman. 'Peace be upon you.' By the time he was on the tube, Jan was in a coffee bar at the top of Baker Street called Bar Linda. She needed to find somewhere quickly while her memory was still fresh. Well, she could hardly have got her phone out and recorded everything, could hardly have taken notes, could she?

She ordered a flat white and began to write down everything that Rashid had told her, from it being just an ordinary day to one that would bring death to innocents at the hands of some crazy man in overalls and a balaclava. A balaclava with a flag of St George embroidered on the back. He particularly remembered that.

It was such a vivid story that she quickly forgave herself for not asking him why a white boy would be called Rashid and was working in the bookshop of a Mosque.

12

SAUL AND TOM

TOM scanned the bloke's flat, which they had reached via a steep hill leading up from a road on the north side of the park. He had dumped the hoodie in a bin on the way, making him less conspicuous. At the crest of the hill, the area turned into what was probably a trendy little enclave of neat roads of terraced townhouses that would have been home to a single family in the days before huge property prices, but were now divided into apartments. The man, Saul – strange name – lived on the first floor of a two-storey house.

The flat was small but tidy and Tom immediately liked its compact cosiness. He suddenly felt safe for the first time in two days. Its front door at the top of the stairs opened on to a short, carpeted entrance hall with a toilet off it and led into a narrow sitting room that looked out on to the street below from a bay window, in the curve of which stood a desk and two dining chairs at either side, with a faux leather office chair facing the window. The beige-carpeted room also had a plain brown three-seater sofa, a matching armchair and a coffee table, both aligned with a TV in a corner, near which rested an acoustic guitar, neck upright. He liked the look of that. A couple of rugs, in burgundies and oranges, gave the room colour and warmth.

The walls at either end gave an intimate feel to the room, both being full of books in shelving that encroached into the space and went from floor to ceiling. Among them were several shelves full of old vinyl records and CDs to go with a Bang & Olufsen turntable and sound system. Impressive.

Tom couldn't yet see what else there was, but two other doors led off this room, one he presumed to a bedroom. Through the other, Saul entered the living room with a tray carrying a pot of tea, small milk jug, sugar bowl, two mugs and a plate of Rich Tea biscuits – boring – and set them on the coffee table. His arrival startled Tom, who had his head in a book he had taken down from the shelves. He quickly closed and replaced it.

'Right, Thomas Judd come and have some tea,' said Saul, sitting down.

'Please, Tom. I hate Thomas.'

'OK, understood,' said Saul and Tom tentatively joined him on the sofa, sitting at one end, careful to keep a space between the two of them.

'Where are we exactly?' Tom asked.

'An area called Primrose Hill,' Saul said.

'It's really nice round here.'

A silence, of both relief and realisation, descended upon them as they sipped tea, Tom dunking and gulping down three biscuits as he contemplated what had just happened. In their flight after the shooting, they had lived on adrenaline, done what they both had to in order to survive. Now, as both relived the events of the afternoon in their thoughts, it was beginning to dawn on them separately the seriousness of what they had both experienced.

The question in Saul's mind concerned what exactly it was they had escaped from and where they went now. The potential dangers of bringing the kid back to his home now became real and provoked a momentary shiver. But then, he had been following an instinct of compassion, rekindled by the celebration of human spirit shown these past few weeks. Besides, the boy had saved his skin and he still felt he owed him.

The umbrella in his cocktail of emotions remained the dilemma of what he should do next. Yes, the kid, Tom – solid name – looked vulnerable and incapable of murder, but it seemed certain he was mixed up in all this somehow, so should he turn him in? Should he have protested more about him getting rid of the hoodie, told him to keep it? It might be – well it would be – evidence. No, getting rid was right. They just had to get away from the vicinity of a crime scene without drawing attention to themselves and worry about the next steps later. After all, he wanted to find out the real story before he rushed to judgment.

Feeling increasingly certain he was in no danger, he decided to bide his time, to let matters unfold.

'You enjoy the Olympics?' Saul asked.

'Great, yeah,' said the kid.

'I liked the opening ceremony,' Saul continued. 'Everything that is best about our country... the NHS, the role of immigrants in our modern history. Bowie and *Heroes*. Excellent.'

'Right, yeah,' Tom replied. 'I liked that kid Adam Gemili. Good sprinter. Big future.'

Their different wavelengths produced another silence, leading to Saul pouring more tea. Saul could see a shake developing in Tom's hands as he grasped the mug.

'You OK?' Saul asked.

'What do you think?' Tom snapped back. There was a pause. 'Sorry,' he added. 'I haven't had a cigarette since this morning and I'm feeling a bit strung out.'

'Sorry can't help there. Gave up years ago,' said Saul. He now knew that to hit the boy with a barrage of questions too soon would be to scare him and probably send him into a shell. Best to tread softly, to distract him even, before pushing. Best to establish some trust, though he knew it would have to be earned.

'You like Springsteen?' Saul asked, noting the kid had been leafing through Dave Marsh's biography.

'Bit dadrock, but wrote some great songs,' Tom replied.

'You into music then?

'Could say that.'

'You a musician?'

'Not really. Just play a bit of guitar, write a few songs.'

'Then you are a musician.'

Tom liked the sound of that. It was the first time anyone had said that. His mother thought he was just messing around, finding excuses since leaving university for not getting a proper job. Why was this bloke being nice to him, though?

'You play the guitar?' Tom asked Saul, pointing to the acoustic.

'No. Strum a bit. Need to learn properly.'

'Maybe I…'

'Yes?'

But Tom stopped – best not to get too forward and friendly – and they went back to sipping tea in silence. Saul was not the best at conversation, having lived on his own for so long, and certainly not with a lad in his early twenties. He stole a quick look across the sofa and saw the boy deep in thought.

Tom was unsure of this guy. Did he think he was taking some rent boy back to his flat? Was he that sort? Tom had heard of this kind of thing and he guessed he did look like some kind of waif or stray who had fetched up on the streets of London from some point North. Someone in trouble. Someone who could be bought.

He was starving, despite foraging the sandwiches from the back of that cafe at closing time last night, though the couple of cigarettes he had ponced this morning had dulled his appetite for a while. His clothes were now dirty and he felt filthy. He had wanted a wash in the toilets by the gardens on that circular road inside the park, but had thought it would draw attention to himself. He wished he could have slept in one of the cubicles, but it had been too risky. He had heard people shouting as darkness fell last night, alerting anyone left that they were locking the park gates, and just stayed put.

'That wash…' Tom said.

'Let's have something to eat,' said Saul. 'Then you can have a shower before bed and I'll find you some clean clothes.'

Saul saw the look on Tom's face, a mix of relief and suspicion.

'Look, I'm not some dirty old man or something,' he said. He knew that the innocence of doing somebody a good turn without scepticism, of times when older men could take sons and daughters swimming and not feel conspicuous when playing intimately with them in the water, were long gone. 'I just wanted to help.'

'I think you're forgetting that it was me who helped you,' said Tom.

'Fair point.' Saul replied. 'And I'm grateful. But I have the feeling that I may well have helped you out of something too. Anything you want to tell me? How come you're living rough?'

Tom knew that this guy was holding the aces all right. Tom may have dragged him out of the gunman's path, but he needed this sanctuary and dared not risk the bloke either kicking him out or going to the police with a description.

'I wasn't really living rough. I just spent a night there.'

'And that was, for why…?'

'You've got a lot of books. Never seen so many. Except in the uni library.'

'So you went to university?'

Tom thought it unremarkable information to venture and it might even throw the guy off the scent of why he had been in the park overnight.

'Yeah. Loughborough. Why do you keep all these books around the place? You could have a Kindle these days.'

'Can't beat proper books,' said Saul. 'I love the smell of the new ones, the feel of the old ones. I love the covers and the designs.'

'You sure you're not a dirty old man?' Tom joked. Saul smiled, pleased that the lad was relaxing a little.

'I've been in the publishing trade most of my life. The trouble with Kindles and being in the trade is that you see people on tubes or buses reading them and you can't tell who's reading what and what the market is doing. There are plenty of figures and statistics out there but I've always preferred the evidence of my own eyes.'

Tom was feeling more at ease. The guy was asking some questions he didn't want to answer, but was not pressing for responses, was happy to go off on tangents. He could talk to a bloke like that. Gradually.

'I've not read a book since I graduated this year,' said Tom. 'I think it may take me a while to read for pleasure again after three years of reading stuff I was told to. Don't get me wrong, I enjoyed some of it, but too many dead poets for my liking.'

Saul smiled. 'What did you have to read at uni then?'

Tom offered that he had done a French degree, got a 2:1. He had enjoyed Camus, modern material that seemed relevant to him. He had found something in *L'Etranger* that had appealed to him, admired Zola and his noble view of the working classes and thought Montaigne a clever and perceptive bloke. It was just all the old stuff and guff from centuries ago. Worthy no doubt, but tedious.

'Perhaps you could write some songs in French,' Saul suggested.

'Yeah, my brother says that,' Tom replied. There was a faint smile, until his expression turned much darker. In the silence that followed, Saul quickly sensed the mention of a brother had provoked something disturbing in the boy.

'An older or younger brother? 'Saul asked.

'Older. But I don't want to talk about him. I don't know him any more. Don't even know if I have a brother any more. Enough about me. What about you?'

'What? What about me?' said Saul, taken aback.

'What do you do? Where's your family?'

Saul stuck to the first part of the question. He had been a book editor on the staff of a publisher but now freelanced in semi-retirement. The book collection was testimony to his life's work. They were ordered in sections, like a library, he told Tom. There were travel books, reference books, music books, the odd sports book and novels – divided into literary and commercial fiction.

Tom interrupted him. 'What's the difference?'

'Well, in commercial fiction, characters want something and get it. In literary fiction, characters want something and don't get it.'

He smiled at his own aphorism but Tom didn't seem to appreciate his cleverness.

'And family?' Tom asked.

It was nearing 6pm. 'I think we need to see the news, don't we?' said Saul.

He turned on the television and they watched the lead story about the gunman shot dead in Regent's Park after a rampage that had killed three people and injured another two. The gunman was now being identified. He had a name of Asian heritage and came from the East End of London. The victims were also named, all of them men – white men – aged between 20 and 40. Two of the three dead were tourists, as was one of the wounded. The other two were Londoners joining them in enjoying this late summer, the park still looking magnificent even on this grey day. Three of the men were with their families, including children, one was with his partner and the other on his own. Witnesses talked of several more shots but also of the gunman having stopped when he had hit five people. Given that, the report said, and the fact that all the victims were male, police were treating it as an act of retribution for yesterday.

Saul watched with eyes ever-widening, eyebrows raising ever higher. He was stunned, and infused with the survivor's mixture of relief and guilt. He shook his head, occasionally looking across at the boy, who betrayed little emotion until the second item came on. It told of the hunt for the mystery flamethrower who seemed to have disappeared into the ether of the city. There was an interview with the Mosque's director who urged an end to reprisals on both sides, as did the Prime Minster. The two were standing together in solidarity on the steps of 10 Downing Street.

Tom felt a tear dribble from his right eye and tried furtively to wipe it away before Saul saw it. He failed. Saul was convinced more than ever now that he was not sitting alongside a murderer. The boy was involved somehow, however, and he needed to find out how soon, to persuade the boy to tell the police what he knew. It seemed that they both had secrets that would not be given up readily.

13

DEENA

DEENA sat in the corner of the Butcher's Arms at the back of the station nursing her orange juice. It was one of those spacious old London pubs, with rooms going off at all angles and polished wood and frosted glass panel partitions helping to break up the size and give intimacy, making it easy to hide in a corner. It was just past 5.30pm and the drinkers among the office workers were coming in, pretending that they were waiting until the rush hour was over and the trains out of Paddington were less crowded. In reality, they needed, deserved, a drink after what they insisted was a stressful day.

If only they knew about Deena's day, not that she wanted to share it with anyone who wasn't in the job and therefore who wouldn't understand. And not over a drink; of alcohol anyway. She didn't drink it. She liked clarity, to feel everything, even if right now she didn't want to feel this pain and sadness. She knew, being from upright stock, that booze was the devil's brew and solved nothing.

Deena was proud that her grandfather, 82 now, had come over from Jamaica on the *Windrush* in 1948, and the depiction of the suited and suit-cased immigrants arriving from Kingston in the opening ceremony of the Olympics had brought tears to the family's eyes. Mum and Dad were Pentecostal Christians. They believed in industry and abstinence, Dad a bus driver, Mum a teaching assistant in Kennington, and they did not waste money on fripperies.

Such was the family work ethic that brother Kyle, two years her senior, even had two jobs, as a solicitor's clerk and a semi-professional footballer for Tooting and Mitcham. Mum was delighted about the first, Dad enjoyed watching the second. They were proud, too, of Deena, if concerned about what she might encounter on the streets of the capital, and she respected them deeply in return.

She stared at the juice, twiddled the glass and wondered why she had allowed Darren to talk her into coming here. The Paddington Green day shift would be knocking off and here soon enough too and she wanted to avoid them. All she wanted to do was get on her train and home. Daz wasn't even bloody here. Better not let Mum hear her use language like that.

Finally, he appeared, wanting to know if she was ready to break the habit of her soon-to-be-over teenage years after a day like this with a proper drink. She replied with a firm 'no' and watched him get his own pint of lager.

'Bastard of a day,' he said sitting down quickly, needing a long gulp as quickly as possible.

Deena suddenly got up to leave.

'Something I said?' said Darren.

'No, I just don't feel very sociable, sorry,' Deena replied.

'Oh come on. Stay a bit. What you gonna do? Go home and stew on it?'

Deena felt guilt at her mood. People had been burned and shot to death and others were fighting for their lives. Here she was, dragging her personal dark cloud everywhere with her just because of a ticking-off from a superior officer. Grow up girl, she told herself. Get over yourself.

And yet. She was worried by what the bigwig had said, she told Darren.

'He said I endangered public safety,' said Deena. 'I released information that could have caused panic and provoked more violence through another revenge attack.'

Darren doubted it. The gunman was dead. The only problem in talking to the papers was that they had the information an hour or two earlier than they might have. The powers that be hated info being given out by anyone apart from them. If PCs started giving it out, they couldn't justify their jobs could they? Senior officers liked ordering press officers about. Press officers – and God knows there were enough of them these days – liked timing their releases to give them power over journalists. Way of the world, Deena, he said with the benefit of his six months' more wisdom in the job than she had.

'Anyway, you might have done everyone a favour,' Darren added.

'How come?'

'Releasing that early gave everyone time to absorb the info and calm down. Release it later in the day and more people will be around to take to the streets.'

Deena smiled. 'Thanks Daz. But early release might also have given people longer to arrange street protests...'

'Yeah right. There was people who'd been in the park tweeting pictures of the bloke within half an hour,' he said. 'Fuzzy pictures, granted, from a distance but you could sort of make out he was Asian. I just don't get it. They're taking pictures on their phones as the bloke is coming at them? Then when they do get away, they put a picture on the Internet? Desperate to be on telly is one thing. Desperate to go viral is another.'

'I don't think I'm cut out for this job,' said Deena.

'Cobblers,' said Darren. 'You're a natural. Trust me. Dedicated. Loyal. Good with people and an eye for a criminal.'

'Saw enough of them where I came from,' she said.

Deena thought aloud about what she could do. Shop girl? Office work maybe? They're jobs rather than careers, though, aren't they? But maybe that would be better. No responsibilities. No real potential to mess things up. Certainly not to put people's lives at risk. Maybe Dave had a point.

Darren had no need to say anything, sensing that she just needed to vent. As she paused for breath, he reminded her of something.

'Thought you wanted to be a detective?'

'Some chance of that after today,' she said.

'Well, if you're going to give up after the first setback, then you're not right for it are you?' said Darren, feigning disgust. 'Fair enough. Quit then. That gutsy woman who chased that tea leaf round that Bayswater estate with me that night is not the person I thought she was.'

Deena smiled. The door to the pub opened and in piled half a dozen more of her colleagues but lethargically, at odds with the enthusiasm they might have shown on a dawn raid when there was a door to be negotiated. Normally they would have been in high spirits at the prospect of a couple of drinks at day's end but the last 36 hours had drained them. This was a time for camaraderie, for a drink to commiserate, not to celebrate.

One of them noticed Deena and Darren in the corner. 'All right boys and girls?' said the booming voice of desk sergeant Bill Joyce, walking over. It was a question that did not require an answer. 'Hear you got a bollocking from the Chief Super today. Welcome to the club. Makes you a proper copper in my book now.' He grinned and headed for the bar.

'See?' said Darren.

Deena managed a weak smile. She knew they were right. She may not have been in the police long but it was long enough to have discovered she was made for this life. Obeyed orders well, used her initiative when it was right. What about the time when that Detective Sergeant had given her a 'Well done Constable' when she noticed a tooth pick in the street just outside the house where they had found a body and they had used the DNA from it to find the guy and help convict him of murder?

Her head may have been messing with her but in her heart she knew that she couldn't quit now, that it would be an insult both to her parents and herself. Darren was right. What loser gives in at the first sign of trouble? She finished her orange juice and thanked him.

He smiled back and she touched his arm as she rose. She went to the bar and thanked Bill too. He seemed bemused. It was everyday conversation, he reckoned. He had said nothing special. But he had.

A proper copper. That had done the trick for Deena. It was a simple phrase but one that told of respect she had earned. Often the most basic sentences are those that offer the most consolation and encouragement.

She stepped out into the street. The day's weather had begun dull and never recovered. Tonight was sultry and sombre. London had had its joy sucked from it. People were scuttling back to their homes, not to watch the Olympic Games tonight but to be amid the safety and warmth of the people they loved. What choice did anyone have anyway but to carry on as the city always did in adversity? In the real world, the clocks didn't stop. There was a selfishness to it, but one that also said that people had not died in vain. We would not be giving in.

Yesterday's killer was still at large, though he might be long gone from the city. At least everyone hoped so; civilians that was, if not the authorities. Today's assassin was dead and people were glad, it had to be said, as they would do on the late night phone-ins. Nobody felt in immediate danger from those sources but it was the tension between communities that troubled everyone: Muslim against Christian, Asian against Anglo-Saxon. Deena was only on the way home on the understanding that her phone could ring at any moment calling her back to work. The sense tonight, though, was that the death of the gunman, a 25-year-old man of Pakistani heritage from Bethnal Green, had sated the bloodlust of the white racists and would suppress any lingering Islamic resentment. For now. We would see.

She headed for the Circle Line at Paddington Station, contemplating its inconsistencies, and how busy it might be at Victoria, where she would change for Stockwell. She felt another flutter of butterflies in her stomach, the fear worse than chasing any crook up the Harrow Road, as she looked at her watch and realised her boyfriend would be ringing in an hour. She would not be ending her career but it was time to end something else.

14

SAUL AND TOM

SAUL made a meal of fish fingers, mashed potato and baked beans. He had his speciality dishes, made fine scrambled eggs and roast dinners, but his repertoire was limited. He also hadn't had time today to do any shopping for something fresh. Tom didn't care. He would have eaten anything put in front of him. The fact that it was comfort food, reminding him of less troubled student days, made it all the better.

A full stomach loosened his tongue as the two of them sat at opposite ends of the sofa. That and Saul putting on Springsteen's *Born to Run* album, on vinyl of course. After the privations of the previous night spent outdoors, Tom was just grateful to be inside and in the warm. His nicotine cravings were passing and he was feeling less snappy. Bruce sang 'Jungleland' and they sat listening, full, contented, as the lyric unfolded through images of barefoot girls, hoods of cars, warm beer and summer rain.

'I didn't do it, you know,' Tom said. 'That stuff on the news.'

There was a silence.

'I didn't think you did,' Saul replied. 'You wouldn't be here if I thought you had. But I do think you know something about it.'

Tom ran through it all, or most of it: driving his brother down to London from Birmingham – that's where he was from, he said – dropping him off at the front of the Mosque and parking round the back. Being stunned as his brother emerged from a back entrance, peeling off a balaclava and running towards the car. The argument. His brother driving off at speed.

If he'd known Jason was planning something bad – yes, that's my brother's name – of course he wouldn't have been anywhere near this. And he knew as soon as he came out of that Mosque that it was something bad. Something very bad. But until he saw the TV news tonight, he hadn't known just how bad. Evil, even.

'Why didn't you just get out of there? Why hang around?' Saul wondered.

'I don't know London. I didn't know where to go. I couldn't see any tube stations or bus stops in the park. I checked a map on my phone just before it died but it looked miles to a tube station and I didn't know which direction to head for. I thought that police might be checking people at them anyway and I knew some people had seen me near the scene. I didn't know if they would have told the police. They might have a description of me. Looking back, I don't suppose anything would have happened that quickly but I wasn't really thinking straight.

'Then I thought that if I mingled with people in the park, I'd be safer. I guessed the police would soon be all over the exits so I thought I'd be best right in the middle of it, where people had nothing to hide and where they weren't looking for someone.'

'The eye of the storm,' said Saul. 'Safest, quietest place is in the eye of the storm.'

Bruce sang of lawmen chasing criminals and kids living in shadows.

'You looked frightened when I first saw you,' Saul added.

'Really? I was going for intimidating.'

They both smiled, even though they knew there was nothing amusing in any of this. But to smile, however weakly, was for Tom a small stab at coping with the shame. Though he didn't recognise it, it was also a denial of just how serious it all was. To acknowledge that, though, would be to crumble. And he couldn't crumble just yet. As for Saul, his own smile was supposed to reassure a kid he could see was in pain.

'What was your plan then?'

'I didn't really have one. I just thought I would lie low overnight, give it 24 hours until they thought anyone connected to it was long gone and try and find a main road and some public transport and take it from there. Problem was, I only had a few quid in cash. I was expecting to collect some money off someone. Jason actually. I have a bank card in my wallet, and I guess there was just about enough in my account to get me back to New Street. Then my mobile died so I didn't get to find out what had really happened. Well, I was expecting to be back home by the time it ran out, wasn't I? Which reminds me... You have a charger for an iPhone 4?'

As it happened, Saul did, having fallen victim to the latest version himself at the end of last year, and told Tom it was in the small table in the entrance hall. Tom found it and plugged in his phone.

'What was it like in the park overnight?'

'Spooky. Cold. Damp. More wildlife around than I thought. Rats mainly. A couple ran across my feet. Loads of Squirrels. I kept hearing noises so I had to stay hidden behind that shelter. Heard the odd car nearby.'

Saul told him that they closed the park gates at night so it must have been Royal Parks police patrolling.

'I didn't know that. I did think about trying to get away to signs of civilisation in the early hours but I thought I might stand out. I also thought about getting out to get some rolling tobacco or to scrounge a couple of fags but then I realised I'd probably be caught on CCTV. Everywhere these days, isn't it?'

'Not in the park. Yet. But yes, most other places. It's there to catch the guilty and protect the innocent...'

'Yeah right. There to spy on us.'

Actually, Saul agreed with him, as with speed cameras. Not so much to quell speed but to raise revenue.

'Why didn't you just go to the police? You haven't done anything wrong have you?

'I'm an accessory to murder.'

'Unwittingly.'

'Not sure they're going to see it like that. And besides. What am I going to do? Grass up my brother?'

'Yes. Of course you are. Look what he's got you involved in.'

Tom paused. He knew there was logic to this. But this bloke didn't understand. He lived on his own. Didn't understand family, obviously. Nor could he know just what a massive thing Jason had done for him once upon a time.

'He's my brother. He's been there for me all through my growing up.'

'That was his job, as your older brother, to look after you.'

'He got me out of bother once, right? Big bother.'

'Bother?'

There was a pause, broken by Tom trying to avoid having to explain.

'Look, I don't want to see him any more after this but I just can't turn him in to the police. How do I live with that?'

'How do you live with not turning him in?'

'He must have had his reasons…'

Saul found himself growing angry. 'Reasons? For setting people on fire? And what might those reasons be?'

Thinking long and hard in the cold last night, Tom guessed why Jase had done something bad at that Mosque. Five men, of Asian background, had raped Rachel. Now he knew that five men had died in the Mosque. This was pure revenge, though Tom was not ready to share that with this man just yet.

But why had that horrendous night provoked Jase into vengeance? Every time Tom thought of Rachel being raped it seared into his soul. The coldness with which he'd treated her afterwards was something else he couldn't bear to dwell on too long. But he couldn't work out why Jase seemed so much angrier than him about it and would do something as outrageous and extreme as this. Afghanistan must have done something desperate to him.

Bruce sang passionately on, telling of secret debts being paid in his 'Jungleland' world.

'It's called dark loyalty,' said Saul.

'What's that?'

'It means we stay loyal to people or situations even when it's not good for us. Family often. People who have a hold on us. Staying in places because we are frightened of the alternative.'

'Where do you get this stuff from?' Tom asked.

Saul waved towards the bookshelves. 'Everything is in there,' he said. 'I get it from books. And experience of life.'

Tom thought it was time to change the subject, deflect attention back on to Saul. To get some of the benefit of that experience.

'Are you Jewish?'

'No, why?'

'Saul's a Jewish name, isn't it?'

'Yes. But my parents liked books, too. Passed them on to me. It's after Saul Bellow. American writer.'

'Yes, I know. I read one of his once. *Seize The Day*. I liked it. It was short.'

Saul was impressed. Tom was grateful for his compliment. He was getting to like the old guy.

'What was all that with offering me the socks?'

Saul smiled. 'It's something I do. I thought you were homeless. I don't like to think that if I give them money it might end up in the profits of drinks' companies. And plenty of people give them sandwiches. One homeless guy once told me that he hated wet feet and that clean socks were a real treat. So I give out new socks.'

That made sense to Tom and he started to move from just being grateful to the guy, though retaining some suspicion about his motives, to having some respect for him.

'Why are you helping me?' asked Tom.

'Because you look as if you need some help,' came the reply.

That was for sure, Tom thought. Now he wanted to change the subject away from himself.

'You not got any family then?'

Saul was immediately uncomfortable. It had been a long time since he had talked to anybody about this sort of stuff. The boy had opened up to him, though, been honest. He deserved something in return. Just as Bruce told of lonely-hearted lovers, Saul spoke.

'Not any more. I was married, house in the suburbs. Finchley. We grew apart. It was the silences that killed us. Didn't even row any more. She left me. Said that staying would have driven her mad. Her going drove me mad but I got over it. She remarried.'

'Any kids?'

'No. Never happened.'

'You not had a girlfriend or remarried since?'

'There was a woman a few years ago. She died, sadly. Leukaemia. Now I function better on my own. I like my privacy, my own world.'

'Blimey. You are a sad bastard, aren't you?'

Saul couldn't help but laugh.

'Sad *and* unlucky.'

And Saul laughed louder.

'You don't know quite how unlucky,' he said.

Beginning to enjoy sharing conversation in a way he had not for a while, he ventured to Tom that he had prostate cancer. The lad was silenced at first, then interested, said he had heard of it but didn't know anything about it.

Reassuring Tom that it was OK to laugh, Saul told of the spot check by his doctor that he had been dreading, the insertion of a latex-gloved and gel-lubricated index finger into his anus while he lay on his side, knees raised up to chest, and that it had not been painful, just uncomfortable. He explained to Tom that the prostate was a gland the size and shape of a walnut – in its shell, rather than out – and situated beneath the bladder. And ironically, walnuts – out of their shell, rather than in – were good for prostate cancer.

(He then glossed over the bits about the urethra tube, through which men passed urine and semen and which helped in the filtering of one and production of the other. He also thought it a bit soon for describing how the prostate grew enlarged, causing pressure on the urethra and forcing the frequent urination but only allowing a slow flow. As for the blood test that revealed a high-enough reading – a PSA level, standing for Prostate Specific Antigen – of 6.8, or rather a high-enough increase of 10 per cent in a year, he didn't want to bombard the kid with technicalities.)

Saul added that his test results from his local health authority's overstretched laboratory suggested the need for the subsequent, confirming biopsy, which Saul now enjoyed describing in comical detail having previously formulated it in his head.

Tom laughed again, particularly enjoying the tale of the nurse and her interest in the rectal wall, before enquiring whether he should get checked out. Saul insisted he had plenty of years before he need worry about that.

'Hopefully by the time you're my age,' Saul said, 'they will have developed a pill that will kill the cancer for your generation.'

Tom was initially less amused when he heard about the treatment involved, specifically that Saul needed to go tomorrow and Tom had better stay in the flat out of sight. He protested momentarily but he quickly ceased, knowing how selfish he sounded after all that he had been told. And he knew Saul was right. They needed to work out what to do, see what developments tomorrow would bring.

Saul broke the subsequent silence.

'And your family?' Saul asked. 'Mum and Dad? Any other brothers or sisters?

'I live with Mum. Dad left after I was born. Met another woman apparently. Never seen him since. Sent us money, to be fair, and we grew up in a nice house in Edgbaston. Leafy. Bit like here. Just me and Jason. That enough?'

It was, Saul replied. And he didn't want to press any more for now. Finding out about this 'big bother' would have to wait for another time.

'You going to turn me in? Or Jase?' Tom asked.

Saul pondered for a moment.

'Do you think he'll kill again?'

'Doubt it. No, I'm sure he won't. I think he's done what he set out to do.'

'Then no, I'm not going to turn you in right now. Or him. But you are.'

He stared Tom in the eye as Springsteen sang his climactic lines, of shots echoing and ambulances pulling away, of streets on fire. When the music stopped, Tom heard the beeping of a message coming into his mobile that had now been powered back to life, grateful to be able to move away from the old man's gaze.

He walked over to the hall table and read the text. It was Rachel. 'Where are you?' it read. 'Your Mum said you'd gone to London. You OK with all that stuff happening down there?'

Saul seemed concerned.

'Who's that?'

'Someone I used to know.'

'Not your brother?'

'No.'

'You have a girlfriend? Or boyfriend?'

'No. I did have a girlfriend. Don't want to talk about it.'

His phone rang with a voicemail. It was his mum, wondering whether he was safe in London. He sent a quick text message back to say he was fine and there was no need for her to worry.

It was a sign of his life, he told Saul with a rueful smile, that there was nothing else on his mobile. Just two communications.

'Help me sort out this sofa bed,' said Saul, looking to cheer him up. 'At least you'll have something softer to sleep on tonight.'

They unfolded the sofa, Saul went to fetch some bed linen and they made up the bed. Saul provided a towel, a clean, plain white T-shirt and pyjama bottoms and Tom went to shower.

He felt better, refreshed at least, but after bidding Saul goodnight, he lay awake, faintly hearing the radio news coming from the bedroom. He could hear that there was tension again tonight on the streets of London and other major cities but so far no violence nor looting. Police had the situation under control, with a show of unity between various religious groups so far paying off. Celebrities were also appealing for calm, which was helping.

Tom wondered again about Jase, what he had done and what his motives were; where he was now. He thought about Rachel and wept quietly for a few moments. And he contemplated this dark loyalty that Saul had talked about. When he stopped thinking about that being a good name for a band, he asked himself whether it was indeed clouding his judgment and whether he should be going to the police.

PART III

WEDNESDAY
AUGUST 15TH
2012

15

JAN

THERE was a new spring in Jan's step as she breezed through the revolving front door that responded only to the barcode on staff passes, and smiled at Donna on reception, who waved at her. She chirruped 'thanks' to Tony from features on the 'nice work yesterday' compliment as she moved through the atrium to the cafe stall to get her usual morning double espresso before taking the lift to the news room floor.

More compliments came from those around her as she sat down, though it was still not like the grand old days. A scoop on the website still lacked the cachet of a front-page byline, and the reaction did not approach the old times when a real once-a-year exclusive would have brought a round of applause. No sooner had she settled at her computer screen and taken a hit of the coffee than Vickers was across from his desk.

'Got anything today yet?' he inquired.

'Yes, I did do well yesterday, didn't I?' she replied and smiled.

Vickers ploughed on. 'If you have, let me know before conference, OK? Need to put it on the news list.'

He went to go back to his desk at the centre of the news hub but turned back.

'And if you've got anything you need to chase out of the office, you need to run it by me, all right? You got away with it yesterday but those fucking warnings aren't going away.'

This time he did trot off, Jan muttering 'Just fucking jog on' under her breath, and she watched him seek out his next victim, some rookie who had not been able to stand up a story yesterday and who might as well have had the word 'terrified' tattooed on his forehead. As she watched the boy disappear towards the toilets after the exchange, she thanked her lucky stars she was well beyond the need to take herself off to a cubicle and cry. Instead, she recognised in Vickers's implied permission to go out on the road again, like a proper, traditional reporter, the stirrings of a compliment. Well she never.

Jan did indeed have something for tomorrow's paper but she would not be letting on just yet. To do so would be to have to file it all now and see it on the paper's website before lunch-time. Every Twitter account with too much time, too short an attention span and too little information would be tweeting it, every media outlet in the world would then be carrying it. Just a few would credit the paper for the piece, fewer still would acknowledge her as the writer. By the afternoon, it would be overtaken by every major TV, radio station and paper assigning their own reporters to the tale and their byline being all over it. It would make the paper tomorrow morning, but somewhere deep into the 'book'. Certainly not on the front, turning to a spread early on.

And so she waited for her moment. The evening conference was at 6.30pm. The later she alerted them, the more dramatic its impact would be. In fact, it would be an old-fashioned scoop, a coup, a late front page to get the adrenaline going. For some-one whose instinct was to want to tell people things they didn't know, who took pleasure in it and could hardly resist it indeed, sitting on something all day was going to be some task.

She had been right about what had made up today's paper. The front page was mostly taken up with a picture, released by the police, of the man who had committed the revenge rampage (and one day, if she ever got a relationship, a proper life and a house, she told herself, she must stop thinking in tabloid speak), under the banner:

THE FACE OF EVIL

Inside were stories on the killer's background – Yousuf Ahmed, a young Muslim aged 26 of Moroccan extraction who lived in Bethnal Green, East London – and the follow-ups to her story on the number of dead and injured: three of the former and the two with gunshot wounds still surviving. There were pictures of the victims too, accompanied by cameo biographies. In addition, there was a spread on the tension in British cities with reports from the major centres. Birmingham and Bradford were particularly troublesome, with white racists looking to move into Asian neighbourhoods, but there had been only a dozen arrests in both as police managed to keep a lid on things.

It helped that it had rained last night, clearing the air after the hot weather of the previous week, though more of that was forecast over the next few days. Indeed, Jan's journey in on the tube had been a sweaty one. She was credited as part of the team, jointly bylined on the casualty figure tale, and listed later in the crowd of 'additional reporting by' names. She was satisfied with that.

More detail about Monday's Mosque atrocity was postponed until page nine, giving more credence to Muslim leaders who had spent the previous night on TV and radio saying that they were not defending the indefensible but the story of the gunman had taken over from the first offence and the police had now taken their eyes off the ball, even though the retribution was a solved crime and 'theirs' was not.

A police spokesperson denied it, insisting that it was understandable that officers had to deal with the most immediate, shocking event but that many more were still searching for the flamethrower murderer, and that they had leads they were following up. They were, they said, working on witness statements and checking roadside cameras in London for the dark-coloured Honda (so they still hadn't identified the actual colour) but added that it would take time.

His next statement confirmed to a practised journalist like Jan that they were not getting very far.

'The unfortunate element of the latest sad and shocking event,' said the spokesperson, 'is that it did not help our hunt for the perpetrator who fled the Mosque. It may have given him more time get further away. All stations, ports and airports are being monitored, but we still need a proper profile of the man and a picture, since closed-circuit television shows only a man in a balaclava. We would appeal to any member of the public who knows anything about him or this horrendous crime to contact us.'

Jan had hurried back to her one-bedroomed flat in Maida Vale last night after writing down every word of the 'interview' with Rashid that she could remember. Once inside, she had unscrewed the top of a bottle of red wine, settled on to her sofa, followed every cough and spit of Sky News during the evening, taken out her laptop and worked on the piece.

First, she googled the Mosque and found his picture and a short biog on the 'About Us' section of the official website of the London Central Mosque Trust Ltd and The Islamic Cultural Centre. Rashid Johnson had 'reverted' to Islam from Judaism a year ago and worked in the bookshop. It just got better and better. This was the gift that kept on giving. He had gone to a comprehensive school in Stanmore, Middlesex and had a degree in business studies from London Metropolitan University. Unfortunately, it didn't give his age. Why didn't people understand the basics?

She wrote up the interview, around 1,200 words that she knew would make a two-page spread inside the paper. Then she wrote a 500-word potential front-page piece along the **MY VISION OF**

HELL variety that would turn inside after a few intro paragraphs. And for good measure, she added a 700-word backgrounder on the nice Jewish boy who had bizarrely, in her mind at least, converted. For her readership, that was the word she needed to use.

Such was the Internet these days that she could find references to him here and there and built up a picture of a model student who had achieved good A levels. After doing his business degree, however, something had happened to force him to want to change his life but she could find no obvious explanation for it. There seemed to be a bit of a gap between leaving uni and working at the Mosque but not a long one. Her paper was fond of headlines that asked questions, though she had been brought up on local papers to believe it was her job to find answers to them for readers who led busy lives and couldn't. This, she felt sure, would play as something like: **What made a model Jewish boy turn Muslim?**

Now at her desk, she browsed the wire services – Press Association, Reuters – finished her coffee, took out her laptop and opened it, preferring to work on that rather than a big screen on the desk. They handed out gongs at awards ceremonies for newspaper teams these days but they were just ways of rewarding editors and sub-editors who were never by-lined for their contributions. Actually, teamwork was limited. Rather, papers were more a collection of individuals and rivalries that were as much internal as with competing press outlets. She did not want her material being seen and pinched by a so-called colleague. It had happened when she was green. She had left a story up on a screen when she went briefly to the canteen and later found the story in the paper filed by another reporter, almost word for word. She was sitting on pay dirt now and she wasn't going to share this.

Suddenly a voice was in her ear and she jumped. 'Well done yesterday. We oldies strike back.' It was Neil. He was still here, in his early 50s, because he used to drink with the editor, had started as a reporter with him, but wanted little more, unlike his ambitious mate.

Jan quickly shut her laptop. If ever there was a byline bandit it was Neil Rushman. 'Less of the old. Speak for yourself,' she said. Neil moved on. She could only hope he hadn't been at her shoulder long enough to see the contents of her screen.

She needed to get out of the office. She couldn't pretend to do nothing all day and guard her secret. She was too twitchy. She went over to Vickers.

'Where are we with Monday's killer?' she asked.

'I need one of you to tell me that,' he replied.

'Well, we know he was driving a Honda Accord, yet to be found.'

'Perhaps it's in South London. Everything gets lost in South London,' said Vickers. It was as near as he would ever get to a joke.

'I thought I might nip out to meet a contact of mine. See if I can find out more.'

Vickers went to his default position, pointing out that there was a voracious monster called the website that needed regular feeds but he stopped himself. He was clearly recalling that Jan had taken herself off yesterday and delivered.

'OK then. But I want you back here by late afternoon to see where we are. And I want something from you today. No resting on laurels. That's not what makes us the best news team in the business, yes?'

Only as good as your last story, Jan thought. The what-have-you-done-for-me-lately culture. She smiled, knowing that she was even better than her last story. Having something in hand took the pressure off, like fuck-off money in the bank gave you the freedom to do what you really wanted to do with your life. She looked forward to that day.

She walked off the news room floor, out into a corridor and scrolled down the contacts list on her mobile until she came to the name of Frank Phillips.

16

TOM

TOM returned the sofa bed to being a sofa, folded up the sheet and duvet, sat down in the pyjama bottoms and T-shirt Saul had lent him and wondered what to do next. The guy had been good to him, for what reason he still wasn't sure, and he liked it here, felt safe in this cosy, tidy, manageable living space. For now. But where to go from here? How was he ever going to get back to a normal life after what had happened over the last two days? Get back to a normal life? Finding any life would be a start. What sort of life could even be up to the police and the courts.

He made himself another mug of tea. Had a bowl of corn-flakes. Washed up the cup and bowl. He had another look around the bookshelves and went through the CD and record collection. He picked up the guitar, played some chords, sang a couple of songs he had written. He was rusty.

He had been into Saul's bedroom last night to get to the shower but not lingered. Now that the guy was out, he ventured in properly. He felt a bit guilty for his intrusion but his curiosity was only natural, he told himself. The same beige carpet as in the living room. A double bed with plain white linen, a wardrobe, chest of drawers, a leather tub chair and a bedside table on which sat a digital radio, a half-finished *Daily Telegraph* crossword and a book, *Ordinary Thunderstorms* by William Boyd. He read the synopsis on the back cover. Sounded like a good story. Might have a read of that when Saul was finished. If he was still around when Saul was finished.

Tom wandered back into the living room, paced around uneasily, and looked out of the bay window into the street below. Late-morning empty. Another bright sunny day to replace yesterday's cloud cover. It was then that the craving hit him. He had somehow resisted the urge to leave the park that night and find a 24-hour shop to buy some tobacco and what with everything else happening yesterday afternoon, he had not worried about it too much after having scrounged those couple of cigarettes to keep him going in the morning. Boredom, the enemy of an addict looking to quit, was kicking in.

For a while he resisted. He made himself another mug of tea. Found an Arcade Fire LP, *The Suburbs,* and put it on the turntable. It did sound better on vinyl. The guy was going up in his estimation. But he remained restless. His mobile whooshed with a text message. 'You there Tom?' it said. It came from his mother. He suddenly felt guilty. His heart raced. He knew he should ring but what was he going to tell her?

He got his story straight in his mind and phoned. He was just staying with a mate in London for a few days, he said, taking in a couple of gigs. Yes, he should have let her know. He was sorry. No, he hadn't been caught up in any of that scary stuff of the last couple of days. London is a big place, Mum. Been miles away from that. Jason? No, not seen him. It was certainly plausible he hadn't. His brother had his own flat and his own life.

'Rachel has rung the house,' his mother added. 'Said you're still ignoring her texts and messages. She sounded upset, not surprisingly. Why don't you call her?'

Tom felt bad all over again. Bad enough to know that he would have to face her and her pain sooner or later. He agreed he needed to talk to Rachel, he said, but would be home in a day or two and should do it face to face.

He hated lying to his mother about what had happened and about Jason but justified it by telling himself he didn't want to alarm her and was protecting her from the horrific truth that would shatter her. He knew her world would come crashing down soon enough once the police were on to Jase but he wanted to be with her when it happened. She seemed reassured by the time he said goodbye.

He had barely ended the call when the phone coughed up another a text message. From Jason. Jesus. 'Where you?' it said. He threw the phone down on the sofa as if it was a hot potato and paced the room quickly and randomly, like a buzzing fly, all the while staring at the device. What the… What did he want? He thought he would have been far away by now. Abroad even. Should he text him back? Tom felt sick to his stomach every time he thought of him but there were so many questions he wanted answered. Hesitantly, reluctantly he tapped back a message.

'Place called Primrose Hill. Where you?'

The reply came within a minute.

'Meet me Chalk Farm tube station. 1 hr.'

Tom convinced himself that he now really needed nicotine. He went to the kitchen. His trousers and T-shirt were now dry having been in the washing machine overnight and he changed into them. He washed the dirt off his white trainers with a kitchen cloth. He began to scrabble around the flat for some keys. Surely Saul kept spare ones around the place? There they were, in the drawer of that little hall table. There were two Yales, one surely for the door, which he tried and turned, and the other for the building's front door. The same with the two mortice keys, one of which worked for the flat.

He bounded down the stairs and tried the other two keys at the front door. They fitted. The door clanked shut behind him, causing him to grimace as he turned around in regret at making such a noise. He noticed a woman, an elderly woman, peering from behind a ground floor curtain at him. She quickly closed it as he made eye contact.

Instinct having taken over, only now he was out in the street did he recall Saul's words about staying in. He felt he had no choice, though. He needed to know more from Jason. That call had changed the situation.

Tom had no idea where he was going but at the top of the street, out of sight of the woman, he checked the name of the road, keyed it in to the maps app on his phone as his starting point and Chalk Farm Underground as his destination. It showed a walk of six minutes, giving directions. He checked the time on his phone. He would be early but he badly needed that roll-up.

He walked down Saul's residential street on to Regent's Park Road and saw a Post Office and newsagents. It would do cash. Dare he withdraw money? The police might be on to him by now. Might be monitoring his bank account. Better not. He checked his pocket. He had £3.86 in change. He went into the newsagent and bought the cheapest tobacco, Cutters Choice, just 10 milligrams, and Rizla cigarette papers. It came to £3.58. That was a relief, but he would have to do without filters, though he could tear the cap from the Rizla packet and use the cardboard as a roach.

He turned right and walked back to Primrose Hill itself rather than left to Chalk Farm and found a park bench as far as possible from anybody. He sat down, gazed over the cityscape below and rolled a cigarette. He lit it and drew deeply, savouring the nicotine, enjoying watching the smoke. Now he could take in the view – Canary Wharf to the east, the skyscrapers of the City, the London Eye and the BT Tower. He began to get his bearings. Then he recognised the Mosque's minaret down to his right, and shuddered. The breeze blew up and he felt a chill.

It had been 30 minutes since he received the text from his brother. Having taken his walk to the hill in the opposite direction, the map now told him it was 10 minutes' walk to Chalk Farm. He rolled a few cigarettes to kill time now and save time later. Should he keep the meeting, he now began to wonder in the cold light of day? As he thought of Jason, the anger welled inside him, at what he had done, at how his brother had abandoned him like that. But he was still his brother, still his saviour. And Tom was, he had to admit to himself, curious at what this was all about.

Tom got up, looked down at his phone and turned back towards Chalk Farm, following the blue dot that was tracking his movements. He felt guilty, and worried that he looked guilty. But just as at the newsagents, nobody even gave him a second glance. Just another kid out on the street during the day. There were plenty of them, out of work, just mooching.

He began to relax about being recognised and apprehended, having more confidence in his belief that there were no cameras around the park on Monday. He grew more nervous, however, as the dot on his phone representing him drew closer to the red pin that was his destination. He walked past twee shops and cafes, over a railway bridge, where he slowed down, and looked at the tangle of tracks below, so as not to arrive too soon at the tube.

He felt conspicuous standing outside the old-fashioned tube station whose brown tiles appealed to his eye, and smoked another cigarette. He looked this way and that, watched people come out of the station but nothing. He checked his phone. Five minutes till the meet. He turned to scan the road again and drew deeply and comfortingly again on his roll-up. There was a minicab office 20 yards away. That could be useful.

The tap on the shoulder came a couple of minutes early. He turned to see Jason with his arms spread wide. Tom had no choice in the matter of the hug but he was not going to return the gesture. He just stood there being hugged, arms at his side.

'Good to see you, bruv,' Jason said.

Tom's tension took over. He was not going to be easy for his brother. Not this time.

'Good to see me? What the fuck? After what you've done?'

'Shh,' Jason replied and grabbed him by the arm. 'Keep it down will you, for fuck's sake. Let's go and talk somewhere.'

Tom said he knew a park and walked him back to Primrose Hill. As they walked he wondered why Jason had wanted to meet him here. 'Northern Line,' was all he said, apart from: 'Now shut up in case anyone overhears anything.'

The peak of the hill was filling up now with tourists taking in the view, as recommended to them by the guidebooks and concierges in search of a tip, so they moved to an empty bench away from the crowds. Tom lit another soothing cigarette.

'That'll kill you, that shit,' said Jason.

'Says the expert in killing,' Tom replied.

Jason let out a brief laugh and shook his head. Tom recoiled in horror at how Jason could laugh at the mention of the word killing. Jason wanted to know how Tom had ended up here. He told his brother how he had hung out in the park for a night and this guy had befriended him. How he was holed up in a flat near here.

'Really?' said Jason. 'Interesting. Is he an arse bandit or something?'

Disgusted, Tom realised he had already said too much. There was a silence. There were more pressing, important questions. He plucked up courage to ask them and they emerged in a torrent.

'What the fuck was that all about Jason? The car? Why did you do it? Where are you hiding?'

Jason sat in silence for what seemed to Tom like an age.

'It was for Rachel.'

'Rachel? Why?'

'After what those fucking dirty Pakis did to her. Worse than the Afghans.'

Tom sat there stunned for a moment. He never had Jason down as a racist. Not like that.

'I was sickened too, Jase. Fucking outraged. Sickened to my gut. But I would never have thought of taking revenge like that.'

'So how would you have taken revenge?'

Tom didn't know. He actually hadn't thought about revenge, though he wanted the rapists brought to justice.

'Exactly. You didn't have a clue. Police weren't doing anything. Somebody had to do something.'

'But something so… so radical? Jesus. Jason. Killing innocent people. And with a flamethrower for God's sake? That is not revenge. That is just… barbaric. Where the fuck did you get a flamethrower from?

'Found out how to put one together on the Internet. Surprising what you can find. There's even an instruction video on YouTube. Bought the materials at various shops round Brum.'

Tom was shocked to see that Jason was now enjoying recounting how he had planned and executed it all.

'Did you like the overalls? People never stop blokes in blue overalls. Think they're workmen. Also picked a balaclava with the St George emblem on it. Make them think I might be attached to some right-wing party. Throw them off the scent.'

'And that car?'

'Nicked it. Over Bordesley way. During the night, Monday.'

'Where is it now?'

'Dumped it. Back street just south of the river somewhere. Found a tube station near.'

'But why do this in London? If it's revenge you're after, why not do it in Birmingham?'

'People only take notice of things that happen in London, don't they? The media, and all that. Once they link it to what happened to Rachel, might get these people found and prosecuted.'

'So why not go looking for those five?'

'How can I identify them if Rachel can't and the police won't? Need the DNA and everything.'

He leaned conspiratorially across to Tom.

'Reckon the coppers are sitting on it because they're frightened of upsetting Muslim leaders in Brum and it all kicking off there.'

'So what you doing now? Where you staying?'

'This is where you come in,' Jason said. He told how he had arranged a safe house in South London a week ago, got the keys of the flat off a bloke who was an old squaddie mate. Or at least he thought he was a mate. Turned out, the bloke had run off with the £2,000 Jason had stashed in a holdall under the bed in the spare room where he was staying.

'Can't fucking trust nobody now,' said Jason.

There was a pause before he added: 'This bloke you're staying with, Tom... he got any money?'

'Fuck off Jason. Jesus.'

'You are my brother,' came the guilt-trip reply, followed by a menacing: 'And you owe me.'

'How can I forget it? But this is just something, something... on another level. Another planet.'

Tom looked into Jason's face. Behind the bravado and toughness that his No. 1 cropped hair sought to portray, it was pleading. Desperate. He had never seen him looking so vulnerable. He would have to be desperate to take the risk of leaving his bolt hole and travelling the Underground.

'They're going to get you sooner or later, Jase. Why are you running?'

'What have they got? Me on CCTV in a balaclava. No one who can identify me. A car nicked in Birmingham with hundreds of different prints all over it. Made sure of it. The car will be on cameras in Central London but I could see them and I covered my face. They won't have a clear image of me.'

'But if they do make the link with Rachel,' Tom reasoned, 'you and me are going to be questioned...'

'I'll be long gone by then.'

'What about me?'

'Weren't you that did it, was it?'

'Where will you go?'

Jason said nothing and for a moment Tom was silent too. He was coming to acknowledge something that he had never thought would happen, however guilty, ashamed even, it was making him feel. He wanted his brother out of his life now. Eventually he broke the silence.

'Look, I'll see what I can do.'

'Good kid,' said Jason and got up. It was time for him to get out of here, he said. Tom said he would walk back to the tube station with him but Jason warned him against.

'You should get back indoors too. Just in case. And take this.'

He got some money out of a pocket and offered it to Tom. 'It's not the full fifty but it might help.'

'I don't want your money. Anyway, thought you didn't have any?'

'I've got enough to get by but not to get away.'

Tom looked down at the cash – two £10 notes. He then looked Jason in the eye, torn between disgust – for both of them – and sympathy. With the embers of brotherly love thrown in. He grabbed the money, to his shame, but couldn't bring himself to hug his brother. He set off abruptly in the direction of Saul's, turning just once to see Jason standing, hands in pockets.

When he got back to the house and turned the keys in the front door, he noticed the old woman again looking at him from behind the curtain before she recoiled when he saw her. What he didn't see was his brother standing 50 yards up the street behind a tree and watching him.

17

RASHID

RASHID felt unsure of himself and worried about doing something wrong. This would be his first Muslim funeral, one that would see five burials in one service, and so he would be leaning on Omar. As a boy, Omar said, he had been to his grandfather's funeral, though he remembered little. Rashid was not to worry, he added. The important thing was that they should attend. They had been at the scene of the murders, after all. They wanted to respect their fellow Mosque users and honour the dead. They needed to be part of a community of mourners.

It had taken two days to get to this point of a midday ceremony, delicate negotiations having taken place between Muslim representatives and the police, all conducted in the glare of media attention and national interest.

The police had told the board of the Mosque that it was unlikely they would be allowed to use the site again this week. Naturally this provoked arguments, gratefully reported by the media. Print journalists were happy to be assigned to the proper, frightening news of the last couple of days, to dig for information about the murdered and to interview experts on Islam, racism and right-wing terrorism rather than have to fill the front of the paper with the celebrity trivia that market research too often dictated now. Radio and rolling TV news had something to get their teeth into beyond phone-ins and massaged government figures and press releases.

The Mosque, the police had reasoned, was a crime scene, and forensic work needed to be painstaking. It was, the board counter-argued, a holy place, and it should not be denied to its users for a moment longer than was necessary. They were especially keen to have it open for Friday prayers, which were attended by thousands. State and Church had often clashed in the past, but this was a new twist, one for which the Metropolitan Police had no training, even if they did individually take day courses in how to respect and interact with the Muslim community.

The families of the five men who had died in the Mosque had wanted them buried as soon as possible, even on the Monday itself, in accordance with the teaching of the Prophet Muhammad. 'Hurry up with the dead body,' he had written. 'For if it was righteous, you are forwarding it to welfare; and if it was otherwise, then you are putting off an evil thing down your necks.'

The police just could not allow that, however, with post-mortems essential in such a murder case. Five different senior pathologists had been brought in to perform the examinations as quickly as possible and the arguments had continued all day on Tuesday. Such delays and procedures had always been contentious and the Muslim Council of Great Britain had been working with the authorities for some while. A body should not be tampered with, according to Islam, but they accepted the law of the land while continuing to negotiate to see if a non-invasive procedure like an MRI scan could be used instead.

In the end, under growing pressure from politicians and religious leaders, and with the Prime Minister personally speaking to the Met Commissioner, the police had relented by the evening as the glare of the news spotlight intensified: they consented to the funerals being held on the Wednesday. Reporters standing outside the revolving New Scotland Yard sign also advanced the theory of the nebulous 'some people' ever present in news reports who were saying that they wanted public debate to cool down before the bodies were released.

They were also making plans for funerals that would inevitably be high profile and potential flashpoints for clashes of extremists, of whatever political or religious persuasion. Why, after all, would a post-mortem be needed when the cause of death was obvious? The police insisted they might glean more clues about the type and model of the flamethrower from the nature of the injuries to the corpse and match it to those sold recently. Of course, Muslim leaders replied, we want the murderer brought to justice and will co-operate.

The compromise deal meant that while the bodies were released, the Regent's Park Mosque remained closed for now. And so the five were taken to the East London Mosque at Whitechapel to prepare them for burial in the tradition. One of the largest mosques in Europe, it was also able to accommodate 7,000 people at a time. More than that number wanted to pay their respects and pray, and queued to do so.

In private ante-chambers on the Tuesday night, the families had come to perform the *Ghusl*, the washing of the bodies, and the *Kafan*, wrapping the bodies in white shrouds, comprising three pieces of cloth. They were tasks that wives were permitted to undertake but only one of them could stomach it, given the blackened state of the bodies. Instead, brothers and cousins had fulfilled their duties for the other two parts of the ritual, the funeral itself, the *Janazah*, featuring the central *Salat* prayer, and the *Dafan*, the burial itself.

Ordinarily, the funerals would have been conducted at a Mosque but such was police concern, not only about conflict between right wing groups and Muslims, that they insisted the ceremonies be conducted at the same place as the burials, the Garden of Peace in Hainault, an Essex suburb of the sort to which East-enders had aspired to escape for generations, ceding their old homes to new waves of immigrants, first from Europe, then from Asia. It would be easier to keep order there, said the police. While that was true, it clearly had something to do as well with not wanting East London and its commercial activities to grind to a halt. Access would be easier for all, they pointed out. It was, after all, the largest Muslim cemetery in Europe. Today would be far from easy, however.

Omar had driven from his own home in Kilburn to pick Rashid up at Stanmore at 10am for the midday ceremonies. It should have been about an hour-and-a-quarter around the North Circular Road and up the A12 before cutting up towards Fairlop tube station towards the end of the Central Line, giving them plenty of time to park up and prepare themselves. Omar had worked it all out. After sitting in a queue of traffic for half an hour with a couple of miles still to travel, however, and with the funerals due to start in half an hour, Omar decided to turn into a residential side street and park his Mini.

On the main road, they joined a column of similarly pressed-for-time Muslim men – all men; only women family members could attend the funerals, if not the burials, and they were already at the cemetery with the hearses. Rashid was smartly dressed in white *kurta*, cotton trousers and black *kufi* but many simply wore jeans. He and Omar followed them down what would be the main road leading to the Garden, Forest Road. There, at Fairlop station, where hundreds more Muslim men were arriving, Rashid could see that police had closed the road ahead to traffic. They clearly wanted an exclusion zone but it didn't help latecomers such as Rashid and Omar.

The whole area was tense and large numbers of police had been deployed in response to Internet anger and message boards, particularly those among the English Defence League threatening to turn out in force at the entrance to the cemetery. It was as well, with so many walking along Forest Road, that a line of police, two every 50 yards or so, stood as sentries.

The road was flat and they passed playing fields on their left and a sailing lake on their right. After 15 minutes, Rashid saw people turning left 100 yards ahead into a side street, Elmbridge Road, and the main entrance of the cemetery. He was sweating by now as the heat of the day reached its zenith. The informal procession slowed as they reached the entrance due to the volume of people and Rashid realised – and heard – why he could see a huge police presence.

All morning, the web and Twitter had been abuzz with details of the funerals' location and invitations from white right-wing organisations to attend a demonstration against yesterday's killings in Regent's Park. They seemed to have overlooked Monday's massacre, which prompted and provoked the retaliation.

In the event just 50 or so men – all men; this was deemed not to be women's work – turned up to spew bile. All but the hard-core knew they would be outnumbered and their bravery did not extend to this scenario. The potential for violence, indeed mayhem, was high but they were kept at bay on the pavement opposite the road into the cemetery around double that number of police, who had in fact given them this controllable area as a sop, to stop a wildcat appearance elsewhere. There, the police could also form a guard for mourners at the entrance to the Gardens. This was a thick blue line. All was being monitored by TV cameras – and police cameramen, too, for their records and any potential inquiries.

Rashid and Omar glanced in the direction of the 50 as they passed but had no desire to look directly at faces screaming abuse about filthy foreign hypocrites and murderers. Rashid was sure in a previous life he had read something in the Bible about motes and beams but would not be reminding them of it, nor engaging any in conversations about no religion being able to legislate for the misinterpretations of individuals or the hatred and personal agendas of lone wolves. He certainly did not want his face to be remembered. Later, there would be no police guard in a residential street two miles away when they returned to the car.

The pair had made it just in time as the service was about to start. It would be in the open air in the car park next to the prayer hall of the copious complex and people crammed around the shrouded bodies lined up on the ground at the back of hearses with their rear doors opened. Men spilled on to the bridge over the water feature that led to the burial ground, sought vantage on every path. One or two younger men tried to climb on to the roof of the wooden tea bar, closed today, until their fathers told them to get off.

There would be no preferential treatment, though naturally the families were given room to stand at the feet of their dead. Rashid and Omar were at the back of several thousand people, though thankfully for them, the prayers of the five Imams were to be relayed on loudspeakers.

With their backs to Mecca, they went through the *Salat* funeral prayers as ordained, calling out all four *Takbeers* and two *Salaams*. They took in the *Thana*:

> *Glory be to You Oh Allah, and praise be to You, and blessed is Your name, and exalted is Your Majesty, and there is none to be served besides You.*

They said a *Dua* for each man:

> *Oh Allah! Forgive those of us that are alive and those of us that are dead; those of us that are present and those of us who are absent; those of us who are young and those of us who are adults; our males and our females. Oh Allah! Whomsoever You keep alive, let him live as a follower of Islam and whomsoever You cause to die, let him die a Believer.*

All sought the forgiveness of the dead, to be followed by supplication for the dead and mankind as a whole. Rashid was fascinated. He did as others did, moving his arms when the more experienced did, turning his face towards the right and left shoulders when appropriate. There was neither bowing nor kneeling, however. Weeping among the women of the family could be heard but there was no wailing. It was decreed, frowned upon.

The ritual lasted some 30 minutes and the bodies were returned into the hearses, the crowds parting to allow the fleet of five to drive up to the freshly dug graves several hundred yards away where the *Dafan* would be conducted. Rashid and Omar followed the procession, men willingly united in a necessary community outpouring of respect. Such was the size of the burial ground, and the slowness with which so many people moved, that it took 20 minutes to reach the graves, where Rashid was surprised to see a yellow JCB digger, incongruous, at odds with the air of spirituality.

He thought how cold and bleak it would be here in winter, with bushes and saplings still not fully grown, as they passed row upon row of graves, all similar, all simple, just a semi-cylindrical mound of earth no higher than one hand width, each mound topped with a small green marble plaque bearing just the deceased's name and dates of birth and death, in both Gregorian and Hirji calendars. This was year 1433 after the arrival of Muhammad. Displays of adornment were not permitted on the graves in accordance with a general principle of Islam that had attracted Rashid: icons and emblems should not be allowed to come between man and Allah.

The graves, as ordained, were perpendicular and aligned to Mecca, the *Qibla*. Brothers and brothers-in-law took the traditional 40 steps carrying the bodies to the graves from the hearses and lowered them, one by one, with ropes into the neighbouring plots, ensuring that they were placed on their right sides, facing

Qibla. The gravediggers had prepared five sets of three spheres of packed soil, the size of cricket balls, as props for the head, chin and shoulder and the relatives delicately, lovingly, climbed down ladders into the graves and set them in place. Planks were rested on the bodies so that the soil that would later envelop them would not touch the bodies.

For each one, an Imam recited a verse from the *Qur'an*.

We created you from it and return you unto it. And from it we will raise you a second time.

Rashid and Omar were too far away to hear it properly, especially when a dog barked in the back garden of one of the residences nearby or a duck quacked beside the water channel running through the grounds. They knew to join in, though, for a new recital of the *Dua*. Normal practice was for each participant to put three handfuls of soil into the grave according to the Prophet but practically it had to be limited to families, such was the throng.

One final prayer towards Mecca begged for forgiveness on behalf of the men and it was time to depart as the JCB moved in to scoop the banks of earth back into the ground on top of the bodies. There was little milling around, little chatter. Reverence was imperative. Rashid and Omar again followed the throng back to the main road, keeping the silence.

As they all departed, some were willing to talk to the TV cameras about the disgrace of Monday's atrocity, though less willing to discuss yesterday's revenge attack. A few did, decrying the man as un-Islamic and not acting in their name. Some were still angry from Monday. Many called for calm and perspective. Had the first not occurred, had the provocation not been so outrageous, then the second would not have happened but given where we all were here and now, they said, we should not provoke more anger.

Suddenly, one of the TV reporters, his cameraman in pursuit, rushed towards Rashid. Clearly he stuck out, a white boy – though actually one of several dozen – in a sea of hundreds of black and brown faces. Rashid declined the offer to speak and hurried on with Omar, back down Forest Road, past Fairlop station and back to the Mini and the transport chaos that the area would face for several hours. Thankfully, the police had given them space to escape while white, banner-waving right-wingers were retained and restrained in the ire of their pen for the duration of the dispersal.

In the car, as it crawled back towards the North Circular, Rashid and Omar sat in silence, humbled by the day's events. Rashid was a new Muslim and felt he should have nothing to say; indeed, had nothing to say. Or at least he thought he didn't.

18

JAN, DEENA

JAN had not been in this pub for years, even though she lived only a couple of miles away. Had never really wanted to come back after it ended. Too many memories, most of them bad. Too many associations with Frank and his job – and hers – when they used to meet here, it being convenient both for her place and for Paddington Green nick where he was based then. It hadn't changed much, she thought, as she waited for her order of an orange juice and a pint of bitter, half an eye on a TV showing a news report and footage from the Muslim funerals. It was still a proper old backstreet London local, big and untouched by the modern penchant for turning them into tourist bistros.

She took the drinks to a corner table, though it was not so much the corner that appealed as the fact that it was the most private spot in the place, the nearest tables a couple of yards away and its occupants unlikely to overhear their conversation. It had been a while but she guessed Frank still preferred bitter and she thought it would loosen his tongue, well worth the outlay even though she could no longer claim it on expenses. If she did, she would have to name him on the exes form and that could be a sacking offence for him these days in the wake of cases involving so-called corruption of public officials.

Soon he arrived, saw her in the corner and walked over. The pecks on both cheeks were formal rather than warm. Her choice, not his.

He saw the pint. 'I can't drink this,' he said. 'Not any more.'
'You given up?'

'I gave it up a while after us,' he replied. 'Actually it gave
me up.'

'I see,' she said. She was impressed. She watched him pick
up the drink and carry it at arm's length – careful not to spill
any of the beer over his hand – deposit it on the bar and order a
mineral water.

'You bring a girl to all the best places,' said Jan on his return.
'The Butcher's Arms? Something a bit weird about that after the
last couple of days, isn't there?'

Frank didn't get it at first, then clicked and remarked about
what a sick sense of humour journalists had. He hoped she didn't
mind meeting here, he said, given their, um, history. She said no,
it was fine, though it wasn't. Walking back into the place had
given her butterflies in her stomach and she wished she hadn't
agreed. But then again, she was glad she had. She was curious
about him after all this time. And she had a professional reason
to be here, as well. Frank, meanwhile, was hoping that coming
here might ignite some old feelings.

'I've had business at the Green,' he said. 'It made sense.'
That bit, amid the maelstrom of sexual dynamics and emotional
tension between them, was true. And no, he added after her
enquiry, it was not something he could share with her just yet.

Jan smiled. She liked the 'just yet'. It meant that he was here
to share something, just not that, whatever it was. But then she
knew in agreeing to the meeting that he would be throwing her
a bone in the shape of a story that the Met wanted out there. She
couldn't just be here for old times' sake.

'See you got a bit of a scoop yesterday,' Frank said. 'Got a bit
bored. Checked your website. Created a bit of a stink our end…'

'I am guessing that is your way of saying well done? What is
it with men and an inability to give a compliment?'

'Did hear from someone there that you weren't flavour of the month. You must be back in favour after yesterday, surely?' he asked and she shrugged. 'It was nice to hear from you. Been a while hasn't it?'

She knew this moment would come, when he would hint plaintively at the affair, and that it would come early in the piece. She was ready for it. It had lasted almost a year, some ten years ago, and was largely about two people who really didn't want to go home alone after long days at work and short but intense bouts of drinking. At least, that's how she recalled it. She was now having flashbacks of it being more meaningful than that.

Jan stopped herself. 'Different times. Different rules,' she said. 'We can't be seen to be, what shall we call it, backscratching these days, can we?'

'No. But I wanted to see how you were. What you looked like, to be honest. You look good.'

'Thank you. And you look better. Slimmer. Calmer.'

'That'll be sobriety. Not that things are calm at the moment...'

Bittersweet episodes flashed through her mind but she had no desire to reprise them. It had hurt her too much. Even if there was a moment of melting at Frank's softer manner and appearance – with a sheen to his less florid face and sharp features and a smoothness to his salt-and-pepper hair – she had no need for a man in her life.

'I'm in counter-terrorism now. DCI.'

'I heard. Well done you. And you have something for me, yes?' Jan asked.

'Are you on this story then? Am I talking to the lead violinist or just a member of the orchestra?'

'I am not on this story, Frank. I am all over it. At about ten tonight online you will read another rather juicy exclusive. And I intend following it up with more.'

There was a pause. He noticed in Jan a fire in her eyes of a decade ago.

'You've got it back, haven't you?'

She smiled at him. Yes, she had.

'OK,' he said. 'We've found the car.'

'Bloody yes,' she said. 'Where?'

He took a brown envelope out of his pocket and slipped it across the table. Jan picked it up and took a look around the pub before opening it. She noticed she was being watched by a man at the bar, but was reassured when he quickly looked away from her 'not available' eye contact and began staring at his phone and tapping at it. She withdrew the picture carefully. It was of a car, a dark blue Honda Accord, with number plate clearly visible. She turned it over to read the street name and postcode. She tried to look and sound relaxed about the information but inside she was screaming with the anticipation of another huge exclusive.

'Why are you not putting this out to everyone?'

'We are,' Frank replied. He looked at his watch. 'In about two hours. You've got till then to put it on the Internet.'

'And why are you giving this to me? Aren't you going to get into bother if you are found out to be the leak?'

'Nah. They want me to do it.'

'How come?'

'You're back in favour with us too. We're getting a bit fed up dealing with rookies who get the wrong end of a story. And have nothing to give us back.'

'Even though I got that stuff out of the PC?'

'Wouldn't worry about that. Was coming out anyway. There was, shall we say, a grudging respect for it. All a bit how it used to be down the Yard. You and us. Mixture of confrontation and co-operation.'

Jan remembered it well. Frank sipped the last of his mineral water.

'It's not all nostalgia. We like your website. Gets millions of instant hits. Press conference is for more detail and follow-up material. Now make it sing: "This is the car used to drive flame-thrower killer," that sort of thing. Stay in touch, yeah?'

'You can bet on it,' she replied and he flashed her a smile. As she watched him go, she noticed a young black police officer in uniform enter the pub and approach the man at the bar who had been tapping into his phone. She had a quick word, the man nodded towards Jan and before she could move, the police-woman was sitting down opposite her.

There was a tense moment as Deena stared at Jan, who was initially bemused but quickly recognised the woman.

'Remember me?'

'Yes, I do,' said Jan sheepishly.

'You got me the mother of all bollockings.'

'I'm sorry about that.'

'No you're not. You only cared about your story.'

This was true, although Jan did have a pang of conscience about the girl. She knew what bollockings could be like, even if these days she did not let them wield the same power over her that they had had when she was a reporter about this girl's age. As long as they didn't come with formal warnings.

Jan sought to buy herself time, aware that the longer the woman went without speaking, the more likely her anger was to subside. She offered to buy her a drink. Deena thought for a moment and then agreed. Why not take something off her after what she had done? They were good in here. This was a coppers' pub. They accepted police in uniform and nobody grassed on them or bothered them. Not that it mattered with teetotal Deena. She asked for a coffee and one that would put Jan to some trouble.

'Tell Ted I want a proper filter coffee, not instant,' she said.

Jan went to the bar and had to wait as the barman, having rolled his eyes, went to the kitchen to make fresh coffee.

'She's a good kid and she didn't deserve that,' said a voice next to her.

'What's it got to do with you? What do you know about anything?' Jan replied, suddenly defensive.

'I was there. I'm her oppo,' said Darren.

Jan now recognised him too. 'Well, she's a grown woman. She should be careful about giving away things. I told her I was a reporter.'

'Yeah, and you also told her you already had the info. But you're right. She's learned a lesson. Shame that being helpful gets you into trouble, but there you go. She's green but she's good. Popular, well liked. Wants to be a detective.'

A faint smile came on Jan's face and she looked across to Deena, who was checking her messages on her mobile.

Ted returned with the coffee.

'OK, I get the picture,' said Jan, handing over payment to Ted. She picked up the coffee and returned to Deena, speaking first in a further attempt to disarm her.

'Thought you might be assigned to the Muslim funerals,' she said.

Deena saw through it. 'East London and Essex responsibility. What were you talking to Darren about?' she asked.

'I wasn't talking to him. He was talking to me. Or at me,' said Jan. There was another pause, Jan now in an unfamiliar position. Normally, she waited for interviewees to fill an uncomfortable silence. Deena was not about to let her off the hook that easily, however.

'Is there anything I can do to make it up to you?' Jan asked.

Still Deena said nothing, leaving Jan to stew in a guilt that evoked her local paper days when she had once covered an inquest into the death of a teenager and got the cause wrong because she had been too embarrassed by her ignorance to ask the coroner after the hearing to explain the details to her. The boy's family had been upset that the whole of the community had been misinformed and Jan had been deeply sorry. Just as

Deena was undoubtedly going to be wiser for all this, it had been her own early career lesson. That lesson was to be brave enough to ask the questions a reader wanted answering, so hang your ignorance and pride. She also learned that she should deal with, and respect, grieving families by getting the story right on probably the worst day of their lives.

The reason Jan had not felt this way for so long had been down to a growing insensitivity and a relegation to the Internet fodder of stories that no longer mattered. That and so rarely getting out of the office these days on actual stories that she no longer met the public she was supposed to be writing for. Eventually Deena spoke, calmed by caffeine.

'I can't think of anything right now,' she said. 'But I can see you squirming so at least you have some sense of what it has been like for me.'

Jan did not want to look at her own watch for fear of upsetting the young woman again. She had a story about a car that she needed to file. Instead, she stole a quick look at Deena's wrist. She began to rummage in her handbag and took out a business card and a pen.

'I have to go right now,' she said. 'Here's my card.'

She wrote her mobile number on the back to complement her direct office line and slid it across the table to Deena.

'Contact me on that number if you need anything.'

'Need anything? I can get in more trouble talking to you again. I only risked it because Darren told me you were in here and I wanted to see if you felt bad about what happened.'

'I do,' replied Jan, a little surprised that she did. She liked the kid's feistiness.

Deena looked at her and paused before placing the card in a pocket of her uniform.

Jan smiled, nodded and got up to leave. She offered her hand and though Deena hesitated, she shook it.

Walking out into the hot Paddington afternoon, Jan suddenly began for the first time in a long while to look forward to going to the office. For now, she would sit in that little park on Warwick Avenue overlooking Little Venice and write the car story for the website.

After that, while they were still impressed, she would hit them again with an email to Vickers ahead of the key conference of the day in the Editor's office. She could imagine the Editor purring as Vickers outlined the story she had been holding back for 24 hours now. By the evening, the blue Honda would be all over the TV news but the paper would have an exclusive: the Jewish boy turned Muslim and his account of that hellish day at the Mosque.

Jan may have rediscovered a vestige of humanity but she was ever going to remain at heart a journalist. And she was full of quiet pleasure at being in the centre of a big story again, a big player in her profession once more.

19

SAUL AND TOM

SAUL had barely closed the front door to the building when the door in the hall to Mrs McIver's opened. He said his usual 'Hello, how are you?' to which he received his customary, 'Fine thank you Mr Bradstock and yourself?' and was in the middle of his 'Yes, OK thanks' at the bottom of the staircase when he was stopped in his tracks by an unfamiliar question.

'Would he be a relative perhaps?' she asked.

Saul was stunned and could say nothing momentarily as he continued to look up the stairs. He felt a racing of his heart. His being motionless gave Mrs McIver the opportunity she was seeking to press on. Now nearing 70 and alone, Mr McIver having died 10 years ago, leading to her converting the top floor and selling the apartment to Saul after his divorce, she welcomed the stimulation of curiosity amid the routines of her life.

Saul turned to face her. His shopping bag was heavy and he wanted to put it down on the floor but to do so would be to suggest to Mrs McIver that he was willing to stop and chat for a while.

'The young man. Coming and going from your flat today?' she continued.

Coming and going? Saul had explicitly told Tom not to go out. What the hell was he playing at? He could not let Mrs McIver see either his anxiety or his annoyance, however. Instead he smiled.

'Thomas?' (Best to give his real name now to avoid tricky moments later.) 'No, not a relative. My Godson. Son of an old friend from years ago. Not seen the boy for years but he was in London and in need of a bed so I agreed to put him up. About time I fulfilled my duty, I thought.'

Saul looked her in the eye. Mrs McIver's expression betrayed scepticism but Saul knew it was a plausible explanation and was pleased with himself for thinking it up on his feet. Perhaps a little guilty for her nosiness, she assured him she was only concerned about his flat as she had not seen the lad before. He thanked her for her neighbourliness.

'Shocking week, Mr Bradstock,' she said. 'I hope all these people are finished now and they don't keep attacking each other.'

He smiled again, said 'Indeed' and thanked her once more for her concern about his flat. As he walked up the stairs, he heard Mrs McIver's door close behind him.

Once inside his own home, he found Tom sprawled on the sofa glued to a TV news channel. There was footage of the Muslim funerals from earlier that Saul had also seen while at the Marsden. Saul stood there for a moment as the picture flicked from a group of angry young white men, to a less angry young white man wearing a black skull cap and white tunic and cotton trousers, offering a polite smile but shaking his head at a request to talk to the reporter.

'Really sad,' said Saul.

'Yes,' said Tom, suddenly sitting up, embarrassed by his own slovenliness. 'How did your, um, treatment go?'

'It's radiotherapy and it went OK thanks. How was your day?'

'OK. Not done a lot. Been watching the news mostly. I've been worried there might be another incident out there somewhere today but it seems quiet so far.'

'That's the British for you,' said Saul. 'In every area of life, a crisis occurs and they pull back from the brink. I'm hoping sense will prevail now. Tea?'

Tom said yes and thanked him for his kindness. Saul disappeared into the kitchen, set his shopping on a counter and turned on Radio 5 Live as he put the kettle on. He would normally have been listening to Radio 4 in the late afternoon but he wanted to hear any breaking news. He was also wanting Tom to tell him that he had been out today, rather than confront the kid and force it out of him.

Tom followed him into the kitchen and watched him as he went about making the tea. There was a silence between them and Saul knew that the boy was brooding, preparing to say something.

'I'm a bit worried,' Tom said finally. The radio intervened.

Some news just in. A newspaper website is reporting that the Metropolitan Police have now found the car used by the man who burned to death five Muslim men at the Regent's Park Mosque on Monday. The dark blue Honda Accord was discovered among some derelict warehouses off the Old Kent Road in South London early this morning. Police are now examining the vehicle for clues as to the identity of the man who committed the atrocity.

Tom and Saul stared at each other intently for a moment, shocked, before a panic gripped Tom.

'Jesus. What the fuck am I going to do?' he blurted out.

'Go to the police?' said Saul.

Tom bolted into the living room, pacing the room. 'No. No, I can't.'

'But they'll find something to connect you. It's only a matter of time. It'll work in your favour if you go now.'

The firmness of Tom's reply startled Saul.

'I just fucking can't, OK. Not now. And anyway, what's it going to look like for you if I do? Harbouring an accessory...'

Saul thought about it. The kid had a point, though that wasn't going to stop him pushing Tom into doing the right thing. Now just wasn't the right time.

'All right, take it easy,' Saul replied. 'Did you wear gloves when you drove the car?'

'Course not. What is this? The golden age of motoring or something? What reason would I have to wear gloves? And in summer?'

'Have you ever committed a crime? Been fingerprinted by the police?'

'No… Well… No.'

It was the 'well' word that alerted Saul.

'What does that mean?'

Tom spoke softly, in his embarrassment. 'I once nicked some cider from a corner shop.'

Saul let out an involuntary laugh.

'All right, all right,' said Tom. And couldn't help laughing himself. The tension, the seriousness of the situation, would not dissipate that easily, however.

'Did you leave anything of yours in the car?' Saul asked.

'No, nothing. I only had my phone, wallet and tobacco. I thought I was driving straight home again.'

'Then there's nothing to connect you with this, is there? Besides, they haven't mentioned a second man yet, have they? They're just looking for the man who did it.'

Tom began to calm down, went back into the lounge and sat back on the sofa. Saul had by now turned down the volume on the radio and TV so they could hear themselves talking and he could see a man talking to a newsreader on the news channel as the news bar at the bottom of the screen repeated: '**MOSQUE MURDERER CAR FOUND…**' They cut to a police press conference that was about to start.

'Cake, I think,' said Saul, needing to find some normality

again. He went to his shopping bag and fetched out a coffee and walnut cake, serving it to Tom with his tea.

'I'm going to put a beef casserole in the oven for supper,' said Saul. 'Come and sit in the kitchen with me while I'm doing it and we can talk.'

Tom obeyed, and followed him into the kitchen, sitting on one of the two chairs and setting his tea and cake on a small table in the window that looked across the small back gardens of the neighbouring flats and houses. He was growing ever more grateful to this man. He had felt on edge for most of the afternoon after the appearance of his brother and his demands for money. He had to broach the subject with Saul at some point but his heart pounded every time he thought about it. He ate the cake, sipped sweet tea and felt better.

Saul had wanted him in the kitchen to get him away from the TV and the news, away from the worry. He still didn't quite know himself why he was helping the kid. Tom was right. The boy was an accessory to murder and Saul was leaving himself wide open to perverting the course of justice. He was less worried for himself than for this sorry, hapless figure, however, and justified his sheltering of him by telling himself that he might actually be helping the situation in trying to persuade Tom to go to the police and talking, rather than scaring him into flight, and so ultimately bringing about justice. The authorities would surely understand that when it came to him being charged with anything.

In truth, in a place he sensed but did not yet properly acknowledge, Saul was enjoying the company despite himself and his professed love of silence and solitude. The crowds could indeed be maddening and he often thought about going to live in Dorset to be far from it. These Olympic Games, though, had made even him question whether he was an island.

He had told himself that he was content about the many days when he went without hearing an adult voice, apart from on

147

the TV and radio, or a shopkeeper or Mrs McIver or a publisher on the end of the phone wondering when the corrected proofs would be ready. A sociable adult voice, that was. He had come to feel comfortable with his daily routine at the Marsden, where he was on first-name terms now with receptionists and radiographers. But then he would retreat to his man cave again, glad he was not exposed to the crassness of Jolly Jack with his fear-concealing laughter for more than half an hour a day.

Tom – Saul realised, lying awake last night – had also given him a purpose, a cause. He read, he walked, he listened to the radio, he watched TV and he thought plenty. It was a safe enough existence. But it didn't have a goal, a product, and the boy had provided him, a father manqué, with somebody to care about, something to worry about. And he realised he had missed a bit of worrying. However, complications always arose, he knew. People had this annoying habit of not behaving how you wanted them to. Or dying on you. It was why he had avoided friendships and relationships for so long. Somehow, he felt more inclined with this kid to risk his life of routine and familiarity being disturbed so dramatically.

He knew he had to ask Tom about him going out today. Not quite yet, though. He first pan-fried the stewing steak in the casserole pot, adding salt and pepper and flour, an Oxo cube and boiled water to form the gravy. Tom watched intently.

'You cook, Tom?'

'Just stuff like eggs and frozen chips. My mum or Rachel always did the proper cooking.' Tom quickly clammed up.

'Is she the girlfriend you mentioned?'

'Was. Not seen her for a while.'

'Want to tell me what happened?'

Tom didn't really but the old man had shared his stuff about his ex-wife. And he needed to give him a picture, to understand about Jason, so that he could maybe sweet talk him a bit to get some money out of him and get Jase off his back.

Saul put the meat in the oven and began preparing carrots and leeks. He might even ask Tom to peel the potatoes for the mash.

Tom's story stopped him in his tracks, though. He told of the night of the rape. Of having a drink with Jason and receiving Rachel's text. Of the police station and the scenes. Of how scared and brutalised Rachel was and how, to his shame, he couldn't handle it and how he hadn't been able to see her since. And how full of rage Jason was.

'I'm so sorry, Tom,' Saul said softly when he was finished. 'I can hardly begin to understand how you feel. What an ordeal. Poor girl. Poor you.'

He let his words hang in the air for a while, until it felt appropriate to ask the question that had occurred to him.

'Why would Jason be so angry?' Saul asked.

'I wondered that myself,' said Tom. 'He felt for me, I suppose and for her. He liked her, I think.'

'But to murder for something that happened to your brother's girlfriend?'

'I know. We're obviously more different than I thought. He was always angry, volatile, but this is something else.'

'Is he a racist? Got something against other people's religions?'

'I never thought so but he was a soldier in Afghanistan for a while. I guess he saw some stuff out there, though he never really talked about it. Least not with me. Picked up on the odd remark lately that shocked me. About the Taliban, calling people Pakis, that kind of thing.'

'You love him?'

'Of course. He dominated me when I was young but he always looked out for me.' Tom stopped, contemplating the day it happened, after which he knew he would forever be bonded to Jason and in his debt.

'He loved me too,' Tom continued. 'I know he did. Does. He always preferred my bikes and toys, though. Said I got better ones than him because I was brighter. Mum loved me better he reckoned because she always wanted a clever son. I just think she worried about me a bit more because I never had a dad. At least Jason had one for a few years.'

'You blame yourself for your father leaving?'

Tom grew sheepish. He had obviously thought about it.

'No. Maybe.'

'It wasn't your fault, you know,' said Saul. 'He left because he felt he needed to, for whatever reason, and nothing you did or said caused that. You do know that?'

Tom did with his head but was unsure in his heart. It was deep in him not only that he had lacked a father figure, but that his very birth had caused his father to leave. Rejection at both an initial and ultimate level. He at least liked Saul acknowledging that it might have crossed his mind. Saul broke the silence again.

'Why can't you go near Rachel now?'

'I don't know really. She feels… tainted to me.'

'And to herself, I suspect. Poor, poor girl.'

'It sounds horrible, I know, but she feels… dirty to me. I hate myself for not supporting her, but I also fucking hate the idea of those men having sex with her. I know she didn't choose it and she did nothing wrong but I just can't seem to forgive her.'

'As you said, she did nothing wrong so what's to forgive?' said Saul, not expecting an answer. 'Anyway, forgiveness is for ourselves, not for the other person.'

'How do you mean?'

'If we don't forgive, then it's us who suffers, not them. Our bitterness and resentment will eat us away eventually.'

Tom hadn't looked at it that way. He would need to absorb that. 'You know,' added Saul, 'life really is an echo chamber.'

'What's that mean?'

'Everything that we do, everything that happens to us in our formative years will carry echoes in our later years. All the experiences will colour and inform our actions. We will feel the same feelings, of fear and pain and anger and jealousy. Shame. Even pleasure, when we get into similar situations. We will hear the echoes. The best we can hope for is that we learn to act and react better, or at least more productively for ourselves and others, when we hear those echoes.'

'OK…' said Tom, not sure that he understood. Saul suddenly grew self-conscious.

'Better do these veg,' he said, turning his back to Tom.

'I need a big favour,' Tom said.

'Oh yes…?'

'Jason's been in touch.'

Saul stopped slicing carrots and turned around. 'Have you met with him?'

'No. Um. He rang me.' 'Really?'

Tom knew he needed to come clean. There had been a growing honesty to their conversations and the guy deserved the truth. He also wanted to tell it. Tom told him of the text summoning him to the meeting at the tube station, the walk on Primrose Hill. And Jason wanting £2,000.

'I think we need to give it to him,' said Tom. 'Or he will dob us both in.'

Saul was angry, both at Tom for leaving the flat and for meeting Jason. And the fact that he was now being blackmailed.

'You are bloody joking,' he said in the way it emerges from mouths even when people are clearly not. And Tom was clearly not joking. 'Two grand? *We* need to give it to him? *WE*?'

'He wants to go abroad.'

'I'll bet he does. Me helping to get you away from a crime scene and working out what to do next is one thing. That's because I believe you are an innocent caught up in it. You are, aren't you?'

Tom said nothing but nodded slowly.

'Giving money to a murderer is something else. And how come you refuse to turn him in but he seems to be willing to turn you in?'

'So you're not going to do it?'

'Of course I'm bloody not. And you need to stay in this flat.'

'Yeah? I do, do I?' said Tom, growing angry at being told what to do, at being controlled. He got up and made for the door, making sure to pick up the spare keys from the hall table as he left.

Saul shouted after him but the door slammed and he could hear the stomp of steps down the flight of stairs into the hall, through the front door and out into the balmy North London evening.

He looked out of the window, watching Tom head up the street, unaware that Mrs McIver was doing the same one floor below, and cursed himself. Saul thought about going out to find him but realised how dangerous that could be if it created a public scene. He feared for the kid and what he himself had got into with him.

20

JAN

JAN poured her third flute of Moet, filled a bowl with Kettle Chips, and settled down on the sofa in her White Company waffle robe to watch the BBC news, first checking her Twitter feed. More than 12,000 followers now; not bad. There was a 10pm embargo on the newspaper front pages being shown and it was the time the papers' websites also began to showcase their best stories.

In the old days of... well, actually not so long ago, the first edition would carry some less attention-grabbing front, a dummy, just so that rivals were thrown off the scent of a scoop. Nowadays, with the potential for a story being broken given that there were so many news outlets, it was about being first, getting it out there. She still had trouble understanding why papers spoiled their own front pages, mind, by putting it out on the Internet and thus maybe killing sales in the morning, but it was all about hits and clicks now, traffic to show to advertisers.

'Cry havoc and let slip the dogs of war,' she mouthed, enjoying the thought that right now, in newsrooms across TV, radio and papers, not to mention the la la land of the websites who played at being newsrooms, reporters were being stung into action by her story, forced to follow up as she so often was with other outlets' material. She liked this feeling of doing unto others before they did unto her, as one of her old editors put it. She came over all nostalgic.

Congratulatory emails had filled her inbox in late afternoon just ahead of the Met's press conference after the appearance of the found car story. Vickers naturally basked in the glory of the Editor's rare praise for him. Jan was one of his staff reporters after all. He had deployed her, he told the Editor... He just had an instinct, he said. Just call it good old-fashioned newspaper work.

The piece on Rashid, the Jew who became a Muslim and had witnessed the full horror of the Mosque attack, had prompted something even rarer. The Editor had emerged from his office in early evening when her copy dropped, strode across the editorial floor and deposited on Jan's desk a bottle of Moet tied with red ribbon, still chilled having been sitting in his office fridge.

'This,' he said in a booming voice, turning to the troops, 'is for a proper fucking reporter. Read her piece tonight and weep. And none of you bastards leak it to any of your mates on other papers before it's on the site, right? Instant sacking offence.'

Jan feigned modesty. She accepted the peck on each cheek from a man who had once tried and failed to grope her at a Christmas party. Her survival when Vickers had threatened final warnings had not just been because she had something on the Editor, though, but because of days when she had delivered, like today. Even though it had been some while. And when allowed. She smiled and enjoyed the plaudits from those colleagues secure enough in their own abilities to congratulate her and endured the silences from those envious.

Probably the most treasured moment came from Vickers.

'I'm glad I sent you back out there,' he said. 'But you still had to pull it off and to be fair you did.'

'Thanks,' she replied, knowing that there was bound to be something else. It was Vickers's attempt at a joke.

'Next time,' he said, 'see if you can get him on video for the website. On your phone will do.'

He smiled. She didn't. She wanted to remind him of how she had kept telling him what she had learned in her training: that news is people and came from talking to them, not from sitting at computer terminals. No need, though. She was in a strong position now. Why start an argument? Keep powder dry. Best also to gloss over the fact that she had to fight – even risk the sack – to be allowed off the leash and back out into the world. Vickers made or broke you. Fortunately, astutely, Jan had always known how to bend rather than break.

Instead, she asked Vickers about maybe getting those warnings expunged from her record, so that she wasn't so vulnerable to the sack. 'Let's not get ahead of ourselves,' he had replied with a grin. The bubbly was now finally medicating the anger that discretion told her she should stuff down at the time.

Some poor duty reporter on the BBC's '10' had indeed been forced to assemble a hasty piece about Rashid's account of seeing a man wielding a flamethrower working his way through the Mosque. To give it gravitas and immediacy, they had the reporter doing a question and answer with the newsreader about whether the witness's account might now help with the killer's capture. They even had to credit Jan and her paper. No avoiding that with an exclusive like this one.

Naturally the BBC couldn't lead on it. Didn't have time to prepare. Their top story was the funerals of the five dead Muslims and more detail about the white people killed in the revenge attack. Besides, it was somebody else's story, no matter how good, and no organisation wanted to lead on the success of others unless there was nothing else. And there was plenty else.

Jan listened to the reporter quote from her piece, giving detail of Rashid's account of the murderer directing his flame-thrower at the five people then making his escape through the back of the Mosque. And a question occurred to her: Why just five people when there were a hundred around the prayer hall?

Her mobile buzzed to sidetrack her. 'Brilliant Babe,' read a text from a girlfriend. 'Never lose it,' said another.

'To me,' she said, lifting her glass. She decided to fill the 20 minutes before *Newsnight* with a trawl of the Internet. There on the paper's website was her news piece as the lead on the home page. Alongside was a link to the backgrounder on Rashid. It looked good, and would get millions of hits around the world, certainly millions more than the circulation of the paper itself. But still she would never get the same frisson from a computer screen as seeing her name in print, seeing people reading it. Once she would have wanted to scream: 'That's me, that is.' Now, she enjoyed the quieter satisfaction. In the old days, she would be in the pub at the back of the old office just off Fleet Street, nicknamed The Stab In The Back, celebrating with colleagues, swapping war stories. These days there were fewer people left to drink with. Shifts were so long, the Internet so demanding, that by close of play – not that there ever really was one now – tired brains and bodies just wanted to get home and curl up in front of the TV with a drink. For many, Jan among them these past few years, wallowing alone in the soul-gnawing desperation of it all with a bottle of wine seemed a more attractive proposition than weary, feigned camaraderie.

In the rush of today, she had felt an excitement and energy that she wanted more of and for which she came into the business. Getting the story out of Frank, getting it over and on to the website, then applying the *coup de grace* with the Rashid interview had been among the finest moments of her career. After ordering the deserved Chinese takeaway earlier, she had even permitted herself a vision of being at the Grosvenor House Hotel, at the British Press Awards, next March sitting nervously at a table hosted by the Editor expecting to be named News Reporter of the Year.

Now, as the maudlin side-effects of the Champagne region's finest insinuated themselves in her body, she began to suffer from the post-scoop blues, questioning herself, her profession and her *modus operandi*. She had felt it before, late at night after 7/7 when the professionalism of simply getting the story, the stories, out there subsided and the humanity returned. Those poor victims. Being bombed underground. What a shocking way to die, so brutal and terrifying. She shivered at the very thought.

She needed another glass of Moet and reached down to the bottleneck by the side of the sofa. She tried to divert herself again by googling her own name and up came the story, hastily being followed up by everyone. She didn't mind the other papers doing it. It was the game. There was no copyright on news. They stole from each other. There was honour among thieves. And she didn't even mind these sites that were trying to be thoughtful alternatives to mainstream media and their commercial, vested interests that sometimes made you wonder what you were reading, the subtext, and why it had been written with that angle. No, what she detested was all these bloody sites that passed themselves off as news-gathering organisations when all they did was pay kids to rewrite stories they had ponced. The kids needed the work, the pittance, and were desperate for bylines to put in portfolios to get proper journalistic jobs one day. Content fucking harvesting.

She googled Rashid Johnson's name and up came a similar list to that for her name. For the first time that day, she wondered what his reaction might be. But he had said those things, hadn't he? She hadn't made anything up. She just reported them. Should she have told him she was a reporter? She told that young policewoman. But he wasn't a public official. She couldn't observe and overhear and tell everyone that she was working, could she? Being a jackdaw, stealing quotes rather than silver, was part of journalism.

When her mobile rang to startle her, she had to wipe a tear from her eye to see the name on the screen. It was Robert and she picked up. In her paranoia-pissed mood, he was about the only man in the world she would have picked up for.

'Hey you,' she said.

'Hey you,' said her brother. 'Are you sniffling?'

'No. Just a bit of a head cold.'

'You're going to have to do better than that. What's up?'

'Oh you know me. I always get like this on summer nights. Bit lonely, that's all.'

'Well, you've got your work to keep you going, haven't you? Just seen your name on the news. Congratulations.'

'Thanks. Bless you for calling.'

They talked for a while, about what a shocking week it had been in London and about how Robert was glad he was now in Edinburgh. The new job as a theatre manager was demanding, he said, and Gemma had her hands full with the little ones but all was OK. Was Jan?

She was, she insisted, and they wound up the call. Feeling better for the sound of a voice that loved her, her head cleared and she no longer felt sorry for herself. It suddenly came into her head that she recalled having wondered aloud to Vickers about this second man, a driver, something she had pushed to the back of her mind given all the events of the last 36 hours. She found her notebook and pen and began a to-do list.

She was buoyed too, by the buzz of a text on her mobile. 'Class is permanent,' it said. It came from Frank Phillips. Ringing him became item two on tomorrow's list.

In Middlesex, another mobile was taking texts but they would not be discovered until the following morning. Rashid had long since turned it off. The funerals had drained him mentally, physically and emotionally. He had performed *Isha,* the final prayer of the day, at 9.30pm in his bedroom and fallen asleep immediately afterwards, unaware of his new national celebrity.

21

SAUL AND TOM

IT HAD taken Saul a long time to get off to sleep and he was startled to be roused by the noises. Against the backdrop of the midnight news on Radio 4 carrying more detail on the young Muslim who had told his story, he had lain awake wondering and worrying about Tom, having begun to feel almost paternal towards the boy but fearing that he was being lied to. He began to drift off to the geography of the shipping forecast after the ever-soothing strains of 'Sailing By'.

The sounds seemed to be coming from his living room. They were rhythmical, high-pitched emissions punctuated by deeper groans. He sat up in bed, alarmed, and came to realise what the noises added up to. It was sex. A woman was yelping as a man moved inside her, his groans the result of each thrust that provoked her pleasure.

Saul was about to get out of bed to force his angry frame upon the pair, having guessed the identity of one of them, but could not resist listening for a minute. He was partly embarrassed to be hearing it but intrigued too. Once he would also have been excited but the Zoladex designed to suppress his testosterone and injected into his stomach ahead of the course of radiotherapy meant that any excitement was faint. For now, he could achieve a semi-stiffness but he knew that even that would not be for much longer. It was chemical castration, though they were never quite that graphic in describing it at the hospital.

He heard the couple climax and suddenly felt an overwhelming anger. He rose quickly from his bed, threw on his dressing gown and burst through his bedroom door into the lounge. He turned on a light to see a woman lying on top of Tom, spent, regaining her breath. The sofa bed was pulled into position but not made. They had clearly not bothered in their eagerness.

'What the hell...' Saul shouted.

The girl screamed and grabbed some clothes from the side of the bed to cover her breasts and pubic hair before finding her bra and knickers.

'Who the fuck is this?' she shouted at Tom.

Tom scrambled off the bed and dragged on his underpants.

'Charming. I happen to be the poor sod who owns this flat,' said Saul.

'Shit,' said the girl, dressing hurriedly in short skirt and T-shirt. 'Now I know why we couldn't go in the bedroom.'

There was an awkward couple of minutes while she sorted out her clothing and gathered up her handbag. All the while, Saul glared at her but she avoided his eye. Tom sat in an armchair in just his Calvin Kleins, embarrassed. After what seemed like an age, the girl slipped into a pair of flip flops on the way with as much dignity as she could muster, before exiting, her footsteps echoing on the stairs before the front door of the building slammed.

Saul stood staring at Tom, who looked back at him sheepishly. This was not the time to tell the kid that he was relieved to see him, glad that he was OK. It was instead the time first to be angry that Tom had taken the risk of going out, an anger designed to mask his own fears about life without him now. It was then the time to feign anger at Tom bringing a girl to the place, an anger designed to mask his envy of Tom's youth and virility.

'Well?'

'Well what?' said Tom.

Saul was baffled as to how he could pick up a girl and take her to a virtual stranger's flat what with all that had happened but he came to a conclusion about him searching for comfort, about ports and storms. He was going to insist on Tom explaining, though, and Tom ran tetchily through his story. He had met the girl at a pub, they had got on OK and after a few drinks he had asked her back here. She lived with her parents and they couldn't go back there. And she wouldn't do it anywhere out in the open. She was quite classy like that.

Saul wanted an apology for the lack of respect towards him and his home and Tom duly delivered one but they were both going through the motions. Tom was only a bit sorry. He had needed to get out, to drink and smoke, to release some tension. Saul was upset, irked rather than enraged as he probably had every reason to be. His feelings were more about regret.

Tom offered to make Saul a mug of tea. He was getting to know the old man.

'Normally I'd say no as I'd be pissing all night but go on then,' he said.

It was almost 2am and a bleary-eyed Saul looked out of the front window on to the street. The only movement was an urban fox's haughty, cruel scavenging patrol. He sipped Tom's tea gratefully, though could not resist comment on its insipid colour, wondering whether the tea bag and the hot water had exchanged as much intimacy as Tom and the girl.

'What was the girl's name?' Saul asked. 'Kelly,' said Tom.

'Well, at least you were on first-name terms.'

'I only really went out because you pissed me off,' Tom added. 'I wasn't planning that. One thing led to another.'

Curious, Saul told him, how terminology changed a lot these days – wicked meaning good, for example – but young people still used some quaint old phrases, like 'one thing led to another'.

'Well,' said Tom, 'At least you didn't come out with another of them – "what time do you call this?"'

Saul smiled. 'Why didn't you just get away?'

'What, on twenty quid? That's what Jason gave me.'

'Might have got you back to Birmingham. Cheap if you take a slow train from Marylebone. Or you could have hitched a lift. What brought you back? And what's keeping you here?'

Tom had clearly been pondering that himself. There was a silence.

'I thought about it. I could have gone for your sake, really. So you're not involved in this mess. But I like it here. I guess I feel safe. It's weird. I feel like... like, I ought to be here for some reason. What's out there for me?'

They smiled at each other. Saul felt a human connection he had not felt for a long time. It was comforting, warm, but also worrying. It carried responsibility in its undertones.

Tom interrupted the moment. 'Can I ask you something?'

'Sure,' said Saul.

'This treatment of yours... Is it painful?'

Saul smiled. It was funny. He had always thought cancer treatment would be gruelling, as the adjective always had it, and chemotherapy most certainly was, with its needles and cannulas and infusions of heavy-duty chemicals, often for hours, that could strip heads of hair, pubic areas indeed. He had also thought that early in the radiotherapy, he could feel a burning sensation on his hips around the tattoo dots on to which the beams were trained.

'No it's not painful. It just wearies me. And worries me.'

'Are you frightened you're going to die?'

Saul liked the kid's directness. 'Yes and no,' he said.

He sipped his tea and thought about it.

'Sometimes I wake up in the night, or at 6am, in a sweat. Hot flushes are partly a side-effect of the drug I'm on but also due to anxiety attacks. I worry about all the things I may never do, or never do again now. I've got a list of them. They're not big, high-energy, bucket-list things, like trekking up to Machu Picchu or parachuting. They're the achievable things. Like writing a novel.'

'Well, you know a lot about them,' said Tom.

'That may be the problem,' said Saul. 'Readers often make the worst writers. They can get paralysed by knowing too much, get writer's block. Perfectionism can kill creativity.'

'Sounds a bit of a cop-out to me.'

Saul smiled at him, pausing before saying it. 'And sex. It scares and depresses me to think I may never have sex again. That's why...'

He suddenly became aware that he was sharing too much on something so intimate with someone he had met just a couple of days ago. And nearly 40 years younger. And he might also be bringing the boy down when he had so much to look forward to in his life, even if Tom himself wasn't seeing it like that currently. Just now, his life felt empty with few prospects. He was not to know, as Saul did, that things happened, life changed. If you just held in there long enough to allow them to happen and change.

Saul continued, unable to stop himself, having had no one with whom to voice the thoughts that beset him in what the South Americans called the 'dead time', between midnight and 6am when decisions should not be made.

'On other days, I think that I've had a good life and done lots of good things,' he said, 'travelled enough. Been blessed in many ways. And when I think that some people lose their lives instantly, in car crashes – or flamethrower or gun attacks – unaware they are about to die, I can't work out if that is a good thing or not.

'Me? I'm being prepared for death gradually. I get to sort out my affairs, spend my money, though you never know how long you'll live and so how much you're going to need. It's always a juggling act. I can't decide if that's better, though. If it's a good thing that you know it is coming slowly. The honest answer is I am afraid some days, some times of day, and not others.

'The older I get, the more precious I realise life is. So precious that I actually want to be bored and for it to pass slowly, rather than it be exciting so that it flies by. I want to savour it, its sadness and its pain. There is lasting contentment in that, rather than the fleeting attraction of fun. There is almost a disdain for it in the young, a belief that it will just go on and happens to someone else, someone older. You hear about death, you fear it but it is remote. Now it seems closer, much closer. Maybe my fear of death that I carried as a younger man is gradually leaving me and I guess I should be grateful for that.'

Tom took all that in and there was a silence between the men.

'You believe in God?' Tom asked.

'I believe in a power greater than me, something spiritual that wants us to fulfil our potential as human beings. What you're really asking me is if I believe in an afterlife?'

'I suppose I am…'

'Well, then I do. Too many people want tangible evidence, won't believe the teachings of faith, the books written on it, even holy books. But if you look at most religions – Christian, Muslim – they all have a supreme being and an afterlife at their core. Are all the billions of people now and in ages gone by going to be wrong? Takes some kind of arrogance to refute all that.'

There was a silence, broken by Tom.

'Wow,' he said.

'Any of that make sense?' Saul asked.

'Put it this way. I think I might try and remember it.'

Saul felt gratified. And he was pleased with his own insights, wondering where it came from. He was being taught things through the cancer and its treatment, he realised. Maybe that was what it was for. Sometimes he went through a teary 'why me?' stage but here in the early hours, it dawned on him that his predicament might not only be for him to arrive at some peace with himself, but to pass something on. To someone like this kid who had been thrust into his life.

Tom's appearance had also prompted Saul to ask himself whether he would trade wisdom for youth, the moments of knowledge and understanding for the energy that in his 20s and 30s, and even 40s, he could not conceive of ending. To exchange his financial stability and acquired experience for Tom's uncertainty and health. Tough, tough decision, he thought.

'Just two more days of your treatment,' said Tom.

'Yes. I'm looking forward to it and I'm not,' Saul replied. 'It's been good for me to get out but it's tired me out.'

'I'm sorry about today,' said Tom, 'maybe tomorrow will be better, eh?'

'Well, tomorrow is today now,' said Saul. 'And we need to work out what the hell we're going to do with you and how we sort this whole mess out.'

He looked Tom in the eye.

'Tell me,' he said. 'Tell me truthfully. Did you really not know what you were doing that day when you drove your brother to London? Did you not have any idea what he was going to do?'

'I promise. I did not,' said Tom.

Saul did not avert his gaze. He simply nodded his head a couple of times.

Tom actually maintained eye contact too. Shit, that's a bit of an adult thing to do, isn't it? Only when Saul took a sip of his tea, and when he himself began to think about Jason and the money – the issue and argument that had sent him out into the night and not gone away despite the grown-up conversation that had just happened – did he look away. Saul could not know why he needed that money as the next instalment of a lifelong debt.

PART IV

THURSDAY
AUGUST 16TH
2012

22

RASHID

NO MATTER how much the funerals had moved and drained Rashid, causing his early night and swift descent into sleep, he could not let any of that distract him from his duty and the first prayer of the day. He had set the alarm for 4am to perform *Fajr* at the appointed hour of 4.04 and gone through the ritual on his prayer mat in his bedroom, well used now to kneeling towards Mecca.

He tried to get back to sleep and dozed for odd minutes but the images of the previous day repeatedly assailed his mind's eye preventing a return to a deep sleep. He recalled the words of his mother the night before: 'Well, it's your first encounter with death, isn't it? You're bound to be upset.'

When the shafts of August sunlight poked through the gap in the curtains he looked across to the digital alarm and noticed the time: 5.46am. Knowing that he would sleep no more, he performed the next part of his morning routine. While the early prayer may have made him different from the majority of his contemporaries, this one made him similar to most young people. He picked up his mobile from the bedside table and turned it on.

It lit into life, searched then found its network. It rang immediately with the number 121 demanding attention. It also buzzed its messages and whooshed its emails. Rashid was surprised by so much activity. He hastily looked at the texts, mostly of the 'What were you thinking man?' and 'What was all that about?' to 'Did you get any money for it?' Baffled, he went through the voicemails, the early ones making little or no sense, asking why he was speaking to the papers about his ordeal on Monday. Well, he wasn't. He didn't know what they were talking about.

Then he came to a message that had come in recently, around 5.30am. It was from one of the Mosque's board members. They had been allowed to open the office and the library for staff, though not the prayer hall to worshippers yet. Could he please come in for 10am as the director would like to talk to him.

He went to his computer at his desk and googled his own name. He knew the references to both Richard and Rashid Johnson almost by heart, there were so few. Now he was stunned to see that there were pages about him. Chief among them was an 'exclusive interview' with a national newspaper.

He called up their website and saw it there in full. It contained his account of Monday's horror, his words in quotation marks. There it all was: being dumbfounded initially... wondering what this guy in the balaclava was doing... not realising it was a flame-thrower he was carrying... of feeling guilty at failing to stop him... of gazing on in horror as people he recognised – or once did – were on fire... the scene of devastation in the Mosque... the flamethrower man running from the back of the building.

He read his own story with growing incredulity, his disbe-lief increasing when he saw his picture that had been screen-grabbed from the Mosque's website. He wondered where they got hold of all this stuff and racked his brain. He had only really spoken about this to Omar and he wouldn't have sold this to them, would he? Surely not. After all, Omar had been one of the people texting him and asking why he had done this. Unless Omar was bluffing. He suddenly felt bad at his own cynicism and lack of trust.

Then he recalled that nice woman who had spoken to him as he stood gazing across the street two days ago watching the police go about their business. He had been touched by her concern at the time. Now he wondered anew about her inquisitiveness.

He scanned the website article again and saw the picture next to the words 'EXCLUSIVE: By Janet Mason' at the top. Yes, that was her. He slumped forward over the keyboard of his desktop and began to weep. He had let down his Mosque, Islam itself. He suspected that there might be some with doubts about this Jewish boy who had converted – reverted – and there might be some who would want him expelled. Was that the right word? Did they even excommunicate people in the Muslim religion? He guessed that he might well be about to find out this morning.

After another 45 minutes of browsing the Internet and seeing himself all over Facebook and Twitter, as well as media sites, he put on his dressing gown and went downstairs. His shock had given way to anxiety and some green tea might help. His parents would not normally be up before 8am but his mother clearly heard him make his way along the landing and was alerted.

Rashid, his anxiety heightened, turned with a start in the act of putting on the kettle as she spoke from the entrance to the kitchen.

'Rashid, what's wrong?' she asked, addressing him by the name he had requested, hurtful as it had been for her.

He looked at her and tears slowly trickled down his cheeks. He covered his eyes in shame and began to sob.

'Oh my Richard. What is it?' she said rushing across the kitchen to hug her son, instinctively returning to the name she had given him the day she had brought him into the world.

They heard something tumble through the letterbox of the front door.

'I think that might tell you,' said Rashid.

He knew they took the newspaper concerned. They were Middle England – living in a suburb where it was financially still just about viable for newsagents to deliver – and so was the publication.

His mother went to the door, where their paper was looking up menacingly from the mat. She scanned the front page and read its banner:

MY FLAMING HORROR

Beneath was a picture of Rashid and she gasped, putting her hand over her mouth. She continued to stare at it, reading the few paragraphs of text as she slowly walked back to the kitchen where Rashid was sitting with his mug of tea at the breakfast bar. He handed a breakfast tea with milk to his mother. She handed him the paper.

It looked worse in print than on website, where layouts were the same no matter the story – big headline, often long and wordy, then picture, copy running down a page with all manner of cross references and other stories to divert around it. In print, on the front page of a paper, it stood alone. It screamed. It would be on the breakfast table of many, in the hands of many more on trains and buses around the country. And his picture would linger longer in print, would make him more recognisable for longer.

The few punchy paragraphs on the front turned into the paper, on to four more pages. They had made his stolen quotes go a long way, by using more pictures from Monday. There was a story on his life so far, gleaned from his potted biography on the Mosque's website and told of his previous name, Richard, and the details of school and university – with pictures of them. It had him shaking his head that anyone would take notice of such ordinariness. There was another story alongside about a car apparently driven by the killer having been found in South London.

'Some people on the board of the Mosque want to see me this morning,' he said looking up from the paper at his mother and sipping his tea.

'Are you in trouble?' she asked.

He shrugged his shoulders.

'But why did you give the interview?'

'I didn't,' he said tetchily. 'I thought I was talking to someone kind, who was taking an interest. Turned out to be a journalist.'

'I see. I'm sorry,' she said, feeling guilty for having doubted him. 'Whatever happens, you will still be loved in this household,' she said.

Rashid smiled, a brief smile of gratitude, and finished his tea.

'Better go and shower,' he said.

As the water cascaded over him he wondered what he might say to explain himself. His 'crime' had been inadvertent. Surely they had to understand that? And he thought again about the woman from the newspaper and what he might say to her if he ran into her again. In fact, he would make sure he ran into her again. He would ring her, maybe even go to the paper to confront her.

He dressed, putting on a clean, crisp tunic over his chinos. He looked out of his window. Today would be hot, oppressive even. He prayed, for Allah's forgiveness and strength from the Prophet Muhammad (peace be upon him). It was not necessary outside of the scheduled times but he felt the need for as much spiritual help and guidance as he could get today. He felt better, more ready.

Downstairs, he ate some muesli and drank some orange juice, kissed his mother on the cheek and she wished him well, reassuring him that this house was always his haven. As he walked through the door and into the sunlight, a calm came over him, a gratitude at being alive, especially when he recalled those who were not. Not even the double-takes of one or two of his neighbours as they came out of their houses to walk to the tube station, already suspicious at his way of life, could upset him.

He could not fail to be unnerved, however, as he sat on the train opposite people reading the very newspaper that carried his picture on the front. He noticed at least three peer over their paper at him. Or was he just feeling conspicuous? At Wembley Park, he got out of the carriage and walked to the end of the platform and waited for the next train. He hoped to find peace and less embarrassment in an emptier carriage at the back. As soon as he sat down, he realised it was a mistake. More space simply made him stand out more to those already there.

'You're that geezer, aren't you?' said one boy among a group of three teenagers, his voice pregnant with accusation. As if Rashid had done anything wrong. 'On the front of that bloke's paper over there.' He pointed to a man reading the paper, who in turn looked at his own paper's front page then at Rashid.

'What was it like seeing all them blokes frying?' asked the kid, his hair long on top and shaved at the sides, a ring going through his lip. The other two, wearing a similar uniform of baggy jeans, T-shirts and trainers, laughed.

Rashid said nothing but shot glances around the carriage to see that he was now being stared at. Fortunately, only half a dozen people were around to stare but it was enough to make Rashid flush with embarrassment. St John's Wood station could not come quickly enough and he dashed up the escalator past the ornate art deco lampstands and out into the street where he gasped for breath and gulped in great helpings of air.

Rashid bought a bottle of water and sat at a table outside the Beatles Cafe next to the station, watching for a while the young tourists as they headed towards the nearby Abbey Road recording studios to recreate their own version of the LP cover on the pedestrian crossing and hold up traffic, to the annoyance of London cabbies and their own disappointment at the suburban ordinariness of the location. His own mood was now sombre, replacing his earlier eagerness to get this resolved. Anxiety had overtaken anticipation.

He checked his watch. Just 10 minutes to get there now. He got up and headed down Wellington Road towards the Mosque.

His walk was a mixture of pace so as not to be late, and hesitation, concerned by how he might feel at returning to the scene of the crime.

A young policewoman stood at the entrance on Park Road alongside a colleague and he looked at her nervously. He showed her his ID and she smiled at him.

'Thank you,' he said, his humanity overcoming his mistrust of the police these past months. 'And thanks for the smile. It's the first one I've seen since leaving the house this morning.'

'We met on Monday, didn't we after... it?'

Rashid looked at her and remembered.

'Yes we did. Yes... I was a bit out of it. Thank you for your help. My name is Rashid.'

He offered his hand and Deena shook it, puzzled again that a white man should have the name of Rashid and wondering what had propelled him into this community.

'No problem,' she said. 'I'm Deena. Are you feeling better?'

'I guess so. As well as possible, anyway.'

'Yes of course. Sorry.'

'No, it's OK,' he said.

He smiled at Deena, who returned it and ushered him through. Deena watched him go.

'Seems like a nice guy,' said Darren.

'Yes, he does, doesn't he?' said Deena.

As he walked into the reception area, Rashid could see the prayer hall still cordoned off ahead of him and the bookshop closed to his right. To his left, the stairs permitted access to the first floor offices and library, though police officers were still patrolling. He climbed nervously to the top of the staircase where Rafiq at the reception desk eyed him with half a smile and motioned him to sit.

He did not have long to wait. Clearly they were ready for him and wanted to see him quickly. Rafiq ushered him into the room and his eyes took in three men around a table, a fourth chair waiting for him to occupy it.

'Sit down, brother,' said Dr Ahmed Ramaan, the director general of the Mosque, wearing a neat black suit and white open-neck shirt. Rashid had often seen his benign face around the Mosque but now it was altogether more serious, even if his tone was not harsh. Rashid was seeking any signs of their mood. The other two, wearing more traditional Muslim apparel of long flowing white *kurta* robes and *taqiyah* crocheted hats, one colourful the other plain black, said nothing.

'How are you? It has been a difficult week for us all,' said the director once Rashid was seated at one end of the table.

'I am ... well. All things considered. Thank you,' said Rashid.

'Yes. All things considered. Indeed. It has been the darkest time in the Mosque's history,' said Dr Ramaan. 'Anyway, we have had something of a discussion about you. Some agree with me what to do about this newspaper article, others don't, but let us first hear your side of the story.'

Rashid began with nervousness in his voice as words tumbled out. He was sorry. He didn't know who the woman was. He didn't know that she was a reporter. He was sorry...

'Let me stop you,' said the director. 'Please relax. Tell us calmly.'

Rashid slowed down and related how he had been opposite the entrance to the Mosque on Park Road two days earlier watching, grieving privately, when he suddenly felt the presence next to him of the woman. She seemed concerned and asked him questions about himself and he responded in a spirit of openness at her concern.

'The article was very detailed,' said Dr Ramaan. 'It had pictures and personal information about yourself.'

'I didn't volunteer that. They must have found it on the Internet.'

'It is as we thought,' said the director, turning to his colleagues, who both nodded. 'We understand your discomfort with all this and we feel for you.'

'You do?'

'We are not unsympathetic, hardline men,' the director went on. 'And we are aware of what grief does to people. We also seek to be tolerant of modern ways, to understand the demands and methods of the media and life today. The family day on Sunday was part of that.'

Rashid could feel the tension in his body begin to slip from him. This was all very encouraging, though he wondered if it might simply be a prelude to delivering bad news.

'After what happened on Monday, the temptation for us is to withdraw into our world. We are all horrified by what this man did. But then, we have extremists of our own, as we saw on Tuesday. This man did not stand for us or represent us but the public will see it that way. And again we are seen as some kind of crazy fundamentalists instead of the peace-loving people we aspire to be.'

The other two men in the room nodded.

Dr Ramaan paused and rose from his seat, walking to the window to gaze over the courtyard and the remnants of police and their specialists going about their business.

'The feedback to the article from younger Muslims on message boards has already been very positive,' he said to Rashid's astonishment that he, they, would be aware of what was on message boards.

'Far from thinking that you have betrayed the cause, many believe you have advanced it. You spoke movingly and from your heart. You mourned your brothers appropriately. As a Jew who has reverted to Islam, you are a new and modern face for us.'

This had now taken an unexpected turn and Rashid was disarmed.

'We think there is more you can do, if you are willing,' added the director. 'We want you to be an ambassador for the Mosque. How would you feel about that?'

Stunned was how Rashid felt. 'So you're not throwing me out then?' he said.

All three of the board members laughed.

'We do not, to use your word, throw out our own,' said Dr Ramaan.

Rashid thought about the request momentarily.

'Well, yes. What do you want me to do?' he asked.

'Well, since you have the ear of this journalist, maybe you could do another article about how and why you reverted?'

Rashid was unsure. He had been angry with the reporter earlier and did not relish talking to her again after what she had done. He was being asked to rise above it for a greater good, however; being given an opportunity to demonstrate forgiveness and spiritual growth.

'OK,' he said. 'I will do it if it will help Islam and the Mosque. Thank you for using me in this way.'

'Good, good,' said Dr Ramaan. 'We will contact you further. Thank you for your time.'

Rashid took it as his cue to depart and he smiled and thanked them, nodding at Rafiq on his way back down stairs.

'You look happier now,' said Deena as he reached the Park Road exit she was still patrolling.

'Yes, things have worked out well,' he replied, excited, barely slowing down to talk to her.

'Glad to hear it,' she said. She hesitated for a moment before adding: 'I'd be very interested to find out about what goes on here.'

Rashid, by now a few yards past her, suddenly stopped and turned back, walking up to her. He was an ambassador for the Mosque now, after all.

'Really?' he said. 'I'd be happy to tell you, if you'd like to talk more?'

'I would yes. I get off shift at around 2. Want to meet for what – some tea – later?'

Rashid was surprised at his own forwardness, and then hers, but he had learned something this week about seizing life and its moments. He had been grateful for her smile. And such an attractive smile. She wasn't the whole of the police, certainly not the part that had been so underhand with him. He realised he wanted to see her again, and share with her what he had discovered in his time so far at the Mosque. And here was a chance to spread the word of Islam, on a personal level, he told himself as justification.

'That would be very nice,' he said.

She took out a pen, ripped a piece of paper from her pocketbook, wrote her mobile number down and handed it to him.

'Thanks,' he said. 'I'll text you where.' He walked off, contentedly.

Deena turned to a smiling Darren.

'What?' she said as he shook his head, smiling.

She liked the look of the guy all right and her interest after first meeting him had increased on seeing him again. And apart from his name, she was intrigued by something he had said the other day, something he had probably forgotten: 'I was once one of you,' he had said. 'But I wasn't.'

23

TOM AND SAUL

THEY both woke late, Tom not until Saul had brought him a mug of tea. He sat up and drank it as Saul switched on Radio 4 to get the 10 o'clock news, which led on the blue Honda and police carrying out forensic examinations. They shot each other a glance but said nothing. The newsreader noted, with some relief in her voice, that it had been quieter on the streets overnight, the police comfortably able to deal with any vigilantes and malcontents, from both right-wing white and Asian groups. Woman's Hour was quickly into its stride and Tom wondered why Saul would listen to a programme with that title.

'I used to say I liked to know what the opposition was up to,' Saul joked but it fell on deaf ears. 'We'll turn over at half past 10 to get PopMaster on Radio 2.' Saul was expecting the kid to perk up but Tom did not seem to view that prospect as much of an improvement. 'You know, Ken Bruce? It's a pop quiz...' Tom's response was to request a change of station to Radio 6 Music.

With the Britishness of a host, Saul agreed in sullen silence. His acquiescence was also due to an embarrassment about his loose tongue of the early hours and he didn't want the boy to think too harshly of him. Tom had abused his hospitality by bringing home the girl and he, Saul, felt embarrassed? Funny how feelings did not necessarily reflect fact. They sat in the silence for 10 minutes or so, drinking tea. A song came on that Saul recognised.

'I like this one,' he said before the silence between them returned. He wondered now if the kid was thinking again that, rather than a helpful ally, he was some kind of weirdo, a port in the storm that had to be endured in the absence of anything or anywhere else.

'Look, I'm sorry about last night. This morning,' said Saul.

'Sorry?' Tom queried. 'What for? If anything I think I should be more sorry than I was.'

'I was a bit forward. All that love and death stuff.'

'No. Thank you for talking about it. It was interesting.'

'Really? I've been so short of company recently that I don't know what I should share or shouldn't.'

He was relieved at Tom's understanding and to learn that he could have a conversation beyond the banal again with another human being and not be ridiculed. His spirits lifted, it called for some celebratory eggs.

'Breakfast?' said Saul.

'Thought you'd never ask,' said Tom. 'I'll just take a shower first. That OK?'

Saul nodded eagerly, making sure that he heard the jets of water before he turned the radio off in the living room so that he could hear the one in the kitchen tuned to Radio 2, on which Ken Bruce was now making his usual fine fist of being interested in contestants' lives before the two rounds of questions.

He scored a mediocre 18 and 21 points on the questions by the time Tom emerged into the kitchen to wolf down the scrambled eggs and toast. Saul wondered what he might be doing today.

'Not going out,' he said with a smile.

'OK,' said Saul, smiling back, 'so what else?'

Tom looked around the flat. He might, he said, have a play on the computer, if that was OK, watch some TV, listen to the radio. What people usually do. He might even read a book. And play the guitar, write something.

'Look if you need to go out, to get some air or to avoid going stir crazy, then do it. The police don't seem to be on to you or to have connected you to the crime even. They seem more preoccupied with catching your brother, which is as it should be. But when I asked you about what you were going to do, I meant more about your brother, you and the police.'

Tom was annoyed. He knew the guy had been kind to him, and he knew the subject had to be addressed but he was secure here now. Why disturb that? Why did he need to do anything?

'Can't you leave it?' Tom asked. 'Everything's cool right now.'

'Is it? You don't think the police will get this sorted? Find your brother and then connect him with you? But it's not just about that. It's about doing the right thing.'

'Which is turning my brother in, is it?'

'Perhaps. Actually, yes it is,' said Saul with uncharacteristic certainty. 'He has committed a horrific crime and killed five innocent men. He should be brought to justice for that.'

Tom had turned on his mobile and plugged it into the wall to charge. It now buzzed in the other room with a text. He rose abruptly from the table and went to check it.

'Well?' it said.

Jason and his demands for money had slipped his mind amid the events of last night and early this morning. He suddenly felt anxious about getting money off Saul. He liked the man, and did not wish to rip him off, but it seemed the best way to get Jason abroad, and out of his life, their lives. Jason had been closing in on Saul too, simply by knowing the area where Tom was staying, and he didn't want his brother threatening the man. By getting Jason money, Tom reasoned, he would be doing Saul a favour too, doing right by everyone. Saul would understand.

He quickly texted Jason. 'Sorting it. Meet me at tube station 3pm.'

Tom returned to the kitchen. Saul sensed his concern.

'You OK? Who was that?' Saul asked.

'Oh, just that girl from last night. Should never have given her my mobile. Texted her back to say to leave me alone.'

Saul nodded wearily. 'Going to shower and get ready for the hospital,' he said and left Tom alone at the kitchen table twiddling his mobile in his hand.

Tom heard the shower spraying and crept into Saul's bedroom. He saw a jacket hung on the back of a chair. In an inside pocket, he found a wallet, which contained about £50 but more important, three debit and credit cards in one compartment. The front one was a debit card that looked well used; no good. Saul would notice that was missing. The back one was a credit card. Not great – troublesome for getting cash out – but workable if needs be. The middle one was another debit card, an instant access savings account. That would do best, though not without a PIN.

Saul was of the sort and age of a man who might remember one PIN, probably the well-used one, but not three and would thus ignore advice not to keep his numbers in his wallet. Saul would surely be careful about not losing the wallet or having his pocket picked so might be less concerned about keeping a set of numbers in there. Tom rummaged around. There in another compartment was a piece of paper listing numbers to bank cards. He matched the middle one to the relevant bank quickly enough, slipped the card into the back pocket of his jeans and keyed the PIN into the Notes app on his phone. He heard the spray of the shower cease and hurriedly returned the wallet to Saul's jacket pocket.

By the time Saul returned to the kitchen wearing his dressing gown and drying his hair, Tom was sitting at the table.

'That's better. Ready to face the day.'

'Your last but one, isn't it?'

'Treatment? Yes, it is.'

'What you going to do when it's all finished?'

'Hadn't really thought. Hope that life goes on, I guess.'

'It's all right for older people like you, isn't it? You got money, you got a place to live, you're comfortable. No worries.'

'No worries? Cancer not a worry?'

Tom suddenly looked sheepish.

'I'm sorry about that. Of course it is. I just meant…'

'I know. And you're right in many ways. I own this place now, mortgage paid off, with a bit of help from the sale of my old dad's little house. And I was lucky to buy it in the time before this area was this trendy and everywhere in London was so expensive. I tick over on spending money with the odd commission to edit a book. Got some savings and a bit of pension.'

There was a pause.

'But life is always a trade-off,' Saul went on. 'You get one thing sorted and another goes wrong. It's plate spinning, ball juggling. You get some order in your life then your body starts to let you down. When I was young, I couldn't see how it was going to happen – job, house and all that. But it does. Somehow it works out.'

'That's easy for you to say,' said Tom, an edge of resentment coming to his voice. 'That was how it was for your generation. We have to deal with tuition fees and no jobs when we finish uni. With debt and the price of houses, we've got no chance of buying our own place. I want to be a musician but how do you make a living at it these days? People want it for nothing off the Internet. It's not like Springsteen and Bowie and all them. People bought records when they were starting out. My generation will be the one that loses out. Your generation took it all. We just live with uncertainty.'

Saul was taken aback and stood silently for a moment.

'You don't think I live with uncertainty?' he said, his voice rising. 'You don't think I'd trade your uncertainty for mine? Yes, I'm lucky because I don't need money any more. My needs are simple. No car to cost me. I've travelled enough and just want a week away now and then. But I have had a huge health scare and I don't know now, from one day to the next, whether they'll zap all the cancer or whether it will come back and spread. It's living in me and all I can do is live one day at a time.'

Tom was embarrassed into not replying by his own ingratitude.

'Your time will come and soon,' Saul said to Tom, touching him on the shoulder as he turned to go and dress ready for his radiotherapy.

Tom's mobile buzzed with another text. 'No,' it said. Don't want to be clocked in same place twice. Meet me 3.30pm Regent's Park. Cafe called the Honest Sausage. Google it.'

In the threshold of the kitchen, Saul turned and watched Tom read the message, saw the look of puzzlement on his face, not knowing that the boy was wondering why the hell Jason would want to meet in that park, so near to the Mosque.

'And remember, Tom,' he said, 'the loudest voice, the external one that tells you what you should and shouldn't do, and what you should and shouldn't feel, is not always the truest.'

24

JAN

JAN noticed the turn in mood this morning as she made her way to her desk with her coffee. After all the appreciation of yesterday, led by the Editor's public feting, the reaction to her was now more casual. It was partly due to the 'interview' with the Muslim kid and the backgrounder going out on the website last night, along with all the TV coverage surrounding it also dissipating the impact, but down as well to the envy of some colleagues growing resentful of the week of exclusives she was having.

After all, in the eyes of a news editor like Ivan Vickers, her success merely highlighted their shortcomings, giving him ammunition to bollock them. She had been on the end of that logic herself in the past so knew that they might be viewing her with a mixture of resentment and envy. Passive aggression was the default attitude in a newsroom like hers. Except from Vickers. His was aggressive aggression, though at least you knew where you stood, she thought. Besides, newspaper offices did not live in the past, nor even the recent past. Not even the now. They lived, with the advent of the Internet, in the next 30 minutes and then the 30 minutes after that. Tomorrow's paper, once the single, glossy, goal? They would live in that tonight. It was only late morning.

She sipped her coffee and trawled through websites: the big ones, like their own, and *The Guardian*'s and *The New York Times*', the BBC. Had a glimpse at *The Huffington Post* with disdain. A bit early. Not much new doing beyond her own exclusive. No further update on the car. She made a call but got Frank's voicemail. She thanked him for yesterday and asked him to call her as she might have something for him. Her real purpose was to find out from him if he had anything for her but that would not be a sensible way of getting him to call back.

Vickers approached. She could always tell from 10 paces away when she was his quarry. He prowled, casting his long shadow, and she could smell his mood. Today she did not fear him, however. She had credit, money in the bank.

'Editor wants to see us,' he said.

She rose and followed him to the Editor's office, a copious, glassy room in the corner of the building with the best views out, on to the Thames and down river to Tower Bridge. There was a door off it into his own private dining room, in which Prime Ministers had troughed down the years. He was glued to a computer screen and barely moved his eyes to note Jan and Vickers's arrival. Being able to sense presences while carrying on doing the job, a skill Jan had also developed, was part of his armoury. He liked his employees to know they were not his priority, just part of his hectic schedule.

'Come in. Sit down,' he said, gesturing with his right arm for them to perch on one of the black leather sofas. They obeyed.

'How's my star reporter today?' he inquired.

Vickers looked at her darkly. She knew how to play the game.

'Getting good direction from my News Editor,' she said. Vickers approved and looked to the Editor for acknowledgement.

The Editor all but ignored it with a cursory 'Good', knowing bullshit when he heard it and using his preoccupation with his screen as reason for the apparent indifference to her reply. All this stuff had to be thought through. The dynamics of news-papers, now instinct to him and which Jan acknowledged, were important if the right atmosphere of creative tension that achieved results and made the paper pre-eminent in what used to be called Fleet Street was to be fostered.

He rose from his chair suddenly, taking Jan and Vickers slightly by surprise, and walked over to the window to gaze out at the Thames and Tate Modern on the far bank. Another technique: making yourself taller than your employees.

'Vickers had the press officer of the Regent's Park Mosque on to him this morning, didn't you Ivan? I didn't know they had one but I can't say I'm surprised. There's more of them than us these days.' He suddenly realised that what he had said might be misconstrued and added quickly: 'more press officers than journalists, I mean.'

Jan did not like the sound of this. Brilliance was temporary in this business. Bollocking was never far away.

'He said the Director General of the Islamic Cultural Centre wanted to speak to me.'

This was not getting any better.

'I duly spoke to the chap. Well you've got to, haven't you? He's a pretty big cheese by all accounts.'

He smiled at Jan.

'With all due respect,' she said, suddenly feeling a need to stand up for herself. 'I got that interview with the kid fair and square.' Well almost, she thought to herself.

'Pleased to hear it,' said the Editor. 'They seemed to rather like it.'

Jan was taken aback. She knew she had sailed close to the wind in not telling the boy who she was or whom she represented but once he had started speaking, she did not want to interrupt and she had quickly realised this was just too big a story to be dwelling on niceties. She was ready to give her speech, well rehearsed alone in her bed before the effects of a bottle of bubbly had knocked her out, about how she felt the end justified the means. She knew that Vickers and the Editor would privately agree too, even if they could not say so in public. She would accept any rap from the Press Complaints Commission, or whatever was succeeding it now that it was in the process of being closed down following the phone-hacking scandal. You don't get fired for being up before the PCC, she figured. You get fired for not coming up with stories.

In fact, now sitting before him, she recalled the Editor's regular attempt at humour but which carried a pointed message. 'There are eight million stories in the Naked City,' he would sometimes boom across the newsroom when in a bad mood late at night, citing the catchphrase of an old American crime series set in New York. 'And we haven't got a single fucking one of them.'

'Oh they like it? Can't work out if that's a good or bad thing,' she said. 'Are we doing our jobs if organisations are happy?' She smiled, trying to pretend that she wasn't relieved at being able to keep all that bluff and bravado about ends and means in reserve.

'Seems they want you to interview the kid again. About how he converted to Islam from Judaism. What life is like as a Muslim in modern Britain, that sort of thing. I'm in two minds. All a bit soft after we've had the exclusive today but sounds like something we should do for our public image and to keep them happy. They seem to think it will give a human face to their religion after all the grief they get about extremists. I suppose it could be a tale of our times, and you know how fond of tales of our times I am, don't you? You happy to do it, Jan?'

She was. There was something about the kid that interested her and she wanted to know more about his motivations and his life. And naturally she was not going to say 'No' to the Editor.

'Sure. Could make a good read.'

The Editor smiled. He liked that expression. 'Good. If you ring the press officer, he'll give you the young man's mobile number so the two of you can fix it up. Feels like a Saturday morning read to me so needs doing as soon as. I'm off to Chequers for the weekend tomorrow morning so will leave it with you, Ivan, all right?'

He nodded and he and Jan got up to leave.

As they walked back towards Jan's desk, Vickers was straight into her ear.

'The old man's going soft. Or must have got a shag last night. What's all that shit about?'

'I think it could be decent. As he's fond of saying: "Never underestimate the good read".'

'Good read? I want something hard in it. Newsy. See if the kid will sing a bit more about the bloke that torched the place. Get some more colour. I mean, your interview was all very well but it lacked some detail.'

'Do you know how tough that was to get?'

'I don't want excuses, Jan. I want results. And I don't want some fluffy feature about the acceptable face of Islam. The Ed said himself it was a bit soft. What about your police contact? Where are they at with the car? Can't afford to tread water, Jan. Yesterday is history. Actually, today is history. And when the old man gets grouchy later, he'll tell people exactly what I've just told you.'

He turned on his heel as they reached her work station, in search of his next victim.

'Wanker,' she said in a stage whisper as he left.

A young reporter sitting opposite her, one of the few youngsters with some respect for her even before all this, piped up.

'Has there been a day in your working life at this paper with him when you haven't uttered that word?' Ed Orton wondered from across the desk.

She smiled and then rang the press officer at the Mosque, followed by Rashid's number. The kid was not as angry as she expected, so was clearly onside, albeit just a tad reluctant at first. Soon, after she'd said something about getting off on the wrong foot, he'd agreed. He had stuff on till 3pm, he said, and Jan suggested they meet at a cafe not far from the Mosque called the Honest Sausage on the Broad Walk in Regent's Park.

'A Jew who became a Muslim,' said Rashid. 'And you want to meet at a place called the Honest Sausage?'

'Oh God,' Jan replied. 'I didn't think… And sorry for saying God… It's just a cafe. Oh, sorry…'

'No it's OK,' said Rashid, enjoying her being on the back foot. 'That's fine. I know it. See you there.'

Soon after ending the call, a message flashed on her mobile alerting her to a voicemail. She dialled 121 and Frank's voice came through. 'Hi. It's me. OK, what you got for me?' it said. 'I might have something for you. Ring me.' Neither he nor she was going to say too much in messages, not since the phone hacking. With journos even hacking other journos, they were both likely to have been victims of other papers accessing their messages but neither was pressing the matter for compensation. Wouldn't look good.

She knew he was using the same technique to arouse interest as she and she smiled. He had executed it well. She rang back and he picked up after just one ring. 'So?' he asked.

'Don't want to talk about it over the phone,' she said. 'Can we meet?'

'Sure. Butcher's Arms?'

'No. I need to be around Regent's Park at 3. Can we meet somewhere there?'

'OK.'

'There's a cafe called the Honest Sausage on the Broad Walk. Do you know that?' Jan asked.

'I'll find it.'

'Around 4pm OK?'

'Sure.'

'And you said you had something for me?'

'Likewise,' he said. 'Not over the phone.'

'OK. See you later.'

Now all she had to do was find something that she could give him.

25

RASHID AND DEENA

RASHID had been expecting to go home after his meeting at the Mosque but Deena and the meeting with the journalist had thrown off his plan. Not that it was one, really. Instead, with a few hours to fill, he meandered around the park to make the most of such a glorious day, punctuating his stroll by finding a quiet nook to offer up midday prayers, and wondering where to meet Deena for tea. He felt butterflies rising in his stomach as he googled cafes in the Regent's Park area on his mobile.

He thought about those fancy places in St John's Wood High Street but afternoon tea was a whopping £16.50, too much for him even though there looked to be enough for them to share. Just a scone and a cup of something hot was £6 each. He didn't want to ask her to go halves, though she had sought the meeting. Anyway, she was still in police uniform and he didn't want to embarrass her anywhere that was too ostentatious. 'Please do, embarrass me,' Deena might have said if the opportunity had been offered to her.

If Rashid was honest, he didn't want to embarrass himself. That feeling surprised him. He was really looking forward to meeting her, had taken an instant liking to her, but was unsure about her being a police officer after his previous experiences. Then again, he thought, she didn't seem put off by being with a young man in Muslim attire.

In the end, he texted her to suggest the Garden Cafe in the park on Inner Circle. It was not too public and not too far from where she was on duty at the Mosque. Afterwards she could walk down to Baker Street for the tube inside 10 minutes. It was also not too far from the Honest Sausage, through the rose gardens and up the Broad Walk, for his 3pm meeting with that journalist.

He would have around 45 minutes with Deena. That was fine. Long enough if they got on well, short enough if they didn't. He had his next meeting to cite so he would have no need of a feeble excuse to get away. She might want to get away, anyway. She might not feel the same as he, which was, the more he thought about it, an attraction. He was relieved to get a text back from Deena saying 'Sounds good'.

At the sending end of the text, meanwhile, Deena thought in reality that the venue did not speak of flattery towards her but she quickly remembered that this was nothing serious, just a first, informal meeting. At least it was a nice day and the sun was shining so they could sit outside. Even if it was probably to drink tea out of thermal cups and eat a slice of dry cake in cellophane off a paper plate.

'You're sure this is OK for you?' Rashid said when she arrived at 2.15pm and she answered, 'Of course.' They sat outside at stainless steel bistro tables. Sipping tea and munching cake for which Rashid had found the coins, they were an unlikely couple, the PC and the Muslim in the white *kurta*. Unlikely to those who looked and looked away but endearing to anyone who cast a second glance.

They introduced themselves properly, formally – surnames and ages, where they went to school, where they lived – before Deena, used to asking questions and getting quickly to the point, dived in.

'So. You don't look like a typical Muslim to me, if you don't mind me saying. How did that come about?'

He never tired of talking about Islam. In fact, he believed it to be part of his calling. Especially now in his new role. It was important to share information.

Deena was an attentive listener and he was quickly at ease sharing how he felt that there had been something missing in his life and how he had been drawn to Islam, which simply meant 'a simple, total and unconditional submission or surrender to the Will of God,' he told her. He explained why he had changed his name. He thought this was a good rehearsal for his interview with the journalist later.

'We are all brothers and sisters in humanity,' said Rashid. 'We all come from Adam and Eve. In fact, Islam is the only religion that believes in Moses, Jesus and Muhammad. We believe the first two were prophets but that Muhammad (peace be upon him) was the true messenger of Allah, our name for God. That is the first of the five pillars of Islamic faith.'

'Really?' said Deena. 'I didn't know that. I didn't realise you believed in Jesus. Why do you think there is so much conflict in the world then when there are so many similarities between religions?'

'I guess it is to do with differences, rather than similarities. People focus on those too much. Too many misinterpret the words of the Bible, like the eye-for-an-eye thing as justification for revenge. Some do too with the *Qur'an*. They set up courses at the Mosque for believers and non-believers alike so that new and potential Muslims would have access to proper information rather than being left alone with their own interpretations after making the declaration of faith when becoming a Muslim. That is when they can be radicalised and it is dangerous. The idea is to pass on knowledge, not to convert people, as you would say.'

'Glad to hear it,' said Deena. She smiled and Rashid smiled back.

'Some of our faith get it wrong when they are told that Allah is the one true God. They think that means other religions are wrong. What it really means is that we should worship only Allah, not money or material things. And in the teachings of Muhammad (peace be upon him), what we call the *Hadith*, for example, it says: "Do not punish anyone who does not associate with him." If people just heeded that, so much violence would be avoided. We really should be able to get along, given that the message of all religions, of all the figureheads they believe in, is peace and love. I mean, do you know about the Grand Mosque in Paris, during the Second World War?'

'No,' said Deena, warming to Rashid's enthusiasm. He was easy on the eye, too. 'Tell me...'

'Well, the Grand Mosque is in the Latin Quarter in Paris and it has a system of underground caverns. In the War, the rector of the Mosque was a man called Si Kaddour Benghabrit. I have read all about it. It is amazing. In the caverns he sheltered resistance fighters and French Jews from the Nazis. He provided Jews with Muslim identities. He would even give Nazi officers and their wives tours of the Mosque upstairs while refugees hid downstairs. He helped more than 1,700 people, most of them Jews.'

'Wow. What a story,' said Deena.

'And all true,' Rashid replied.

'And is it true that Muslims have to pray five times a day?'

'Yes, it is. It is the second pillar of our religion. The times change according to the seasons but we are expected to pray before sunrise, at midday, mid-afternoon, sunset and nightfall.'

'Really? That must be hard work.'

'Not hard at all. Not work. You just have to make it a priority in your life. Build your day around it. It can be done. We believe in reward, both in the feeling of peace in daily life and the life to come.'

Rashid looked across at Deena to see she had finished her cake and almost her tea, whereas he had started neither.

'I'm sorry,' he said. 'I'm getting carried away...'

'No, no, it's fascinating,' she replied and meant it. She had taken the one-day Met course on dealing with Muslims but this was much more personal. 'You talked about five pillars of faith. What are the other three apart from belief in Allah and prayer then?'

'They are to do with giving to charity, agreeing to fast for Ramadan and to make the pilgrimage, the *Hajj*, to Muhammad's birthplace Mecca at least once in your life.'

Not only was she fascinated by the information, she was also fascinated by him. Many men had hit on her in the past but this one had not. Something about his naivety appealed to her. She was even warming to the fact that he hadn't suggested somewhere posh for their meeting. It showed he was unused to such situations. Not artful. She was also expecting his own question.

'And what made you want to join the police?' duly arrived.

She had her own practised replies, their frequent airing failing to undermine their sincerity. She wanted to help and make a difference, she said, particularly coming from a black community in South London, as she knew kids when she was growing up who had got a raw deal from the police. She was interested in crime, wanted to be a detective, she added.

'Sounds very laudable,' said Rashid. He wanted to hear more about her and her life, thought he was finished about himself, but she caught him with another question.

'What did you mean about once being one of us?' Rashid went silent. 'When I first met you after... after *it*, on Monday.'

'Yes, I know. I remember,' said Rashid. He paused before answering. 'I was in the police for a while.'

'Really? Wow. That surprises me,' said Deena.

'Me too. I didn't know what to do after university. Knew I didn't want to use my business degree. Didn't really interest me. I had this feeling, like you, that I wanted to help people but a month at Hendon showed me I wasn't cut out for it. The culture was a bit too, well, macho...'

Deena smiled. 'Yes, it is,' she said. 'But I like it.'

That was enough for now, Rashid thought. He really didn't want to be getting into the stuff about how he had been targeted by some branch of the police as a potential presence for them inside the Mosque.

'How have you coped this week?' he asked suddenly. 'I guess you've been busy ever since it happened.'

'Me? I was about to ask you the same thing. I mean, I saw the aftermath. You saw the whole thing. I did read the paper, you know…'

'Oh that. Well, I've been OK. The funerals helped in a strange way. They were my first but it was good to be in fellowship with so many people. It's like praying. You can do it alone but it is so much more powerful when done with others. So it is with grieving I think. What have you had to do?'

'On the edges of it all really. Helping out at the crime scene. It was all so shocking. It must have been horrendous to witness. I am really sorry for your Muslim brothers, is that the right word? Were they friends of yours?'

'Not friends exactly,' he said. 'People I knew and saw most days. I'm still making friends at the Mosque and in my new religion. I have lost many from my previous life.'

Deena knew how he felt. Her role as a police officer often left her feeling alone, even isolated in her community. Young black people did not understand that she was doing this out of a sense of duty to her community, and was not their enemy. But she understood their characters in a way white officers could not. She knew, for example, that for black kids, certainly those of African origin, looking down at their feet while they were being questioned was not a sign of rudeness and contempt, as so many white officers assumed and were angered by, but was a mark of respect. Their failure to make eye contact was, in fact, a compliment rather than an insult; they were not making eye contact as they accepted they were subservient to elders and figures of authority.

'I know you have to stay professional but you must have had some personal feelings about this week?' Rashid asked.

She was happy to talk, now relaxed, and feeling no guilt about Dave. She liked that they were talking about proper subjects, not flirty stuff like TV shows and music they might have liked. Even if she would not be averse to a bit of flirting in the future. She told Rashid of how drained she had felt by the experience on Monday night and how she had then been assigned to patrol duty in the park on the Tuesday after the gunman had been shot on his revenge mission.

'He really wasn't one of us,' said Rashid hastily.

'I know that. I think everyone does,' said Deena. 'It was distressing and painful, the whole business, and on top of that I made a mistake.'

'Oh?'

'I talked to a journalist. It was the same one who did the interview with you.'

'Interview? I didn't really do an interview with her.' He told Deena how he felt drawn back to the Mosque on Tuesday but could only watch from across Park Road as it was all cordoned off. He had begun chatting to someone he thought was a nice woman only to find out the truth when the article appeared this morning.

Deena laughed. 'You too,' she said. 'I suppose she told me she was a reporter at least, but she tricked me into giving her some information I shouldn't have.'

Rashid looked at her quizzically and she explained what had happened and that she was sometimes too open for her own good.

Rashid shook his head. 'I've got to talk to her again.'

'What?'

'The director of the Mosque thinks it could be good for us, especially after what happened on Tuesday, if I give her an interview about why I became a Muslim. Actually, I'm OK with it now, I think. I just want to help Islam and my Mosque. And I guess she was just doing her job.'

'But she was deceiving you.'

'Well I'm going to have to forgive her and hope this works out well.'

'You're a better person than I am,' said Deena.

'I doubt that,' said Rashid.

Deena became embarrassed. 'Look... I'm going to have to go soon. Promised Mum and Dad I would cook tonight and I need to get some shopping on the way home.'

'No problem. Me too. I'm meeting the journalist soon.'

There was a silence for a few moments and they both looked at a man who sat down at a nearby table with a cup of tea and eyed them a little warily. Deena thought she vaguely recognised him but was diverted by Rashid spilling out a sentence.

'I was wondering...' 'Yes?'

'What shift are you on tomorrow?'

'Same time. Early. Due to finish around 2.'

'Would you like to meet up afterwards? Have some proper lunch? Maybe go for a walk around the park? It really is beautiful and...'

Deena interrupted his waffling. Flirting may be for the future but no reason why that future couldn't start tomorrow.

'That sounds like you're asking me on a date,' she said.

'Well, it doesn't have to be. Only if you'd like...' Rashid didn't make it to the end of the sentence.

'I'd like that very much,' she said.

26

TOM AND SAUL

TOM's heart was racing as he inserted the card into the cash point, even though he knew there was no logical reason to be nervous. It was a common event. He was just a kid outside a bank withdrawing some money from an ATM and there were plenty of kids about. There was also no need for the shifty look around before he keyed in the PIN as he was blocking the number pad and neither of the two people queuing behind him was paying any attention anyway. It was just that guilt took.on furtive forms. And ever since the Rachel episode, he had become good at guilt and getting better at it by the day.

He checked the balance on the card and was taken aback to see that the account contained more than £12,500. Perhaps Saul wouldn't even notice that two grand had gone. When he tried to get money out, however, the screen informed him that he could withdraw a maximum of £450 today and he cursed himself for forgetting that limit. He took it out nonetheless and stashed it quickly in a front pocket of his jeans, so he could feel it at all times and not risk having his back pocket picked, before heading off quickly. His fear was that someone might remember him, or that any hidden camera above the cash point had caught him. To wear a hat or a hood, though, would have looked suspicious and so he just looked down as much as he could. It was probably all going to be fine, but for him, paranoia had become the bedfellow of guilt.

He checked his watch. 3.15pm. Another 15 minutes to get down Primrose Hill and over the main road, past the zoo and into the park to the Honest Sausage. He checked the map on his mobile. It showed nine minutes' walk. He didn't want to be there too early and have to hang about attracting attention. But then he didn't want to be late. Jason would not like that. Tom suddenly took fright at the prospect of triggering his brother's ire.

He hurried down the hill, crossed the bridge and came out on to Outer Circle near the zoo. The queue on this sunny afternoon was stretching more than 100 yards past the fast track entrance that seemed to have been copied from a Disney theme park. Tom walked on the other side of the road and then turned down on to the Broad Walk to the Honest Sausage. When he arrived, there was no sign of Jason and he didn't want to sit at a table and stick out. It was also hot and so he sought the shade of a nearby tree from where he could see comings and goings properly.

He looked again at his watch. It was time. He rolled a cigarette and smoked it. Jason was now five minutes late. He checked his mobile, scrolled through Twitter and his Facebook page, even though there was no activity. Jason was now 10 minutes late. He watched people at the tables outside the cafe, a couple of families, a few people on their own, and a curious-looking couple, an older woman and a young guy wearing a tunic and skull cap. He watched the man get up and they shook hands, before he left and she watched him go then started reading a newspaper. Tom looked at his watch again. 3.45pm. Fifteen minutes late. Tom thought about leaving but the buzzing of his mobile with a text ended that idea.

'Stay where you are,' it said. He looked around and saw Jason strolling up the Broad Walk from the south and going past the Honest Sausage. He watched him sit down at a bench about 50 yards away. He could see Jason texting and shortly after felt his mobile buzz again.

'Get me a coffee and a ham roll and come and sit next to me,' it said. Tom obeyed. He had plenty of money on him now after all. When he reached Jason, he handed over the thermal cup and food. Jason almost bit his hand off in his eagerness to get the roll into his mouth.

'You're welcome,' said Tom.

'Don't get fucking sarky with me,' said Jason between mouthfuls and they sat in silence save for the chomping of food and slurping of coffee.

'Why the fuck are we meeting here?' Tom asked, catching the mood of bad language. 'I mean, you couldn't get much nearer to… to where it happened.'

'See any police?' Jason asked.

'Well, no…'

'Exactly. Given up around here now, ain't they? Got all they need from here. They're all over South London now they've found the car. And I need to get out of there. Here.'

He finished the roll and the coffee. 'Got it then?' Jason asked.

Tom recognised his brother less and less with each meeting, and now each moment of each meeting. He guessed that desperation did this to people. And this was some desperation. Jason was still in the same clothes as yesterday and though his face was washed, they were that bit dirtier. He was beginning to smell. Tom himself had been in this position a couple of days ago. Except that he hadn't killed five people.

'Well?'

'Yes. I've got some money.'

'Some?' Jason snapped. 'What do you mean some?'

Tom knew he would have to face this moment. The butterflies in his stomach had been demanding that he work out a good explanation but there was just no other way of dealing with it apart from offering the simple truth.

'I stole his debit card but it would only let me take out £450 in one go.' He took the cash out of his pocket and handed it over. For all his disappointment at the sum, Jason took it eagerly enough.

'I asked you for two grand, Tom, for fuck's sake.'

'I know you did but what else could I do?'

Jason rose to his feet muttering 'Jesus' and paced around randomly for a minute or so.

'I can try and get you another £450 tomorrow,' said Tom, a pleading in his voice.

'Not good enough,' said Jason. 'I can't hang around here forever can I? I need to get out of this country, get set up with a new identity before they start putting all the pieces together. And it's in your interests that I do, bruv. You're up to your neck in all this as well.'

'But I didn't do anything.'

'You didn't drive me here? You didn't have a grievance against Pakistanis after five of them raped your girlfriend?'

Tom considered the whole scenario again. He knew Jason was right. He was deeply implicated and could expect no understanding from the authorities or the public and, probably most important, a jury for his unwitting role in it all. He nodded.

'OK. I'll try.'

'Still not good enough, little brother. Trying is dying…'

Tom shot a troubled look down the Board Walk where he thought he recognised a familiar figure in the distance. As the man got closer, he saw that it was indeed Saul.

'Look, I'll get it. Text me later. Now just go. Someone I know is coming.'

'Who?'

'The bloke I'm staying with. Whose 450 quid you've got. Now piss off. He'll turn you in if he finds you, even if I won't.'

'You're just trying to get rid of me, aren't you?' said a disbelieving Jason whose doubt dissipated when he saw the man stop near the Honest Sausage then stare at the two of them.

'Seriously. Go. I'm telling you. Stay and you don't get the money. Go and you might.'

Jason pondered it for a few seconds then got up from the bench and turned and made off across the grass towards the trees, not with the run of the unpractised guilty but with the swift, less obvious, step of the knowing guilty.

Tom quickly got up and hurried towards Saul, wanting to waylay him and give Jason time to make himself scarce. He reached him some 10 yards from the Honest Sausage.

'I thought that was you,' said Saul as Tom approached. 'Who was that you were with?'

'Just some bloke I got talking to while I was out for a walk.'

'You think I'm stupid, Tom?' Saul asked a little too loudly so that the woman sitting at that table outside the cafe nursing a coffee turned to look at them. Saul noticed and shot her a smile, which she returned and looked down again at the newspaper she was reading.

Tom looked across. It was the woman he had noticed earlier with that bloke in the skull cap but was now alone.

'That was your brother, wasn't it?' Saul said more quietly.

This time the woman did not look up.

'He's gone now.'

Saul grabbed Tom by the arm and walked him up the Broad Walk, aware now that they might be attracting attention where people were gathering around the cafe. Tom shrugged Saul's hand off his arm after a few yards. Some 25 yards north of the cafe where there were few people near, he stopped and, angry, turned on Tom again.

'OK. So why are you meeting him? In Regent's Park for God's sake? Where it all happened?

'He's calling the shots, isn't he?' Tom replied. 'It was where he wanted. You said it, didn't you? I suppose he reckons it's quietest at the eye of the storm.'

Tom turned to walk away until Saul grabbed his arm again. 'Will you please stop doing that for fuck's sake?' said Tom.

'Look, some time very soon, people are going to work this thing out. And then they will connect you with him. And then you with me. I just stopped for a tea at a cafe and there was a policewoman there who questioned me the other day. I didn't want to get up and leave in case she thought I looked suspicious and she remembered me. That's what all this does to you. You have to live with being edgy. It's not good for me. You really need to sort this out. We do. When are you going to the police?'

'I am handling it. Leave me alone.'

He pulled his arm away from Saul and strode off, Saul quickly in pursuit but struggling to catch up. Today had been day 36 of 37 in his radiotherapy and he was feeling the strain. Lethargy was overcoming him. He had been determined not to give in to it, to walk to and from Baker Street each day to keep his fitness and spirits up and enjoy the park but he would be relieved now when it was over. He was looking forward to the weekend and just sleeping, taking a late breakfast, reading, watching films, listening to music.

He wanted this over now. He wanted to believe the boy but still had his doubts, still wondered if the kid was telling the truth. Wondered again why the hell he was protecting Tom and why he, both of them, hadn't already gone to the police, no matter the arguments he kept coming up with to justify his and their actions. His fondness and sympathy for an innocent kid who needed help were just obscuring the grave reality of it all. And the longer it went on, the deeper he got himself into it, the deeper the trouble. And the longer the potential punishment.

'Wait, Tom,' he said, his breath shortening.

Jan looked up from the newspaper that she had pretended to be reading and sipped the last of her coffee. She turned to watch the two men, one older, one young, clearly exchanging heated words as they walked away then stopped, then walked on separately.

When they were a hundred yards away or more, she saw the older one dash across to a figure wearing a purple top. The colour was obvious, even at that distance. Some words were exchanged before the figure – a woman, Jan could now see – peeled off the garment and gave it to the man. Jan then saw him take out an object – a wallet? – from the inside pocket of his light summer jacket, remove something from it – some money? – and hand it over to the woman. The older man also took something else from a bag he was carrying over his shoulder and gave it to her.

She watched as the two men then headed north, in the direction of the zoo and her pulse quickened as she recalled what Rashid had just told her.

27

JAN

THE two men had moved out of sight before Jan could react properly. What was she going to do anyway, when she thought it through: make a citizen's arrest? Rashid had gone and Frank wasn't here yet. She was on her own. Maybe she should ring 999 on her mobile? But even if the colour of that piece of clothing squared with what Rashid had just told her, the two men didn't quite fit with the narrative of Monday's atrocity, involving a man in his mid-20s. She also knew now, though, that there was another one, a bit younger, that Rashid had suddenly recalled.

What she could do was speak to the woman who had just handed the garment over to the older man and Jan was watching her intently. She was about to get up and walk up to her when her attention was diverted by the seat opposite her being occupied.

'What are you looking at?' Frank asked, the emphasis on the word 'looking' rather than 'you' so as not to sound aggressive. 'You always were a nosy one.'

'Just something going on up there,' she replied.

'All human life in this park, eh?' he said, sitting down.

She smiled at him and there was a silence between them.

'So I'll get the coffees then, shall I?' he said.

She nodded and thanked him, keeping her eyes on the woman all the while as Frank disappeared inside the cafe. By now she was walking in Jan's direction so there was no need to go chasing her and alerting Frank just yet. She needed to process what she had seen. She smiled to herself at Frank's assessment of her being nosy. She had been the child of two drinkers and it had engendered in her a heightened awareness of events around her. Friends joked that she could sense hostility between couples on the opposite side of a restaurant without them even saying a word, or that she could hear repressed, whispered breaths that passed others by. She believed it made her a good journalist, attentive and observant, but she had paid a high price for her acquired skills. Her mother and father's noisy rows at home after weekend drinking were followed by days-long silences when they were coming off it during a working week.

The shivering memories shook her from her reverie and through the open door she watched Frank queuing to order the coffees at the counter before turning her head to see the woman approaching on a limping meander down the Broad Walk. It was an older woman, her hair grey and lank. She looked in her 50s but was probably in her 40s. Her clothes – tattered vest, thin, shapeless patterned skirt and filthy trainers – suggested she was sleeping rough. She carried a couple of carrier bags.

'Excuse me,' said Jan, getting up as the woman drew level with the table.

'You and all? Everyone wants to talk just lately. All very cheery. Must be these sports things that's been going on. You want to buy some of my clothes from me as well then? Some bloke just gave me a pair of new socks out of his bag so you can have them. Two quid?' She took a pair from her carrier bag and held them out towards Jan.

'No, not for me, but thanks for the offer,' said Jan. 'I am willing to give you some money, though.' Taking a crisp £20 note out of her purse, she added. 'I just need some information.'

'Blimey,' said the woman. 'He only offered me a tenner for a top. You could have had that thrown in.'

Jan smiled and asked her about the two men she had just seen her with, what they wanted. Not much, she said, just the hoodie, and they were willing to pay.

So it was a hoodie. As Rashid had said…

Course they could have it, she said, it was filthy anyway after she'd slept in it for a couple of nights. No skin off her nose and saved her washing it in the toilets over by the rose gardens. It was summer and she could do without it. She had only found it anyway.

'Where?' Jan asked.

'In a bin. On Primrose Hill. Couple of days ago.'

'Did it have anything written on it?'

'Can't remember.'

'Try. On the front. On the chest, the left side.'

'Some badge or other. And a couple of letters – L, I think. And U would it be?'

Jan thanked her, gave her the £20 and the woman moved on with a 'Ta love'. Thirty quid in the space of 100 yards. She had once been told the streets of London were paved with gold, as a girl with hopes and dreams years ago, but this was ridiculous. She just hoped the spirit of these past few weeks lasted for a long time yet. Apart from that nasty stuff that had happened in the park a few days ago that she had seen in an old copy of the *Evening Standard* that had been blowing about.

'Who was that?' said Frank, posing a question Jan had heard twice in a few minutes now, as he set the coffees down on the table.

'Just some old biddy who needed a few quid.'

'Quite the Samaritan,' said Frank. 'Hope for us all. I would have thought what's happened this week had done for all that Olympic spirit.'

Jan smiled. 'You old cynic,' she said.

'Me?' he said, chuckling. He quickly turned serious. 'OK. So what have you got for me?'

'You show me yours first,' Jan replied.

And so Frank spilled the story that he, the department, the force, wanted out there. It told of some CCTV footage they had been trawling through for the last 24 hours. A camera had picked up a man in his mid-20s, wearing blue jeans, a black polo shirt and black trainers, walking up the Old Kent Road near the street where the car had been found and dropping some keys down a drain. He was carrying a bin bag that they thought probably contained the overalls, the backpack, the balaclava and gloves. They were trying to identify him and needed some help. They had a grainy face that might be of interest to her, though it was partly obscured by a baseball cap.

She was getting a two-hour start on the TV stations, Frank added, because she had been breaking some useful stuff and had something to give in return. She knew the game, unlike, he said, most of these kid reporters and TV faces too busy appearing on the box every half hour of rolling news to build contacts or develop a story beyond what they were officially told.

He pushed a brown A4 envelope across the desk and she took a quick look in, seeing a DVD and some black-and-white images. Jan sought to conceal her excitement. This was a great beat. The office would go crazy for this. Not only could the story go on the website straight away, it had moving images that the digital content people could post. They could brand it with the paper's name and get hits from all around the world. And those black-and-white images. Raw, rough. Just right for the final, flagship publication, the newspaper itself, and which might restore some of its lustre.

'Interesting stuff,' she said, not wishing to appear too grateful or excited. 'I'll see what we can do with it.'

'And you have what for me?' he replied.

Jan was relieved that she did have something for him after her enjoyable and illuminating interview with Rashid earlier this afternoon. In fact, she had been pinning hopes on it, which was why she wanted to see Frank afterwards, not before. Rashid was a bright boy and once his initial suspicion and hostility had subsided, he had been articulate and passionate about his faith. It had also helped him relax and speak when she apologised face to face for not being open with him about her being a journalist. Privately, she still did not regret it, deeming the exclusive worth it, but she was reassured about some humanity resurfacing in her feeling of sympathy for Rashid at what she might have put him through.

In fact, she was looking forward to writing the interview and pictured it in her head as a double page Saturday human interest read. He was going on to meet a photographer at the Mosque and the pictures in front of the minaret would look great. She also had a news story stirring in her to go with it, to appease Vickers. Some things were beginning to dawn on her and though the two men were long gone, she thought that if they had dumped the hoodie originally in a bin in Primrose Hill, that might be a good place to start. Maybe people up there knew them or had seen them. Not that she would be telling Frank about the two men just yet, or where the old woman had found the hoodie. That could wait until the story had gone online at 10pm. He'd know then. There would be the phone call to bollock her, him shouting that she had subverted a major enquiry but it came with the territory. She could handle it. To tell him about all that now would mean that he just had to call it in, to start the search and ruin her story. And anyway, she was still working out who the older one was. He certainly wasn't the flamethrower. Didn't look physically capable. Best now just tell Frank enough to keep him sweet, about the hoodie itself and the kid. When he did find out the full details at 10pm, it would still give the police plenty of time overnight to organise resources and searches.

'That lad who converted to Islam, the one who witnessed it all on Monday,' she said.

'Yes. Read all about him today…'

'When he came out of the back of the Mosque, the bloke in the blue overalls who did it was gone.'

'Well we know that,' said Frank, an edgy tone now in his voice. 'Please tell me you have something, Jan. Otherwise I can't deal with you any more after what I've just told you.'

'The Muslim lad, Rashid his name is, did hear and see something, though. Or someone. And it's just made a bit of sense to me. You know, I always think you people should go back a few days later to interview people again because their memories improve. They recall things when their shock subsides.'

'Some we do. Of course we do if we need things explaining. But we don't have the resources as a matter of routine to talk to everyone again. And we give them cards don't we? Ask them to ring us. Come on, stop stringing me along, Jan…'

'He said he heard shouted voices before the car screeched off.'

'Yes, we know that too,' said Frank growing increasingly frustrated and impatient.

'And then he saw a kid disappearing into the park. He was too preoccupied at the time with the suffering going on around him. Torn between wanting to go after the killer and the people who were dying. So he went back into the Mosque to help. I pressed him on the person at the park gate opposite the Mosque. The kid was wearing a purple hoodie. He caught a quick glimpse of the letters LU on the front before the lad turned and ran off.'

'What's the relevance of that?' Frank asked.

'I think the kid in the purple hoodie may be key to this. He would have seen the killer. Seen him disappear in the car. Maybe he was even part of all this.'

Frank breathed in and out deeply. 'OK…' he said.

'Purple hoodie? LU?' Jan went on. 'A university. There aren't that many beginning with L… Leeds, Lancaster…'

'It could be American,' Frank said. 'Louisiana…'

'Maybe, but if there is a university in this country that has that colour and design, then we're getting somewhere aren't we?'

Jan told him she would be writing the story for tomorrow's paper as an exclusive – 'Was this a killer's accomplice?'. That would probably be the headline. She told him that, in return for this and other favours to him, she needed him to sit on it, at least with the media if not his colleagues, till 10pm tonight. OK? After all, these images of what might well be the killer were going out this afternoon and the police would surely want the focus on him through the evening's news bulletins, wouldn't they?

Frank nodded slowly. The priority for now had to be the sorcerer and not the apprentice.

'By the way,' he added, 'there is another element to this.'

'Go on,' Jan said.

'The Muslim kid is known to us.'

'Known to you? How? Why?'

'There's stuff he probably hasn't told you.'

And so, Jan trying not to let her mouth drop, listened as Frank told her the stuff Rashid hadn't – the month at Hendon police college, the approach by a member of Frank's department to be an anti-terrorism presence inside the Mosque. And Rashid turning it down.

'We've been keeping our eye on him at all times since Monday. Seeing what he got up to after it. Seeing who he talked to. You were seen interviewing him on Tuesday.'

Jan shook her head and smiled.

'And?' she said. 'What's he been up to?'

'Going to the funerals. Meeting with people at the Mosque. Meeting you.'

'So what am I going to do with this?'

'Well, I'm no News Editor, but I would have thought the Hendon line might make a good way in to your interview? Would appreciate you keeping our failing to recruit him quiet though.'

Jan thought about it. Keeping anything quiet rankled with her. Her instinct was to break news, impart information. But she knew she had good material, what with the DVD and pictures from Frank and the purple hoodie lead. Introducing this in the mix would just confuse things. And there were always trade-offs in this game.

'OK,' she said. 'But you keep me in the bloody loop, all right.'

'Sure,' said Frank. 'With what you've got today mind, you are the bloody loop.'

She smiled again. 'Right,' she said. 'I think we've both got work to do, haven't we?'

28

SAUL AND TOM

TOM's mistake was to take the hoodie out from under his baggy T-shirt as soon as they came through the front door. Mrs McIver must have seen them arrive through her front window since she was waiting in the threshold of the door to her as soon as Saul had turned the key and they were into the building. Saul was breathing heavily after the long walk and the climb up Primrose Hill and paused for a moment knowing he had a flight of stairs yet to negotiate. Already on edge, her voice startled him.

'Are you all right, Mr Bradstock?' she asked. Saul had told her about his treatment during week three, when she inquired about him leaving the house at the same time each day. She and Tom were the only ones outside of the Royal Marsden who knew.

'Yes thank you,' he said. 'Just a bit weary. Be OK when we get settled in and have a cup of tea.'

'Your Godson with you for a while longer?'

'Not sure, are we Thomas?' Tom shook his head and scowled at his longer name.

'Better get on,' Saul added quickly and headed towards the staircase, though not before Mrs McIver had noticed the hoodie under Tom's arm.

'Ooh, that's a nice colour,' she said.

'Thank you,' said Tom, feeling that not to reply would not only be rude but would raise suspicions. Saul was by now halfway up the staircase and Tom felt he needed him to follow quickly.

He knew what was coming from Saul as soon as they got through the front door of the flat and he had set the hoodie down on a chair.

'Why the hell did you take that bloody thing out of your shirt?'

'I didn't know she was going to be there, did I?' said Tom. 'Anyway, she was just as likely to ask me what was stuffed up my shirt, which would have been more suspicious.'

He had wanted to wear it under the T-shirt, tuck up the sleeves and the hood but still some purple showed. Saul had been adamant that they get the thing back from the old woman now that it was back out there and not in some landfill somewhere as it should have been by now. Saul may have had misgivings about Tom disposing of it but they couldn't have someone wearing it around Regent's Park or Primrose Hill and it triggering a memory for someone who might put two and two together.

'OK. Fair point,' said Saul, accepting the logic of the argument and calming down. 'We'll need to get rid of the bloody thing again now, I suppose. Can't burn it in this flat. Smoke alarm will go off. Go and put it in the bottom drawer in my room for now, Tom. It's all getting too complicated. You could end all this now you know. You could go to the police.'

So could I, Saul thought.

The boy said nothing, just picked up the hoodie and went and deposited it in the drawer in Saul's bedroom.

When he returned, Saul was slumped on the sofa, pale yet sweating. Tom offered to make him tea, which was gratefully accepted. He felt a great and sudden sympathy for the man.

'You OK? You look terrible,' said Tom when he brought him the tea.

'Thank you, Tom. You know how to lift a bloke's spirits. I'll be fine soon. I've just about had enough of all this now. It's got to me.'

'The treatment? Or the stress of this... What's happened and me being here?'

Saul smiled. 'Actually, perhaps all "this... what's happened" has kept me going this week. Who knows?' He sipped his tea, impressed that Tom was finally producing a liquid of a better colour and containing the right amount of sugar. 'That's better,' he said, of both the tea and his equilibrium returning.

'I think I'm going to have a lie down,' he said and went to the bedroom. He thought about doing more on the page proofs he was supposed to be correcting and which lay on his bedside table but he was just too weary to concentrate. He had another couple of weeks. So much unfinished business.

'You OK if I play the guitar quietly?' Tom asked and Saul agreed, saying that it might soothe him. It certainly soothed Tom as he began to strum some chords and hum a tune, some lyrics forming in his head requiring him to go and find a pencil and a piece of paper.

Almost an hour and a half passed in the absorption of creativity that was a welcome antidote to the anxiety the meeting with Jason had provoked in him once more. It was five to six, he noticed when he looked up at the clock on a bookshelf and thought it might be a good time to rouse Saul. They had grown used to watching the six o'clock news, not just for the latest, but because it offered a ritual that suited them both, a transition between the restfulness of summer late afternoons and the cooking of the evening.

Saul was already thinking the same thing, however, and emerged from the bedroom. 'Didn't realise I'd slept so long. Your music sounded good. Sent me off to sleep.'

'Thanks a bunch,' Tom replied, smiling.

Saul sat on the sofa and turned on the TV from the remote in time to catch the opening music of the BBC News.

'New lead in Mosque murders,' said the newsreader, voicing the headline on the top story.

Saul sat up. Tom came in with two mugs of tea and sat next to him, alerted by the words on the TV. They both listened to the newsreader, rapt, as they watched the grainy footage – with a newspaper's logo as an identity in the corner of the screen – of the young man walking in slow motion along the street carrying a bin bag.

This is the man police want to interview in connection with the murder of five men at the Regent's Park Mosque on Monday. They believe that he was driving the car that was seen speeding away from the scene after turning a flame-thrower on the victims in an atrocity that has still not been identified as religious, racist or terrorist. The car was found in a street in South London just yards away from where CCTV captured the driver throwing away a set of car keys. Now police need help in identifying the man. James Pearson reports.

The picture cut to a man with a microphone at the spot in South London where the alleged killer had been caught on camera. The reporter had little to add, but it fulfilled television's modern need to show it was live and on the case and he filled a minute or so before giving a number for people to ring if they recognised the man.

'Do you want me to write the number down?' Saul asked. Tom shifted uneasily in his seat.

'Is that the man I saw you with earlier? That your brother?'

Tom nodded. He recognised Jason in the way only someone close to him could. The dark images were almost indiscernible but Tom could see the clothes that Jason had been wearing before returning to the car in the overalls and balaclava. Beneath the black baseball cap, unmarked by any logo, Tom recognised on the TV freeze frame the cut of the cropped hair and the angle of the nose.

'Well, they're closing in on him,' Saul said. 'Which means they're closing in on you too.'

Tom jumped up, growing angry.

'If you're trying to get me to go to the police again, you're wasting your time,' he said.

'Genuinely, I fear for you, Tom. You have been drawn into this by a brother's wickedness and one who has shown little regard for you in all this. The longer you leave it, the worse it will be for you.'

He picked up his mobile from the coffee table and offered it to Tom.

'Ring them. Ring them now.'

Tom turned his back and walked to the front window. Saul pondered making the call himself but still harboured hopes that Tom would do it for himself, would do the right thing. He really wanted that for the boy but he couldn't go on much longer like this, causing himself such anxiety. He set the phone back down on the coffee table.

'You don't know the half of it,' said Tom.

'So tell me…'

Tom thought about it, about the meetings with Jason and the money he had stolen. He remained torn, his loyalties divided.

'In my own time, OK?'

'That's what I'm saying though, Tom. Time may be running out. How long before they put you and that purple hoodie at the scene?'

Tom thought about it again. The man had a right to know, after everything this week.

'He saved my life,' said Tom. There was a pause.

'I was eight years old. It was winter. Cold winter. Icy. I was out playing with some other kids, mucking around. We were by the canal just at the back of our house. One of the kids pushed me and I fell in. Went through the ice. Wasn't too thick but took my breath away and I kept going under. I panicked. A kid ran and got Jason and he jumped in. Pulled me out. I just freaked. He saved me.'

Saul took in the story. 'He did what anyone older would have done. Certainly a brother,' said Saul.

'Maybe. But the fact is *he did it*. He saved my life. Can you see why I owe him?'

Saul could. He understood the dilemma, though he churned over the new evidence of Jason's twisted morality in continuing to control Tom with an incident that had happened more than 10 years ago. It may not have been up there with killing five people, but it was still sick. And not sick, as in kid's speak.

The news item about the footage of Jason had finished. Now they were into a piece about the re-opening of the Mosque tomorrow for Friday prayers, when 6,000 people were expected to attend the most significant prayer time of the week, before moving on to coverage of the funeral of two of Tuesday's shooting victims. They then sat watching an item on preparations for the Paralympics. The editor had clearly decided after the misery of this week that had soured the previous mood of the nation, it was time for something more uplifting.

Saul broke the silence that Tom's revelation had provoked. They were both clearly in no mood for any more intense conversation and the resulting feelings. It had been a draining day, physically and emotionally. They needed some normality, some respite, however brief.

'I'm too tired to cook tonight. Shall I order pizza?'

Tom leapt at the chance of some fast food and went to the kitchen to get the leaflet from a local company that Saul kept on a pin board. He chose a pepperoni with extra cheese. Saul just wanted a margherita and would top it with some olives from the kitchen. Tom rang and placed the order. It would be around half an hour.

They settled down again to watch the London regional news, which contained more on the mystery man in the baseball cap captured on CCTV, or rather more of the same. There was another BBC reporter on the same spot as the previous one, this time a young Asian woman, and her report led into a question-and-answer session with the anchor in the studio that repeated the message and phone number for people to contact if they knew or recognised the man, aimed at those coming in from work. They watched on, through a feature on a victim of the London 7/7 bombings who had lost both her legs and would be taking part in the Paralympics in the Sitting Volleyball.

'What was he like to grow up with, your brother?' Saul asked.

Tom thought about it for a moment before replying. 'I've been going through all the memories in my head and been looking at them in a different way since Monday,' he said. 'The more I think about it, the more he could be nasty to me. Spiteful at times. I always looked up to him as you do with your older brother. After what he did that day at the canal, he was my hero. And he got me out of bother at school if anyone ever picked on me. He did take care of me, I'll give him that. Physically anyway. But I did better than him at school and he didn't like that. I can see that now. It's funny. You never think your older brother would be like it, but I think he might even have been jealous of me.'

Some 50 yards away at the top of the street where Saul's flat was located, Jason's ears might have been burning had he not been more concerned with his next move. It was then he noticed a pizza delivery moped turn into the street and pull up. It was outside the flat where he had seen Tom go in. Jason walked briskly down, watching the delivery kid take the pizzas out of his pillion box and stand on the step buzzing the doorbell.

A couple of yards away now, Jason heard the clack accompanying the sanctioning of the opening of the front door and the helmeted kid stepped inside. Before the door could close, Jason was inside with him.

'Hello mate. Who they for?'

'Bradstock, first floor.'

'Great. I'm the friend he's got the second one for. I'll take them up.'

The kid looked unsure but a crisp £20 note, to include a fiver for his trouble, saw him quickly on his way.

Jason took the boxes and began to walk up the stairs, not noticing Mrs McIver, who had been alerted by the conversation in the hall, poking her nose around the door of her flat and watching him ascend. Neither did he hear her quietly tut-tut as she closed the door, muttering that it was becoming like Piccadilly Circus in here.

Jason knocked on the first floor 's door and it soon opened with an old man thanking the delivery boy and proffering £20. It was brushed aside as Jason pushed past him. He was inside the flat before Saul could stop him.

'Don't worry. They've been paid for. My treat,' said Jason from the middle of the room.

Tom sprang up from the sofa. 'What the…'

'I knew you'd be pleased to see me, bruv.' He stood in the middle of the room and surveyed the scene. 'This is all very cosy now. Just a shame we're going to have to share two pizzas among three people.'

Saul stood shocked, but intrigued. So this was Tom's brother.

'What do you want?' Tom asked.

Saul watched the two of them stare at each other, Tom looking terrified. It momentarily brought out a fear in him too but he could sense one greater in Tom's brother's tired, unshaven face. It was just being masked by the force field of anger around the man that must be gnawing away at his soul. Saul almost felt sympathy for him too. Of course he wanted him caught and imprisoned, but he had always believed in Oscar Wilde's saying that every saint had a past, every sinner a future.

Saul reckoned the lad was still thinking he could yet get away, and get away with his crimes, but even if he escaped physically, the deed would always be with him. In his desperation now, he would not realise that when – if – quiet ever descended on him again, his punishment was going to be for life.

'What are you doing here, Jason? How did you find me?' said Tom.

'Never heard of being followed?' Jason replied.

'So you're Jason,' said Saul.

'Nothing much gets past him, does it?' said Jason, smiling at Tom.

'Why… why have you done all this?'

'Come on. Tom not filled you in on the details?'

He looked across at Tom, who shrugged his shoulders, fear on his face.

'Why?' Jason continued. 'Because they fucking deserved it. After what happened to… After what I've seen out in Afghanistan, could have been a load more than five.'

'But you can't hold innocent, unconnected people responsible,' said Saul. 'Lives are lived singly, not collectively. They're not a number. They're individuals. Anyway, no one deserves what you did.'

'Look, shut up old man. You need to concentrate on how you're going to help me get out of this. And you, Tom, don't half ask some daft questions. What do you think I'm doing here? Have you told him about his bank card?'

Tom looked ashamed. His head bowed and his voice lowered as he slowly told Saul how he had stolen the card and taken out £450 to appease Jason. He was very sorry.

Saul was initially angry, spitting 'What the…' at Tom and shaking his head. He was upset both about his money disappearing and the kid ignoring his advice about not being blackmailed by Jason. But then Saul realised. How could the kid have done anything else?

'So here's the plan,' said Jason, producing a knife from the pocket of a lightweight black Harrington jacket. The blade was black, its handle wooden and Tom had seen it before. It was Jason's British Army seven-inch combat knife.

First, Jason outlined, they were going to give him their mobiles and they obediently handed them over. Then they were going to watch some television and relax for the evening, all comfy like. Jason wondered, looking at all the books and CDs on the shelves, if Saul had any decent American box sets. Saul couldn't help him there and Jason shrugged his shoulders, lamenting that they couldn't have everything, could they?

'Then, first thing in the morning,' Jason announced, 'We are going to your bank. I am guessing your branch is nearby?'

'It's down at Baker Street. A fair way away, through the park,' said Saul.

'Ah well. It should be a nice walk at that time of the morning.' The TV was still on the background and the South East weather forecast was on. Tom pointed to the screen with the knife. 'And look, it's going to be a nice day. Hottest of the year so far.'

The subject turned. 'How much have you got in your account?' he asked Saul.

'My current account? A couple of thousand pounds.'

'Got a savings account? Instant access maybe?'

Saul hesitated. He shot Tom a glance.

'Look. I've killed five people haven't I?' said Jason. 'One more's not going to make a difference is it?'

'You wouldn't, Jason,' said Tom.

'In for a penny...'

Saul admitted that he had a savings accounts with around £12,500 in it.

'Minus £450 now,' said Tom.

'Then 12 grand is what we – or rather you – will withdraw,' said Jason.

'But you said £2,000,' said Tom.

'Meter's been ticking,' Jason replied. 'And of course the more I get, the further away from me you pair get.'

Tom made a motion towards Jason but Saul intervened.

'Leave it. I'll do it. I'll get you the money,' he said, not saying that he would do it for Tom.

'You are lucky you've found someone to look after you finally,' said Jason. 'I got sick of it. Wiping your arse all these years. I even had to look after Rachel for you.'

'What does that mean?'

'You've not worked it out, have you? Me and her. We were fucking each other.'

Tom looked shocked, then pain crept over his face. Tears began to roll down his cheeks. He crumpled on to the sofa, struggling to breathe properly.

'No, no way...'

Saul worked out the next bit first. Tom was too consumed by the soul-burning information he had just received.

'That's why... The Mosque...' said Saul.

'That's why,' said Jason. 'A gold star for the man.'

This time, Tom did go for Jason, leaping suddenly from the sofa. Jason lunged the knife at his brother as he flew across the room. The blade entered Tom around his right bicep and though not deep, the wound was painful enough for him to yelp, and the quantity of blood enough for Saul to shout out for it all to stop. Tom recoiled, holding his arm, blood seeping through his fingers, and fell back on to the sofa.

Saul made a move for the bathroom but Jason stopped him. 'Where you going?' he asked, breathless and agitated.

'Just to get a dressing.'

'OK. Do it. But nothing silly. You both do as I tell you, all right?'

Saul nodded. He fetched a bowl of hot water to wash the cut and began to apply some disinfectant and gauze when there was a knock at the door. All three looked at each other and Jason motioned for Saul to answer it.

'But I will be holding this to Tom's throat,' he whispered, brandishing the knife, 'so be very careful and get rid of them.'

Saul told Tom to hold the gauze over the cut and went to the door, opening it slowly, just ajar.

It was Mrs McIver, inquiring if all was well as she had heard some strange noises.

'All fine,' said Saul, blocking her view as she sought to look into the flat. 'Just a friend of my Godson's. I suppose you're not used to me having company and footsteps echoing down?'

She seemed unconvinced but Saul was closing the door even as he was thanking her for her concern and she had no choice but to retreat. Saul returned to dressing Tom's cut. He winced with pain, his right arm immobile.

'Right,' said Jason when Saul had finished. 'I'm starving. Let's have that pizza shall we? And some music. I'm sick of all this news shit. Let's lighten up, eh?'

Saul suspected, though, that this was going to be anything but a light night.

PART V

FRIDAY
AUGUST 17TH
2012

29

SAUL AND TOM

THEY might have dozed now and then but nobody really slept, and certainly not at the same time. Jason sat upright in the armchair with his knife in his right hand overseeing Saul lying on the sofa with a duvet covering him and Tom on the floor under a sheet, as had been commanded. Whenever Tom was contemplating leaving the flat – though the pain in his right arm from the cut, now dressed, would limit his mobility – Jason always seemed to be awake. Jason also insisted on a lamp being left on to help him avoid a deep sleep.

Saul, meanwhile, knew that to make a move to the door and then downstairs, even if he could do it without disturbing Jason, would have left Tom exposed to the renewed ire of his brother. He sought to engage him in conversation, about Afghanistan, trying to understand what the ex-soldier might himself have suffered, which might inform, though could never justify, his subsequent actions. Saul believed that evil often stemmed from vulnerability and disappointment, often masked it, but he knew how hard that was to believe when you were in its path. Anyway, Jason was having none of it. If trauma was eating at him, it was going to dine alone.

Saul naturally had to get up to go the toilet every few hours, the first time at 1.57am, the red digital figures on the TV told him.

'What you doing?' snapped Jason, sitting up and brandishing the knife.

'I'm just going to the toilet,' said Saul.

'He's got a problem, all right. Leave him be,' said Tom, sharply, and Jason relaxed. He was surprised at Tom's firmness, impressed even.

'OK then,' he said, 'but the toilet in the hall, not the bathroom.' He went with Saul and stood outside.

Otherwise they rested, to ready themselves for what they all suspected would be a decisive day, when they were all either free of this darkness or swept up in its dragnet. As Tom lay awake thinking, a tear came to his eye at what had happened to Rachel, but then he grew angry at the thought of how she had two-timed him with Jason. He curled up under the sheet so Jason could not see him as he suppressed his sobbing. He knew that life would never be the same, that he at least would always be a prisoner of this week for good or ill and it would define him in some way. He had thought over that stuff that Saul had told him, about life being an echo chamber in which events reverberate down the years, and that view was beginning to make some sense. Everybody had touchstone moments that would follow them into old age.

The sun poked through the gap in the curtains at around 5.45am. Still more than three hours to the opening of the bank. At just before 6am, Saul asked Jason if he could go to his bathroom and shower, then get dressed in his bedroom. The old man looked tired and feeble, Jason thought. He had his mobile and the bloke posed no threat. He agreed. Saul trudged slowly to his bedroom and turned on the radio, to Radio 4 and the *Today* programme, keeping the volume low. Soon he was sitting ramrod straight on the side of his bed, listening intently.

The lead story at 6am told of the worldwide outrage now being felt as the death toll in a shooting of striking miners in South Africa had reached 34. The second story was about a United States Black Hawk helicopter crashing in Afghanistan – the Taliban now claiming to have shot it down – with the loss of 11 lives.

Then, just before the suggestion that today's temperatures could hit 32 degrees Celsius, which was 90 Fahrenheit they added helpfully for Saul's generation, came news of a development in the flamethrower murders at the Mosque. According to a newspaper report this morning, the newsreader said, police now believed the killer had an accomplice who had been wearing a distinctive purple hoodie, found in a bin on Primrose Hill, just north of Regent's Park, and were appealing for sightings of a young man who had been wearing it last Monday. He might now be accompanied by an older man, the report added.

Saul sat stock still for a moment, pondering his next course of action, his heart pumping. Should he tell the pair? Should they get away from here as soon as possible? Or should they sit tight for now, until more people were around on the streets and they could lose themselves more easily? Should they get a mini-cab down to Baker Street, or should they walk?

He needed the toilet again. And a shower. It had been a sticky night, airless, breathless. Opening windows had hardly helped. He walked to the threshold of the living room and saw Jason with the TV remote in his hand. He turned on the TV. Saul was going to have to tell them before they saw it on the news, with the noisy panic that would bring. Jason, however, turned on a music channel. Saul did his best thinking in the shower, he believed. He would consider what to do in there.

After the slow, laboured relief of pissing, he stood in the shower jets, arms stretched out, palms pressing on the wall tiles, and let the water hit the back of his neck and run down his body.

He recapped; tried to get things straight in his mind after the shock of the news report. He had grown fond of Tom, believed him to be a good kid who had been enveloped by evil, but Saul was stretching it now, this wanting him to find it within him to go to the police himself about it all. Doing that, he reckoned, would also lessen the punishment that Tom would inevitably face, even once the truth emerged, as an accessory. But then Tom seemed unlikely to do it given this bond between them, this trauma bond – as one way as it was – engendered by Jason saving Tom's life. There was a physical Stockholm Syndrome, Saul considered, and then there was an emotional one.

As for Saul, he knew he would also be facing charges for harbouring someone the police wanted to interview. By comparison it would be minor, however. He could live with that.

He tried to think through the consequences of keeping the news story from them. He suspected the police would be out there soon flooding Primrose Hill and questioning people on their way to work and their daily business about whether they might have seen someone wearing a purple hoodie recently.

If the three of them went out into the street, walked down Primrose Hill and through Regent's Park to Baker Street, they would surely be confronted by a police officer at some point. Jason might panic, might give himself away. Saul could say something, that this was the man they were after. And that would sort it all out and save him £12,000. But then, Jason had a knife, someone was going to get hurt. Maybe a police officer.

Saul wanted to be rid of Jason, this malign influence on Tom, but with no more people getting hurt. Perhaps if he got the money out and gave it to Jason then he truly would leave them alone. Jason knew the twelve thousand quid was pretty much all Saul had so there was little point coming back for more. Perhaps after that, Tom might then agree to turn his brother in. The police would then have a proper description, would surely track him down even if he did make it to another country. And Tom would get some latitude from the authorities.

Saul's instinct was to tell the pair of them about the news report and to work out a plan of action with them. It was safer if they were all in on it. Less room for unpredictable behaviour. After towelling himself down, he put on a robe and went into the living room, where Jason held the TV remote in his hand and was channel hopping, though still only through the music stations.

'We may have to rethink,' Saul said.

'What you talking about?' Jason snapped.

'The police know that you had someone with you on Monday,' said Saul, not wanting to use the word accomplice. 'And that he was wearing a purple hoodie.'

'That's bollocks. You're making this up.'

'Turn on a news channel, then,' said Saul.

Jason quickly did and soon saw a news bar of white type on a red background along the bottom of the screen announcing that police wanted to interview a young man wearing a purple hoodie in connection with the Mosque murders.

'Shit,' he exclaimed.

He grew even more agitated when the newsreaders – grey haired man, comely young woman; the artful TV news mix of authority and attractiveness – began to amplify the story, telling how the hoodie had been found in a bin on Primrose Hill and police were beginning their enquiries in that area of North London.

'Shit, shit, shit,' said Jason, banging the arm of the chair as he watched the news channel use the opportunity to show the dramatic pictures following Monday's mayhem of police rushing about and paramedics helping shocked survivors, footage he had seen over and over in the days banged up in the Balham flat.

Tom had been enjoying the respite from the tension with some Wild Beasts and Blood Orange videos on the music channels but now stirred from his prone position on the makeshift cushioned bed on the floor and stood up, one hand on his forehead, the bandaged arm by his side, rocking from foot to foot, to watch the news.

'I don't know what you're so worried about, Jason. They've turned their attention away from you and on to me now.'

'Fuck this,' said Jason. 'So what do we do, old man?'

Saul paused, to give the impression that he had thought this through and that his wasn't just a knee-jerk reaction. He then spoke softly and slowly, to give the impression of an authority to his suggestion; that it was surely the best thing to do.

'We call a minicab. The police will be all over this area and the park today. We get the cab to take us down to Baker Street. I get the money out and you're on your way.'

Jason thought about it for a moment.

'You'd better not be messing me about,' he said, pointing the knife in Saul's direction. Saul shrugged his shoulders. He knew that if Jason wanted the money, this was the only way.

'I'll happily listen if you have an alternative,' said Saul.

Jason began to pace the room.

'You go alone. You get the minicab and I'll stay here with Tom.'

'But I could just get the police.'

'You won't. For some reason, you won't turn our Tom in. And you won't want to see him harmed.'

'You wouldn't stab your own brother.'

'Er...' said Tom, pointing to the dressing on his right arm.

'OK,' said Saul. 'But the police are going to be in this area. What if they come house to house?'

Jason thought about this and realised Saul was right.

'OK, OK, we go together.'

Saul went to his house phone and keyed the number of a cab firm whose card he kept on the pin board in the kitchen. He ordered it for 8.30am. Earlier and they would be hanging around Baker Street, out in the open, running the risk of encountering police there. Later, and they would miss the opening when it was less busy. This left about enough time to get there in the rush hour.

'OK, that sounds like a plan. You'll be rid of me in a few hours and we'll all be happy,' said Jason.

It did indeed sound like a plan, Saul thought, but he knew there was one potential snag. While in the shower, he had gone over yesterday's events in his mind. He recalled how Mrs McIver had remarked on what a nice colour was that top Tom was carrying under his arm. And Saul knew, because he sometimes heard the television from down below in the still of early mornings, that she also liked to watch Breakfast TV.

30

DEENA; RASHID

DEENA hurried to send off the text just before going into the briefing. 'Really sorry. Something came up. Working overtime. Maybe meet you lunch break?' she wrote. Now, as she sat at the back of the room, one of more than 80 constables gathered, she felt her mobile vibrate in her breast pocket and dared to sneak a look. 'No problem. Just say where and when,' came the reply.

She smiled to herself. The good feeling she'd had about him yesterday was confirmed. It was early days, and nothing was going on – yet – but she couldn't help comparing this with Dave's attitude to her work. He always acted as if its varied nature and the hours were her fault, rather than her bosses and the job itself. He seemed to want her to work somewhere she could be confined and constrained.

She'd finally had the conversation with Dave last night and felt a weight had been lifted from her this morning. Now it wouldn't feel like she was two-timing him, even if this thing with Rashid turned out to be nothing more than just a passing friendship between two people thrown together by a tragic set of circumstances. She liked him, though, enough to want to see him again socially and develop a relationship, and thought he liked her. Anyway, she had needed to make the break with Dave no matter whether there was someone else or not and now it was done.

It was, she had to admit, so much easier to finish with some-one seven hours' flight-time away. With someone like Dave, anyway. Even if he did get on a plane planning to scream and shout at her, as he had said on the phone he would be doing, his wounded pride would probably feel less acute by the time he reached Heathrow. His bark was worse than his bite. He wouldn't be wasting money on flights and losing work to rescue what he surely realised was a lost cause. It would have been altogether different if he still lived around the corner, as he did when he had met her two years ago.

She felt a sharp elbow digging into her ribs as she re-read the contents of Rashid's text, just to check for nuances as the newly enamoured do (there were none; he wasn't like that) and turned to Darren, who smiled at her. They didn't need to exchange any words. The smile captured his pleasure at seeing her looking happier. He had remarked on it when they showed up for the shift 15 minutes ago at 7am and told her that she was bouncing about indecently for this time of the morning. The elbow was to tell her that she had better pay attention. This was important.

'You will each be given a laminated six-inch-by-four-inch picture of this,' Chief Superintendent Ray Symes was telling them as he held up a much larger, poster-sized picture of a purple hoodie. There was a bit of giggling among the 50 plus officers. Were they really going to show people a picture of a hoodie, and one taken off the Internet after an overnight Google search revealed which university's colour was purple?

'You will see a logo on the front and the letters L and U underneath. They stand for Loughborough University,' he went on. 'Now you are probably wondering why we are showing you this, rather than a picture of a criminal,' he said. 'The simple fact is, we don't have one. This is what we have for now. We need you to connect this hoodie to a face and bring in a description if you can.'

CS Symes explained that they believed the killer to have had an accomplice wearing this hoodie and if they got to him, they would then get to the killer. The hoodie, in fact, had been seen just yesterday, he added. They would be given the pictures to take around Primrose Hill and Regent's Park today and while the killer and his sidekick might be long gone, such a distinctive piece of clothing might just jog memories. In the meantime, they would also be talking again to the traffic warden, cyclist and young mother who witnessed scenes at the back of the Mosque on Monday for a possible description.

'OK, let's go,' he added, looking at his watch. 'Want you out on the streets by 7.30am.'

'So who's the lucky bloke?' said Darren as they got up and walked back into the mess room, having each been handed a copy of the picture by a sergeant, who told them their patch this morning would be the southern part of Regent's Park.

Deena grew coy but the urge to share that also overcomes the newly enamoured took over.

'That lad I was talking to at the Mosque yesterday. Meeting him later.'

'The Muslim one? This one?'

Darren picked up a copy of the paper that had been left on a table amid the thermal coffee cups of the now cluttered mess room and turned to page three. There, displayed prominently, was Jan's story of the purple hoodie along with the picture of it, clearly also googled, that they had just been given. There was, too, a picture of Rashid amid it all.

Deena scanned the page quickly and avidly.

'Yes, that one,' she said curtly. She was suddenly annoyed that he had not told her about the purple hoodie. It had been just a social meeting, tea and cake at a cafe, but surely if he could tell a journalist of whom he was wary about it, he could tell someone who was sympathetic and involved?

'You didn't know about this?' Darren asked. 'You came into work without knowing? It was all over the news.'

Deena made a note that she would have to start listening to news radio when she got ready for work in the morning and not music, even if she preferred to be in a good mood rather than depressed when she clocked on.

Darren noted the byline on the piece, with a thumbnail picture of the journalist alongside.

'Isn't that the woman who turned you over?'

'Yes, but it's all cool now.'

Darren passed her a quizzical look of 'really'?

'Really,' she said. 'Come on. Let's see if we can catch these bastards. I just need a moment, OK? Something I need to do.'

*

'LUNCH not good,' said the text. 'On duty in park. Can't get away.' It was the brusqueness of the text that hurt Rashid. There was no 'sorry' or 'maybe after my shift'. Deena's tone had changed for some reason. Yesterday he had felt a stirring of emotion he had not known before, certainly not during teenage crushes at school. Earlier in the week, brutality had disturbed the new equilibrium and ease in his life but last night a heady mixture of mellowness and warmth had been disorientating him too. He liked her, enough to want to see her again socially and develop a relationship, and thought she liked him.

In a state of such heightened sensitivity, he did not take the text well, especially since it came just 10 minutes after the first, encouraging, one from Deena. This on top of all the texts about the purple hoodie from friends, which prompted him to go online to discover himself again the centre of attention. This was becoming too regular. And too much.

Rashid accepted Deena having her work pattern changed and had liked her trying to rescue the situation by offering to meet at lunchtime. He was hoping it could be the start of regular meetings as he would be back at work next week when the Mosque was reopening fully. Why, though, suddenly send another text changing her mind?

He had managed to get back to sleep for a couple of hours after rising for *Fajr* at 4am but now he was agitated and knew he would sleep no more. He could not even lie there any longer in such a state. He got up, showered and dressed, then headed down to the kitchen. His banging and crashing about as he made tea drew the attention of his mother.

'Rashid?' she said from the kitchen door's threshold, startling him. 'What on earth is going on?'

'Nothing,' he said in the tone that makes it plain to people close that there most certainly is.

'Want to talk about it?'

'No,' he replied but he did.

His mother sat at the kitchen table, asking to join him in a mug of tea.

'Fine,' snapped Rashid and dragged another mug from a cupboard.

Its furred-up interior dragged out the boiling of the kettle but the wait was interrupted by the snap of the letterbox being opened and the thump of the newspaper on the doormat. His mother went to fetch it.

He did not like himself like this, when he was short with the mother he adored, not just for her care and concern but for her open-mindedness and courage in accepting his new life while enduring the silent, and thus cowardly, resentment of others in her circle beyond those who had been supportive. The Jews invented guilt and the Catholics perfected it, he had once been told. Now it seemed that some in this Jewish neighbourhood wanted to inflict some of their own on the Johnsons.

She returned with the paper, concern again on her face as she set it down on the kitchen table. She opened it at page three showing its picture of Rashid, the purple hoodie and Jan's story. She offered a half, sympathetic smile and he looked at her anxiously before scanning it.

'I saw it online earlier,' he said. 'She told me she was writing an article about being a Muslim. About what our religion was really about.'

As the kettle heated, so did Rashid and he screwed up the newspaper, hurling it across the kitchen. He began to sob quietly, covering his eyes in embarrassment.

'I'm sorry, Mum,' he said. 'It's been one tough week. I think things are catching up with me.'

'I'm not surprised,' she said. 'The deaths, the funerals. I'm always here but do you think you might want to talk to somebody professional?'

'No, but thanks for thinking of it. I have my faith. I pray. The police have allowed the Mosque to open for a few hours today for Friday prayers so I'll go in for that. And next week, I'll be back at work, around the Mosque all the time. Around people who care about each other.'

His mother nodded. She wasn't quite so easily fooled. 'Is there anything more?'

This surprised Rashid. He thought the big, evil events would be a deflection from the worries of the heart that were also troubling him.

'What do you mean?'

'Well, I understand why you would be sad and angry but I can sense something else.'

Rashid blurted it out. He needed to talk to someone. 'I think I might have met someone…'

'Really? That's nice. Do we know them?' She did not wish to pry as to the gender of the person Rashid had met.

'It's a she, Mum, it's OK,' said Rashid, smiling. She smiled too. 'You thought I might have been gay?'

'Well, there have been no girls since school. I thought you

might have made more discoveries about yourself after becoming a Muslim. I wouldn't mind, you know.'

'I know you wouldn't but it would be a big problem for me. On top of everything else. I'm just a bit disappointed by something she texted me this morning.'

'Go on…'

'First she wants to meet, then she doesn't.'

'Ah, we women eh?'

Rashid shook his head and smiled.

'What's she like?' his mother asked.

'A police officer but an understanding one. I thought, anyway. A lovely smile.'

She laughed. 'I thought you wanted nothing to do with the police after that horrible month you had?'

Rashid shrugged his shoulders.

'Leave her for now. She'll get back to you if it's meant to be. Go to prayers.'

It was sound, simple and wise, and he couldn't argue. He began to calm down, realising that he had overreacted. It was going to be a beautiful day and he wanted to be out in it, not stewing at home about something that had hardly started. Today he would get the tube down to Baker Street and walk up to the Mosque through the park and enjoy some peace and solitude before joining 6,000 people who would be taking advantage of the window permitted by the police for midday prayers. Today, collective prayer would be far more valuable than ever.

'Let's see what the day brings, shall we?' added his mother.

31

SAUL AND TOM

SURREPTITIOUSLY, so as not to increase the tension in the room, Saul checked his watch for about the 10th time in half an hour. It was 8.15am and 15 minutes until the minicab arrived. The time had dragged over the hours since he had awoken and showered. He had made breakfast for them – some scrambled eggs and strong coffee – and Tom had showered too, the pain in his arm easing and his mobility improving, though Jason's continuing lack of trust meant that both Saul and Tom had to endure his presence in the bathroom. Jason dared not risk a shower himself. Even with the time taken for all that, they were ready far too early.

Neither did watching the TV make time move more quickly. Breakfast news cut every 15 minutes to show a reporter on the street outside Chalk Farm station, where people were on their way to work. Jason noted with pleasure that behind him, police officers were getting plenty of shaking heads or people walking on without stopping, as they showed their picture of the purple hoodie.

At first Jason had grown agitated when he saw the camera and police in front of the tube station where he had met Tom a couple of days ago. The pigs were getting too close, he reckoned. He believed the three of them should get out now before too many police were crawling all over the streets but Saul had persuaded him that it was too dangerous, would risk being seen. The minicab, Saul said, would offer the quickest route out of the area. After all, the police were not stopping cars. They were just giving out pictures to people.

Jason agreed the sense of this but wondered why they just didn't go early down to Baker Street. What, Saul asked, and hang around in a cafe or on the street longer than was necessary? Getting anxious, taking the risk of arousing suspicion when they were safe and free from curious onlookers in this bubble here?

What Saul didn't say was that he was worried that the sight of police around Baker Street might provoke Jason into some kind of reckless reaction with his knife, that the guy might even run and he didn't want that. When caught, as he inevitably would be, and he came to tell his story, he would then surely make it worse for Tom by labelling him his accomplice. Saul still wanted to find a way for this to end well for Tom, or at least not too badly, however naive and more remote such an outcome was appearing with each passing hour, and with Jason in the state he was. From everything he had seen over the last 12 hours, and having been told by Tom of his brother's time in the Army, he thought Jason might well be suffering from an undiagnosed case of Post Traumatic Stress Disorder and he didn't want to trigger any more unpredictable behaviour by a man with a knife. Not that it needed much triggering.

'I'm fucking sick of this,' Jason announced, suddenly rising from the armchair and scaring Saul and Tom. He strode over to the window and looked out. It was mixed news. The bad news was that the street was clear; the minicab had not yet arrived. The good news was that the street was clear; there were no police about.

'I think a bit of music might help,' said Saul, turning down the volume on the TV, the rolling news reports from Chalk Farm offering information but also increasing anxiety. He got up to go to the shelves containing his records and was about to search for something soothing but Jason was there first.

'Why don't I choose?' said Jason, fingering the LP sleeves. 'What's with all the vinyl, anyway? Bit of a dinosaur, aren't we?'

'I love it,' said Tom, growing irked by Jason's swaggering control that the knife, which never left one of his hands, produced in him. Tom wanted to reclaim some of his humanity, his role in events. 'I like the feel of them, I like the art on the covers. It feels like proper music,' he said. Saul smiled at him.

'This is a pretty cool cover, I admit,' said Jason, dragging out *Led Zeppelin III.* He examined it closely, staring at the random colour images on a white background, opening its gatefold and turning a rotating card inside, a *volvelle,* which matched images with the holes in the cover. He handed it to Saul. 'Put on the first track on the second side.'

Saul checked it out and did as ordered. In the silence while he went about removing the record from its sleeve and placing it on the turntable, he took a chance to speak.

'Once I've got you the money,' he said to Jason, 'I need to be away for a hospital appointment.'

'We'll have to see about that old man,' Jason replied, prompting Tom to rise swiftly from the sofa.

'You'd better let him,' snapped Tom. 'This is important.'

'Whoa, bruv? What you getting so upset about?'

There was a tense moment.

'It's OK, Tom. Let's see how things go, eh? I'm sure it will work out,' said Saul.

Lovingly, he set the needle down on the outside edge of the record before the track and Jimmy Page's opening acoustic bars of *Gallows Pole* and the aching voice of Robert Plant, the greatest in rock history, Saul believed, took over from the crackle of the bare space. It told of a man seemingly destined to die but urging the hangman to delay while his friends brought gold to pay him off. As the song wore on, Jason sang along and laughed.

When it finished, his mood darkened, though, and he

walked across to Saul, staring him the face. 'The hangman took the money but hanged the bloke anyway,' he said, almost spitting out the words. 'There'd better not be any double-crossing from you today.'

From there, Jason walked back towards the window and gazed down. Saul checked his watch. It was 8.25am.

'Fuck,' Jason said suddenly. 'Filth.'

Saul moved over to the window. Looking down, he saw the minicab. He also saw a police car parked behind it. Two officers had got out of the car and were standing in the street talking to the cabbie. Mrs McIver, arms folded, also formed part of what was to Saul a terrible tableau. Part of him thought this might work out for the best, that the police would simply ascend the stairs and sort this out. But that was being hopeful. More likely, it would develop into a siege, or somebody would get seriously hurt as the police stormed the flat. He tried to think of a way out of all that, literally and metaphorically.

Saul saw Mrs McIver open her mouth and turn, look upwards and point. Her and her bloody breakfast TV. He recoiled from the window, pulling Jason with him. A startled Jason thought that Saul was trying to get the knife from him and pushed him on to the sofa.

'Piss off. Don't you fucking dare...' said Jason.

'What...? I was just getting you out of sight...' said Saul.

'Can't you see he's trying to help you?' said Tom, going to Saul's aid.

'Fuck, fuck, fuck,' said Jason. 'So what do we do now old man? Quickly...'

Saul thought immediately of the kitchen and pointed to it. 'There's a fire escape through there,' he said. 'Come on.'

They hurried out and Saul unlocked a back door, remembering to lock it from the outside once they were out. It led down some wrought-iron steps to Mrs McIver's ground floor garden, a patch of lawn with flowered borders. In the corner of the fence was a wooden door. With Saul leading the way, within seconds they were through and into an alley that divided Saul's street from one parallel.

'Where to now?' Jason demanded, the knife still in his right hand.

Saul thought for a moment, looking north towards a street that would take them up to Chalk Farm station in around 10 minutes, then south towards a parade of shops just 100 yards away. He knew police were at the tube station. He guessed that the shops would be a better bet. At this time of the morning, there would be fewer people there and less likelihood of police and TV cameras. He also thought the three of them would be less noticeable than they would be walking down suburban roads.

'This way,' said Saul and they followed him towards the shops on Regent's Park Road. There, the coffee bars were open but the clothes shops and restaurants still closed, meaning that there were just enough people about for them not to stand out and so enable them to lose themselves. As he looked north again, Saul could see police about 100 yards away. It looked clear to the south. Tom and Jason, who was carrying the knife still in his right hand but had that right hand in the pocket of his Harrington, followed as if led by the nose. Saul had an idea to walk down Primrose Hill and maybe find a bus stop on Prince Albert Road for the trip to Baker Street.

As they walked up towards the Hill, though, they could see two police officers distributing pictures at the entrance gate. Saul diverted them down the side of the green space, following the railings on Regent's Park Road and coming into Albert Terrace. On the main road, about 25 yards away, Saul now saw more police at a bus stop, trying to engage with the rush hour commuters. A bus was going to be out of the question. He thought of Boris bikes. They might be a good form of escape. Only tourists really used them, after all. The only problem was that the nearest docking station for them was in the zoo car park, another couple of hundred yards walk to the east, the opposite direction in which they needed to go.

The zoo. Saul figured that it was too early for it to be open and there would be no queues; thus no police. He led Tom and Jason over Prince Albert Road, through the alley over the Regent's Canal and on to Outer Circle near the zoo entrance. He could see to the west that the 200-metre running track, now busy with early morning joggers and power walkers, was also busy with police, one of their cars parked adjacent.

And so he turned left and led them towards the Broad Walk entrance to the park where few people, and so no police, were gathering. By now, the morning heat rising, they were sweating and not just through warmth. Saul realised that if he was to get them to Baker Street, to sort this mess out somehow without any more violence, or even death, he was going to have to use his intimate knowledge of the park as he had never done before.

32

JAN

JAN had never been a morning person. It was one of the attractions of journalism in the old days: late start and late finish suited her personality and physical regime. Online editions meant a 24-hour operation, or at least something like an 18-hour one, but she was never going to volunteer for the ridiculously early shifts that some of the kids were assigned.

She did make the odd exception to rising later, including to get up for trips abroad, though they were drying up in these more functional, less flamboyant days of bean-counting and expenses being sent back to you even when you were barely covering your costs. Rarer were the times when you could be sent overseas, except for something like the abduction of a British child in a European holiday resort – assuming the kid and family were middle class and wholesome enough for Jan's paper. And if you were, you usually had to be at the airport, often grim Luton, at 4am for the cheapest goat class, budget airline they could find. It was a far cry from the days when you travelled first class, stayed in a good hotel and, if you'd done a good job, found a voucher for dinner for two at the Savoy on your return in your pigeon-hole at work, or a crate of Champagne delivered to your door courtesy of the Editor.

Now, the only thing that would rouse her in rush hour was the scent of a scoop. And she had had good reason to get up early for a few days now. She put on her robe, walked into her kitchen, made a pot of steaming black coffee and settled in front of the TV, watching the breakfast news unfold, seeing her purple hoodie story develop.

It irked her still that the paper was barely credited, let alone her, but you could see her picture byline again on screen when the story was discussed. And the Editor knew, as did her colleagues and rivals. The industry knew. There was, too, the *Schadenfreude* satisfaction of seeing TV reporters paid more than she was being forced out of their pits to stand in front of tube stations, following where she had led.

She had not slept well, despite the half bottle of red wine poured on top of the weary satisfaction of her productive day's work. Frank's phone call, which came at 10.05pm as expected – even though professional and not the needy personal ones of their drinking days – had not helped, used as she was to such confrontations in the course of her work. It was not his angry tone, his accusation of obstructing the police, it was more the twinge of guilt when he said that the six-hour delay before the information about where the hoodie had been found might have given the killer's sidekick and this mystery older man time to get away.

Jan tried to hold her own, though knew she had taken a liberty. At least they had had all night to find out which university sold purple hoodies and to mobilise manpower for an early morning operation, she pointed out. Frank remained pissed off, very pissed off. They couldn't get out on the streets in the dark to interview and search, though, could they?

The Rashid feature was also weighing heavily on her. She had written a couple of hundred words last night and would finish the remaining 1,000 this morning ready for the early-afternoon deadlines. Friday's were always earlier. So many sections of the paper – TV guides, magazines – needed printing. She wanted to do the young man justice and it worried her. Butterflies beyond those caused by a hangover flew unfettered in her stomach. She cared again, mainly about the quality of the piece but also about the reaction of its subject. She opened her laptop and logged on. Plenty would have wanted to know her password, which was her porn star name of middle name and first pet: Alexis (her mother had liked Dynasty) Smoky (it had seemed fitting for the grey rabbit bought for her one Christ-

mas by her parents).

First she checked her Twitter – more than 23,000 followers now. Very good. Except she had attracted plenty of trolls, abusing both her and the paper. Her notifications took ten minutes to read, mostly about some implied criticism in the paper of the Muslim kid, apparently through a headline she had not seen yet of: **'At last – A lead to Mosque murders'**. Some perceived it as having a go at Rashid for not coming forward sooner. Best not to get involved in replying to them.

Then, by googling 'Mosque Murders Purple Hoodie', she could easily see how the story was running on every media outlet imaginable, and many these days that were not. Her own paper's website was now leading on a celebrity marriage bust-up but her exclusive was still high on the home page.

She would go out later to buy a copy on her way to the office – since papers were no longer delivered in Maida Vale – but there was a way for now to see how the tale was projected in the paper. She went to a website called Clipshare, a subscription service paid for by her newspaper, keyed in her user name and password, and there among the images of every page of every edition of every national newspaper was the front page headline of her paper:

THE HUNT FOR THE HOODIE

She enlarged the image and read the six paragraphs of her copy beneath the picture of the purple hoodie. It was quite a compliment that it was still front-page lead the morning after it had gone live on the website last night and she was pleased. What was Frank getting so arsey about? This would surely help find the killer this morning.

After viewing the page three tale about Rashid and the hoodie, she clicked on to the spread on four and five, which offered more chances to use pictures from Monday alongside coverage of funerals for two of the people gunned down on Tuesday. The two wounded were still hanging in there.

Jan poured herself another cup of coffee and watched the news. She saw pictures of the police showing the hoodie picture at Chalk Farm tube station and of them interacting with the public. There was also a van going through the streets with a megaphone and huge images of the hoodie on its sides. It was telling, she thought, that they still had no pictures of the murderer and his sidekick.

Her mobile rang and the name Vickers appeared on her phone. For friends and colleagues she liked, she also used a picture on the display but she had enough of him at work and could not stomach seeing his florid, porky face outside of the office. She picked up.

'So, what have we got today?' he enquired.

'Yes it was another good story wasn't it? Thank you.' she replied.

'OK, OK, nice stuff. But we've been ahead on this story and need to be again. Where are we taking it today?'

'I've got the big interview with the Muslim kid for the Saturday read.'

'Fuck that. I mean news. What news have you got? What are the police doing? Why haven't they got anything on the killer? No images. Nothing. And this hoodie kid. They're both probably out of the country by now and the police have allowed it to happen. I need you to get on their case and ask questions.'

'Don't you dare piss on my interview, Ivan. It's good stuff. The kid was a police cadet once.'

'Really? That's decent, I suppose, but we still need something hard to set the agenda.'

'Look, the Editor wanted this interview. Wants to keep the Muslim community sweet.'

'The Editor wants a front page lead. That's what he wants.'

'If my piece does not get used…'

'You'll do what?' said Vickers.

Jan knew he had the power over her. There was nothing she could do if her interview did get left out. Except these days, this week, she had become the Editor's favourite again and Vickers did have to be careful about offending him. She could always ring the Editor, though he wouldn't much like it on his weekend wining and dining at Chequers with the Prime Minister. Only another event like Monday or Tuesday was worth interrupting him for.

'Listen, it won't come to that anyway,' Vickers added. 'You get me something good again today and we'll get that interview in.'

She hated the blackmail and deserved some time off after the week she'd had, one that had drained her physically and emotionally, but she knew there was no chance of that. Besides, she wanted to see this through. The bit was firmly between her teeth.

In addition, despite the fact that he was one of the biggest shits in what used to be called Fleet Street, Vickers did have good instincts, a News Editor's instincts. He was right about the police. This hoodie thing was something of a sideshow. They still had little or nothing on the two young men themselves at the scene of the crime. It was remarkable, in fact, that her paper was not doing front page headlines along the lines of **POLICE BAFFLED BY MOSQUE MURDERS** with a cross reference to an editorial about shocking police incompetence amid panic and mayhem on the streets of London and opinion pieces about all this new money that was supposed to be coming from a new government, all this manpower, and the Met were still in a mess.

She sat for a moment after Vickers had ended the call, sipped coffee, watched the now muted images on TV and began to think. Why was Frank so keen to get her involved and give her material, both in breaking stuff for the website and supplying overnight pieces for the paper? And why was he so angry with her last night?

She picked up her phone and brought up his contact details. He picked up quickly. That meant something, she thought, especially given last night's conversation.

'You've got some nerve,' he said. 'Anyway, bit early for you, isn't it?'

'None of the pleasantries please,' she said. 'What have you got for me today?'

'You are joking. After you've been withholding? I thought you might have something for me, by way of an apology.'

'I'm beginning to think you might need me more than I need you.'

'How are you working that out? We've given you some great stories this week.'

'But you're no nearer finding these people are you? You're pissed off about last night because you've got nothing else. You're all over Primrose Hill just because you found out – from me – that a hoodie that a kid at the back of the Mosque was wearing was dumped in a bin there. He may well be involved but he's had four days to get away, so I don't think six hours yesterday made much difference. And you've had two days to catch a killer – let's call him what he is, for fuck's sake – a terrorist, that you've got CCTV footage of. You're clutching at straws Frank. Pinning hopes on me. Admit it…'

There was a silence on the other end of the phone. Jan filled it.

'In other circumstances, my Editor might be bringing a shit-storm and a half on to you,' she continued. 'Bungling coppers and all that. You know he's not your biggest fan with the Establishment turning on newspapers and him serving on the Press Complaints Commission.'

'We are not part of the Establishment. Have you seen us joining in the bashing? That's government, MPs caught on the take, celebrities with their pants down, all that shit.'

'Well I don't think the public will see things your way. They will see well-funded Knacker of the Yard and his mates failing to bring to justice a cold-blooded murderer who is stoking racial tension in this country, while a potentially racist police force looks on, maybe even lets him get away.'

'That is bollocks, Jan, and you know it.'

'Do I? Perhaps I do. But it is amazing how late afternoon editorial conferences see things. Especially when they want a good strong Saturday read to turn over the Sunday papers. And I have to ask myself: the material you've been giving me… is it to deflect Britain's most influential tabloid newspaper – one read by those middle classes the politicians panic over when it comes to election time – from giving you a hard time?'

Still nothing came back from the other end, though Jan thought she could hear the whirring of brain cells. It was, to the experienced reporter with the instincts of a honey badger, confirmation that she was touching one giant, raw nerve.

'So what do you want?' came Frank's voice finally.

She told him that she wanted a full update on where the police were. She had to take something significant back to the paper this afternoon.

There was another pause.

'OK,' he said. 'Where are you?'

'At home. You?'

'At the Yard.'

'Let's meet halfway then,' Jan suggested. 'I'll get the tube in from Maida Vale to Baker Street.'

Frank agreed. 'Where exactly?'

'Cafe at the top of Baker Street. On the right going up to the park. Called Bar Linda?'

'OK. I've got things to sort out here. It won't be for another couple of hours.'

'Plenty of time for my News Editor to get the leader writers sharpening their pencils… Try halving that time.'

'All right. All right,' said Frank, his agitation easy to feel down a phone line. 'See you in an hour.'

33

SAUL AND TOM

IT WAS the most beautiful August day and the temperature had already reached 22 degrees Celsius by 9am. The park was resplendent, its greens beneath the blue of the sky giving lie to some fashion belief that the two colours should never be matched. Joggers were out in numbers, along with the Boris bikers, and already people were reclining in deckchairs, some even drinking Buck's Fizz. It was Friday after all, Saul noted as he, Tom and Jason made their way down the Broad Walk: POETS day – Push Off Early Tomorrow's Saturday.

Some 100 yards ahead, his antennae alert and his anxiety heightened, Saul could see two police officers showing a picture and he stopped in his tracks, the other two following his lead. Saul guided Jason and Tom over to the right, on to the grass and to some empty deckchairs. They sat down as he instructed them. His breath was growing shorter and he needed to rest.

'I think we'd better split up,' said Saul when able to speak.

'Don't try that one,' said Jason. 'I'm sticking close to you.'

'Look, the police will now be looking for three men. They will have descriptions from Mrs McIver. More police will be drafted in from across London to this area. And they won't just be showing pictures and asking for information. They'll be looking for suspects. Us.'

Saul paused to catch his breath. He was running on instinct, still trying to string Jason along and discern a way this might end well, or at least without any more bloodshed.

'If we go singly, and meet up somewhere after I get the money, we might just get away with it,' he added. 'If we keep walking like this to Baker Street, no matter how much we go through the trees or across the grass away from the path ways, we are going to get spotted.'

'He's right,' said Tom.

'OK, OK, I'm thinking,' said Jason.

'Don't think too long,' said Saul. 'A park keeper will be along for the deck chair fees soon and he will remember us, for sure. Anyway, you really want to be captured on CCTV in a bank with me? You want to wait outside like a sitting duck? At some point, if you want this money, you are going to have to trust me.'

'All right,' said Jason. 'Here's the deal. You go get the money. Tom comes with me.'

'Why?' Saul asked.

'You think I'm stupid? We go singly and what do I have on you? The both of you just piss off. You look as if you've developed some kind of weird friendship. I don't think you'll screw me over if he's with me.'

Saul and Tom looked at each other. They had indeed become close, though neither had acknowledged it openly. Saul knew it, Tom had just come to.

'OK,' said Saul. 'But you run the risk of being recognised, the two of you together. What with the hoodie, the police are looking for two young men now.'

'Nah. They may have descriptions from that old bat but they don't know what we're wearing today, do they? And they're more likely to think we've all gone our separate ways. Won't be looking so hard for two together. I'll risk it old man. Just you get that money. Now, two questions: where should we walk to from here and where should we meet?'

Saul thought quickly. He was torn. He wanted rid of Jason but he wanted him caught. He knew that he should tell them to walk down towards Great Portland Street and get out of the park as quickly as possible then to wait somewhere around there, the Pret A Manger or maybe that Turkish cafe at the back of the station itself. If he did, though, the chances of Jason escaping increased.

'Tell you what, if you walk through the rose garden there, and past the Open Air Theatre, you'll reach a cafe,' he said, pointing to a route. 'It's tucked away a bit. Not so many use it. It's called the Garden Cafe. I can meet you there in about 45 minutes.'

Jason pondered, then asked the question Saul was concerned about. 'Really? Shouldn't we be getting out of the park?'

Saul had to come up with an answer quickly.

'What?' he asked, throwing it back on to Jason to think for himself and buying himself time. 'And go into areas where all the street cameras are? You've been lucky so far and all they have to go on is that dark image of you after you dumped the car. This country and this city have more cameras than any other place in the world and now they have a better description of you and know you are still around, they'll be using the pictures from these things, putting all their manpower on it straight away. There are no cameras in the park. You're better off here. Why risk all that until you need to. Until you have the money?'

Saul was surprised at his ability to think on his feet, impressed even. It was remarkable how desperate circumstances had seemed to bring up the resourcefulness not needed in him for so many years. 'Courage,' he thought, recalling his Shakespeare, 'mounteth with occasion'.

Thankfully for Saul, Jason was also impressed as he thought it over for some seconds. Agitation and desperation were clouding his judgment just enough for Saul to be in control, even if Jason was convinced by his knife that he remained so.

'OK, fair enough,' he said. 'But let's get on with this.'

Saul was relieved that they all appeared to be comforted by the logic, however justified, of their own ideas and plans of action.

'You'll need to be patient with me. It might take me a while to sign forms and get the money out. Would you like me to take a mobile so I can keep you in touch?'

'Yeah, like I'm going to trust you to do that.'

'No different to letting me go on my own. I can easily blow the whistle in person.' Not that he would, not with Jason possessing both a knife and Tom, whom he had already wounded.

Jason saw the sense anew and took out one of the three mobiles in his pocket. 'You can use Tom's,' he said. 'That way, you don't have all your contacts stored. My name's in there.'

Saul took the phone. 'You're quiet, Tom. Are you OK with all this?'

'As OK as I can be,' he said, his voice a mixture of contempt for Jason and fear for Saul. 'Let's just do it, shall we?'

Saul nodded. He saw a park keeper about 50 yards away and got up, the other two following him.

'Right,' he said. 'You go that way.' Pointing to the west, he sent them on their way towards the rose garden and the cafe and headed south east to take a circuitous, less populous, route towards Baker Street. He kept them in his sights for a while but stopped suddenly in his tracks as he saw a police officer approach them.

He was riveted by the scene as it unfolded around 50 yards away, watching and worrying that Jason would panic. Instead, Saul saw him calmly shake his head as the officer thrust a picture towards him. Tom shrugged his shoulders and the officer quickly moved on to his next targets.

Saul began walking again, more quickly now, though the tension was provoking a weariness in him and the effort involved was taking an ever greater toll. He would be glad when this day, this final treatment, was over. He envisaged the sanctuary of his flat, his radio, his records and books. And bed.

Reality would not be escaped that easily, however. The mobile buzzed and he checked its face for the message it was bearing. 'Piece of piss this. Coppers got nothing,' it read. 'Get a move on.'

He walked down through the English Garden, sweating with each step, not able to stop and enjoy today's appeal of blooming colour. The heat, now approaching the 80s, was getting to him, along with the hot flushes that the Zoladex had invoked. He wanted to stop, to sit down and drink water, but he was scared to delay.

He took the path parallel to the southern side of Outer Circle, crossing York Bridge, the road to Inner Circle, then walking beside the bottom tip of the lake, where there gathered herons, egrets and mottled Canada Geese, deformed by their inbreeding. At Clarence Bridge, towards the back of Regent's College and the bandstand where an IRA bomb had gone off 30 years ago, killing seven bandsmen, he turned left towards the Clarence Gate exit for Baker Street.

There stood two police officers, a young black woman and a young white man. Saul stopped briefly but realised that to linger would be to raise suspicion. To change direction now would also be to alert them that something was amiss, that he was trying to avoid something. Jason and Tom may have got away with it but he did not want to tell a lie.

'Excuse me, sir,' said Deena. He recognised her. She had been here earlier in the week. And in the Garden Cafe yesterday. He hoped she didn't recognise him. She didn't, so preoccupied in the work was she, but what if she had? He used the park a lot. So what? Guilt was playing tricks with his mind.

'I wonder if I might just show you this picture?' she asked.

He looked briefly at the picture. He had, of course, seen the purple hoodie. And he had just realised that the police had probably found it in his flat by now. There had been no time in the panic of leaving to think about getting rid of it. What would have been the point anyway? The police were on to them already.

'Sorry. In a hurry,' said Saul, fortunate that two young people at that moment came between him and the picture, one remarking how cool the hoodie looked.

'You selling those? Might buy one. Give me a leaflet,' said one of the kids. Deena smiled.

By now Saul was crossing Outer Circle by the pelican crossing and Deena thought about shouting out to him – where have I seen that guy before? Was it yesterday? – as she watched him go. But there were more and more people now coming into the park on this gorgeous day that was only going to get more gorgeous, all of whom had to be asked about whether they had seen a purple hoodie. She was beginning, even having been here just an hour and a half, to wonder if she and Darren were on a fool's errand but they had been told to stay here until further notice.

Saul pressed on the 100 yards down Baker Street to his bank on the corner of the Marylebone Road. It had been open just 15 minutes and fortunately when he arrived in the entrance hall, there were just a few people inside, either accessing or depositing money, and just one person occupying a teller.

The beaming smile of a young woman wearing grey trousers and a white blouse, jacket already discarded, her brunette hair cut into a bob, welcomed him. It was her turn, as part of her shift, to be a greeter, her role to look and sound helpful. It struck Saul as depressing work but then he was thankful on her behalf that she was in work when so many young people were not.

'Can I help you, sir?' she asked.

Saul said that yes, as a matter of fact she could as he wanted to withdraw a large sum of money from an account he held there. She asked his name, he obliged and she left him for a moment while she went to an office away from the hall. He could see through the glass frontage that she was talking to a young man just a few years older than her. Saul felt discussed and scrutinised as they turned to look at him. He concentrated on not looking guilty.

The man emerged and greeted him with an equally shiny, bouncy manner and asked Saul to accompany him to an office. Inside, sat down at the man's polite urging, Saul outlined his request: £12,000 in cash from his instant access ISA immediately please.

The young man tried to look professional but Saul discerned in him a surprise. It might have been his own discomfort though, as he looked for signs that someone might be seeing through him. The man could not have known his circumstances and why he wanted the money, surely wouldn't be getting in touch with the police? It was a lot of money to Saul but not to the bank surely? This was a wealthy part of London. Surely they got others in here wanting their cash?

The paranoia of the anxious assailed Saul. Surely it was too soon for the police to have issued a picture of him, to have alerted ports and airports and stations and banks that he was wanted for questioning? No, he had been watching too much rolling news lately.

'All right, Mr Bradstock. As you'll be aware, that is a large sum of money to be taking out.'

'But it says on your website that I can withdraw my money at any time,' he blurted out.

'Indeed, but that is by Internet transfer. This is cash so we have to go through certain procedures. Certain forms to fill in. I need to speak to a colleague.'

Saul leaned forward on to the desk and he spoke more quietly but also more forcefully. He hated playing the cancer card but if not now, when?

'Please,' he said, seeking to enlist sympathy and deeming it less alienating than the modern aggressive 'look'.

'I have a cancer. Today I finish my treatment. I would like to take my money out now to do with as I see fit. I don't think that is too much to ask, do you?'

He hadn't lied but had conveyed his urgency. It was surprising how people reacted to the word cancer. Everyone had a relative or friend who had suffered. Everyone feared it themselves. Like an intro to a great song that had everyone up from their seats and on to the dance floor, its very mention got people moving.

'Just give me a moment,' he said.

Saul watched him, through the enveloping glass, disappear into another office where this time he spoke with an older, female, colleague. Again they glanced across at him, again he felt under suspicion and scrutiny. He pretended he hadn't seen them and tried to look casual.

That was not easy with the side effects of this medication, however. Saul began to feel hot again, a flush coming over him in response to his growing anxiety. He took out his handkerchief and mopped his forehead. He helped himself to the water on the desk, gulping it down. As frequently as he could without making eye contact, he shot glances across at the pair who held his immediate future in his hands.

Soon, they were marching back towards him and sitting themselves down opposite him. His heart skipped a beat as he wondered if he had been rumbled. Then the older woman introduced herself and smiled and he relaxed just a little.

'I am of an age,' said Saul, trying to lighten the mood and ease his own nervousness, 'when I can remember the slogan of this bank being "the bank that likes to say yes".'

The two of them smiled at him. She remembered it, while the young man had heard it on a training course.

'Well,' said the woman, logging on to the computer in front of her. 'Let's see whether we can.'

34

JAN

SHE KNEW she wouldn't have to wait long, which was why she had already bought Frank his old caffeine hit of choice, an Americano with hot milk on the side, to go with her flat white. Once he was here, she didn't want to be getting up again and interrupting the dynamic. And she was right about the eagerness and urgency likely to be fuelling him, such was the speed now with which events were moving. He was there in the threshold of Bar Linda looking for her this way and that within a couple of minutes of her sitting down and taking a sip of her coffee. Within another couple of seconds he was sitting in a chair opposite her, trying to regain his composure.

'Thank you for this,' he said as he poured the hot milk into the Americano.

'You're still drinking that, then?' Jan said.

'Yes. Only more of it these days,' Frank replied with a forced smile. He was nervous, Jan thought. She was probably right – and Vickers too, it had to be admitted; several lorry loads of excrement were surely hitting large industrial fans at New Scotland Yard.

'Right, niceties over,' she said.

'That constituted niceties?' Frank wondered. Jan ignored the question.

'So where are we with all this? What do you have exactly?'

He went through the car and the image of the figure who had abandoned it.

'That hill of beans,' Jan remarked disdainfully, 'does not have much of a gradient. Let's start with the car. Where was it registered? Who to?'

Frank told her that they had checked on stolen cars around the country and it matched one that had gone missing in Birmingham last Sunday. It was carrying false number plates. The owner had been checked out and was not in the frame.

'No fingerprints?'

'Plenty. Hundreds of them in fact. But from tens of different people. Bloke was using it as a minicab. The guy who stole it must have known. Clever. Checked out plenty of them and a couple have criminal records but Brum police questioned them and they have alibis.'

'And the image?'

'We've blown it up, enhanced it. Bloody councils put in such cheap cameras these days. Cut backs. Not been able to identify him at all. No prints, so no pictures of a criminal that we can match up.'

'The guy was wearing overalls and a balaclava...'

'No sign in the boot of the car. Must have been in the bag the bloke was carrying and probably burned. We've been checking shops in Birmingham. Loads of overalls sold but only a few balaclavas. One paid cash but no description of him. Type of shop where nobody notices much and doesn't ask many questions.'

'What about the hoodie? I gave that to you on a plate.'

'And that was about all.'

'Hardly. Even without the other stuff about the two men and Primrose Hill, you had the info on that yesterday afternoon. So who does it belong to?'

'Give us a break. We've been working on it. And we're out on the streets asking for help.'

'To identify people long gone...'

'We're checking out students who went to Loughborough

who bought them over the last five years. Anyway, we don't think they are long gone.'

'What?'

Frank recounted the tale of the phone call to the 0800 number they had got the TV stations to flash up early this morning from a Mrs McIver in Primrose Hill, of the three men in the upstairs flat and them legging it down a fire escape and via a back alley.

'The hoodie was found in a drawer in the flat,' he said.

'Bloody hell,' said Jan, 'so I was right about all that. And you've got something at last.'

'You want to go up and interview the woman? I'll give her to you first. She seems to be enjoying the attention from our lot. Very chatty. Human interest and all that.'

'Are you trying to get rid of me?' Jan asked.

'Why so suspicious all the time? I'm trying to do you a favour. As I have been all along.'

Jan smiled at him and he smiled back. He knew that she had clearly worked out how badly the police had been struggling to make a breakthrough and that they needed the help of a proper, old-fashioned reporter. She had all the human interest she needed in the Rashid interview.

'Give the woman to the TV. They'll love all that. I'd rather be in on finding these guys.'

'Well it's one guy really,' said Frank. 'There's the killer and someone who drove him. It looks like this bloke in Primrose Hill has been hiding them. They've all got questions to answer but of course we want the murderer above anybody else. He could do it again. Nothing to lose.'

Jan nodded. 'When did all this happen?'

Frank looked at his watch. 'About an hour ago.'

'So they still could be gone?'

'Yes, I guess so. They could be on trains already and we've alerted transport police. We have people at all the nearest ones –

Paddington, Marylebone, Euston, King's Cross. St Pancras and the Eurostar. But they won't have got to a port yet, or an airport, so we have a chance.'

'Got descriptions?' She was fishing for confirmation that two of them were the pair she had seen buying the hoodie from the woman yesterday.

'Basic ones,' Frank replied. 'One lad mid to late 20s, the one we think was on the CCTV. One early 20s. He's called Thomas, according to this woman in Primrose Hill. Bloke about 60. Name of Saul Bradstock. Still getting more background.'

'Hair colour, that sort of thing?'

'The old bloke was grey and we have a picture of him from the flat. On the other two, the woman was a bit vague. Longish dark hair, the younger one. Tall. Short cropped hair the older one. Few inches shorter. We're working on it.'

'Can I have the picture of the older bloke?'

'Soon. But not exclusive. No deals now. It's all kicking off. We need to get it out to everyone.'

He got up to leave.

'Where you going?'

'Back to the office. Easiest place to co-ordinate it from.'

'I want to know any leads. I gave you that hoodie. That's what's broken this case open.'

'A given, Jan. A given.' He recited her mobile number. 'See. I know it by heart.'

They both smiled.

'And that picture?' '

Will email it to you.'

'And you're telling me all you've got now? Don't hold out, Frank, if you want me and the paper to keep helping... My News Editor seems to be in a particularly bad mood today.'

He paused for a moment and sat down again. 'There is one other thing,' he said slowly. 'Another reason why it has taken us so long to get near the guy.'

The way his expression grew so dark, so quickly told Jan that this was serious.

'Go on,' she said.

'We've been working on the principle that this was a terrorist attack. Some sort of extreme right-wing white supremacist, racist or religious act. We're thinking now it might well be a revenge attack.

'But they were random people, not linked in anything but being Muslims and in the Mosque.'

'The car was stolen in Brum. A couple of months ago, five men of Asian origin raped a young white woman in the city. At least we think they did. We've sent detectives up there to talk to local bobbies. The girl came in to the station to report it. For whatever reason, it wasn't logged as a crime.'

'So how do you know about it?' Jan asked.

'A young copper up there was told to keep quiet about it. He was shocked. Got on to the police complaints people. They were looking into it. One of the blokes in our team was checking out recent incidents in Birmingham on the internal system and this came up. We have access across all departments. His eyes lit up at the link between the number five and the word Asian.'

'And why for Christ's sake would a crime like that not be logged?'

'Some forces, where we have the odd Neanderthal, have a policy of not logging unproven crime. Helps keep the figures down. Makes them look good.'

Jan looked shocked. 'Jesus, Frank…'

'I know,' he replied. 'But what can I tell you? This new government wanted that. Some forces are fighting against it, others going along with it – where the Chief Constable's under pressure or a freemason. The girl came back in 72 hours after reporting the rape and was interviewed. She'd been examined on the night, apparently, and she was in a bad way but West Midlands reckoned that since she couldn't identify the blokes who did it, there was no realistic prospect of a conviction and so the crime wasn't logged. What with the stolen car, and this case, we're starting to believe it was no coincidence that the Mosque killer stopped at five.'

'Holy shit. They didn't follow up that rape? If they had, they might have stopped what happened on Monday...'

'I know, I know. The presumption in rape should be that a crime has been committed and work from there. The guys in Brum didn't. They also feared a race incident so dragged their heels on it, thus avoiding publicity.'

'But why didn't he take his revenge in Birmingham?'

'Who knows? We won't know until we catch him and ask. But I'm prepared to guess that if he was going to do something as shocking as what he's done, he was going to make sure the whole country took notice. Power of London and all that. And easier to get away with when the two events aren't automatically linked.'

'So you must now know who it is? Someone close to the girl, right?'

'We only found all this out late last night. Made the connection in the early hours. Our people up there this morning are interviewing the girl and finding out about brothers, boyfriends, someone young who might have done this.'

He got up again to go. He had said enough. More than enough for Jan to get to work.

'This is fucking outrageous, Frank, you know that, don't you? From the West Midlands police's behaviour to the Met being so far off the pace they've been lapped.'

'Yes, I do know,' he replied, growing angry. 'Of course I bloody know. And you'll have plenty of sticks to beat us with once this is over. But just for now let's catch this bastard, yes?' He got up again, this time to text.

'Who you texting?' Jan asked.

'My driver. He's round the corner.'

'You have a driver?'

He smiled at her. As he left, Jan sipped the dregs of her coffee and grimaced at its chill. She needed another. She needed to think about her next move and her next piece. There was plenty of material, after all. It was early in the day, however. Not quite 10am. There would still be much to unfold. It was then that the bloody website insinuated itself back into her thoughts. She was beginning to think in the new, rather than dwell in the old, and she wasn't sure whether it was a good or bad thing that she was being dragged into modern, tiresome and tiring, journalism.

She already had the information about the three men and the nosy neighbour and thought she had better get on to Vickers and file it. For that, she definitely needed another coffee and some contemplation time. She knew the danger was that in being sidetracked by the individual pieces of the jigsaw, and the need to satisfy new media by filing regularly during the day, she could lose sight of the bigger picture on the box and how it all fitted together. It was the curse of modern journalism.

Once back at her table, her laptop out of her bag and the coffee pushed aside to make room for it, she logged on and thought she had better ring in. Vickers was pleased with what he was being told about the three men in Primrose Hill and the heroine basking in her morning attention, Mrs Violet McIver, who was now being named on the TV, but he would have been even more pleased, ecstatic even, had he known what Jan did about the rape and the West Midlands police.

She was not about to impart that yet, however. That was a trump card for later in the day.

'I'll put over 500 words for the website,' she said gazing idly across Baker Street towards the queue at the Sherlock Holmes museum – definitely shorter than before the events of this week, which had badly affected tourism – when her attention was suddenly attracted by a red-faced man walking just in front of the window of the cafe heading north towards the park.

'Ivan,' she said. 'I'm going to have to ring you back.'

35

JAN, RASHID; SAUL

JAN slammed her laptop shut with a force that attracted looks from a couple of tourists – two of the braver ones who had not cancelled their trips since Monday's atrocity and its follow-up on Tuesday – sitting at the next table. She stuffed it in her bag and rose quickly, knocking over her coffee cup and skewing the table, noisily, to the shout of 'Hey' from the guy behind the counter.

At that moment, it didn't occur to her to alert Frank, or to call 999. The story was in her nostrils and that aroma was too heady, too powerful to allow in any other scents, or sense. She dashed out on to Baker Street and saw the guy not far away, maybe 20 yards. He was not walking very fast. She was about to set off in pursuit when she felt a tap at her shoulder.

'I knew it was you,' he said.

'Rashid,' she replied. 'How are you? What are you doing here?'

'I'm taking a slow walk through the park to the Mosque for Friday prayers,' he replied, momentarily forgetting how angry he was with her. It didn't take long to return, however. 'I'm glad I've bumped into you. You didn't tell me you were writing a story about that hoodie. I barely even mentioned it. I thought the agreement was that we were doing an interview about my reverting to Islam.'

'What? Well, yes, we were. It's going in the paper tomorrow. I hope.' She grew agitated, watching the man getting further away now. He was at the pedestrian lights at Allsop Place now.

'So why am I all over page three of your newspaper?'

'It was a news story Rashid. I had a duty to publish it.'

'But it makes it look as if I withheld information from the police. That I was not co-operating with them.'

'Well you withheld information from me, didn't you? About being a police cadet. And the security services trying to recruit you?'

'How do you know that?'

Jan shot another anxious look north. The man was now turning right at Outer Circle at the top of the road.

'Look Rashid. I would love to stand here and debate this with you,' she said in that British way of meaning the opposite of what she was saying. 'But I really need to follow a lead here. You need to trust me.'

'Trust you? Oh, please…'

'The hoodie story has helped the police close in on the man that killed five of your friends. You did a good thing by telling me.'

Rashid pondered this. Jan continued sharply.

'Now you can come with me or go away. Either way, I have to go.' She began to run. For a few seconds, Rashid watched her go then followed, catching her up easily.

'What's all this about?' he demanded.

'I think I've seen someone I recognise from yesterday,' she replied. 'Somebody connected with all this. Stop talking, if you're coming with me.'

They ran together and reached Outer Circle. There, Jan looked right and saw a group of people at the crossing, the traffic lights red, the man Jan recognised, whom she believed to be this man called Saul Bradstock that Frank had spoken of, at the back of them.

'OK. I've got him. Let's not get too close now,' said Jan, and they followed at a safe distance as the man passed through Clarence Gate and walked up on to Clarence Bridge, where he paused and they stopped, watching as he took something from inside a jacket.

*

SAUL needed a rest. He was sweating and breathless. He had also felt the buzz of a text. Needing a support, he leant on the balustrade of Clarence Bridge and carefully removed the mobile from the left inside pocket of his jacket, where it nestled next to one of the envelopes. He didn't want one of those falling out of his pocket. Money, certainly cash, definitely piles on paranoia, he mused.

'Get a fucking move on then,' said the text from Jason, sent a few minutes ago in response to his own of 'Got the money' when he left the bank. He must have missed the first buzz then in his anxiety to get to the Garden Cafe as quickly as possible. He couldn't get a move on, though. His legs had ceased to function for now. He just needed a few minutes...

It had been hard work. All the forms to fill in, all the phoney smiling to cover up his anxiety, along with the thoroughness of the woman, had played on his nerves. But he had done it and now had two envelopes containing £6,000 each in denominations from £10 to

£50 concealed in two inside breast pockets. The slim, new notes stuck together in their crispness, causing him to reflect how little space £12,000 actually took up.

Saul looked at his watch. It was now 10.10am. He was shattered and might have to indulge himself today and get a taxi to the Marsden for his final treatment. He had wanted to see out his routine of walking through the park and back every day, take the tube, not give in, but there were such things as stubbornness and folly.

Thankfully, he noted, the police officers had by now departed from the gate to the park and he could see them mingling with the public and showing their picture away to his right down towards the southern end of the boating lake. He pressed on and crossed Clarence Bridge, sweating profusely. The temperature must surely now be in the 80s, he thought. He rested on the bridge for a moment, wishing he had stopped at Bar Linda for a bottle of water. It was the cheapest place at the top of Baker Street and he had used the cubbyhole of a cafe opposite the Sherlock Holmes museum for years.

He had toyed with the idea of texting Jason to request him and Tom to come and meet him on the bridge but the two police officers could easily walk back this way from towards Inner Circle while he was waiting and they might recognise him from earlier. Besides, he needed that drink and it was only a couple of hundred yards to the cafe now. He turned left from the bridge and took the path that wound around the perimeter of Regent's College, past the bandstand and came out on Inner Circle opposite the Garden Cafe.

Each step was now a struggle and, his lips dry and his legs heavy, he wondered a couple of times whether he would make it. He rested again momentarily at the railings of Inner Circle, but he now had only to cross the road. They were there. He could see Jason and Tom sitting in the window. He saw Tom rise, then Jason grabbing his arm and pulling him back down into his chair. Saul could see the worry on Tom's face but he smiled weakly, waved lamely, and made it over the road and in through the door of the cafe. It was less than half full and there was nobody too near Tom and Jason's table.

Breathing heavily, the airlessness of the cafe increasing his sweats, he made it to their table and almost fell into a chair. The three of them were now absorbed in their own priorities. One was concerned about money, one about his health, and the other caught once again in the middle.

So pre-occupied were they, indeed, that they did not notice the two people who had come through the gate opposite a minute or two after Saul, one a young guy wearing a skull cap and tunic and one a woman on the verge of middle age in white T-shirt, blue jacket, fawn trousers and court shoes, carrying a heavy bag over her shoulder.

'OK, let's get out of their eyeline,' said Jan as they looked across at the cafe, 'I'm sure that's them in the window.'

'They are the men who did this on Monday?' Rashid asked. 'I'm going in there after them.'

'No. Let's not rush into this,' she said, grabbed his arm and led him behind a row of trees across Inner Circle, near the entrance to the Garden Cafe.

'I need to be sure. We have to be smart about this. And careful. If we charge in, it could be dangerous for us, and all the people in there. I'll phone somebody I know at New Scotland Yard. We need police here. If it is them.'

'I could phone Deena,' said Rashid.

'Deena? You know a Deena? In the police?'

'Yes. I met her at the Mosque. She was on duty. We have become friends.'

'Well, well, well. That's nice.'

'At least I think we're friends. We were going to meet at lunchtime but she texted me saying she was on duty in the park this morning. And she told me about how you used her as well. I haven't forgotten about this story today, by the way.'

'OK. OK. Now's not the time, right? Let's get this out of the way then talk, eh?'

'But I think we should call 999,' said Rashid. 'Thinking about it, I don't really think we should get Deena involved in this.'

'Listen, she'd want to be. My contact at the Yard will sort out all the mob-handed bunch. She can just be in on it. You said she was on duty in the park this morning. So she must be somewhere near, right?'

Rashid nodded. After they had made their calls, Jan spoke with a firmness that brooked no objection.

'Right,' she said. We are going in there. All casual for coffee like, OK? And please take off that skull cap.'

36

TOM, SAUL, JAN, RASHID, DEENA

'GIVE him a moment, Jason, OK?' said Tom as his brother asked for the third time about the money and Saul regained his breath and composure. He nodded, tapped the breast pockets of his jacket and Jason momentarily relaxed.

'I'm not getting the envelopes out in here just now,' Saul wheezed. 'Wait till it's quieter. Tom, I wonder if I might ask you to get me a bottle of water.'

Jason motioned for Tom to go. He went to the counter and stood in a queue behind a couple of people. As he waited, he turned around to take in the room. It was idle habit, but the edginess of his situation, the whole episode, added a watchfulness to him. He noticed two people walk in through the door, an older woman and a younger, black-haired man, wearing a tunic that Tom thought looked cool. He did a double-take at the pair, thinking he might have noticed them somewhere before, then realised he was getting too worried about anyone he saw. He faced back to the counter, his turn having come, while the two people stood in line behind him.

'The hottest of the year so far, they reckon,' Jan said, before worrying that the weather might be too obvious a topic of conversation. 'So what are you going to have?'

'I'll take a green tea, please,' said Rashid. The kid in front bought his water and went back to his table, handing the bottle over to the older man, who drank gratefully from it.

The cafe was beginning to quieten after earlier busyness, the sun's heat having lured many people out early in the day. Most tourists were still taking breakfast in hotels but a smattering, at the cheaper end of the market where breakfasts were extra and expensive, had made it here for coffee and pastries. Most wanted them to take their orders away, either to the tables outside or to eat amid the idyllic scene of the rose garden.

At the till, a young boy and girl wearing black polo shirts and aprons looked harassed, she taking orders, him making the drinks.

'Busy morning?' said Jan to the girl, having ordered her coffee and Rashid's green tea.

'Give me the winter any day,' she replied. 'Still, shouldn't wish your life away, should you? Getting quieter now, thankfully.'

Jan looked around the room. It was L-shaped. She pointed to Rashid to take a table in the half opposite the three men, next to a table with a tactile young couple besotted with each other. She figured that she could see across into the other half of the cafe without looking obtrusive and intrusive; the young couple would absorb any attention from other people, either embarrassed by or pleased for them.

Jan sat with a view of the whole room, Rashid with his back to the men so it would not look as if they were both watching them. She tried to take them in without staring. They fitted Frank's profile all right, and the oldest and youngest could well be the two she had seen from a distance yesterday. The older man had almost finished the bottle of water the youngest had brought him. Yes, they were definitely the ones in the park yesterday buying the purple hoodie. The middle one, his hair cropped, seemed to have one expression, which was a scowl.

'It's got to be them,' Jan whispered to Rashid, who was sipping his tea.

He nodded, still restraining himself, in keeping with her wishes and against his baser instincts to turn around and attack these men, one of whom was surely the filthy terrorist.

'I'm going to have to do something soon,' said Rashid.

'Don't,' said Jan. 'Just text Deena again if you're worried about her and tell her to wait outside until help arrives.' She had made him call Deena to get here with some back-up to ensure she had got the message. Thankfully, she had taken the call, despite Rashid saying she seemed off with him. This text was just to keep him occupied. Thankfully, too, Jan was right about Frank still being in his car on the way back to the Yard when she had made her call. But where were they now? Just a few minutes had passed but it was beginning to feel like a long time since they had spoken to Deena and Frank.

She looked across at the trio in the other half of the room but turned away when the youngest one shot her a glance. She suddenly grew worried. What if the kid recognised her from yesterday outside the Honest Sausage? And Rashid? Their pictures had been on the news. In the papers too, though Rashid's fortunately with him wearing a skull cap.

'What should we do?' Rashid asked, his text sent.

'We should keep calm and wait for the police to get here.'

'But it might be dangerous for Deena. The guy turned a flamethrower on five people remember.'

'That's why I told you to tell her to wait outside until my police contact arrives with all his crew.'

'What if they leave before the police get here?'

'Well, the older guy's in no state to go anywhere at the moment. Let's just see, shall we?'

'By the way,' added Rashid, 'I know you'll use that about me being in the police for a while. But please, not some unit trying to recruit me, eh? Even if I turned it down, the people at the Mosque won't trust me anymore.'

Jan smiled. She felt sympathetic. Rashid was a good kid. It may have been a good new angle for the profile, and one she had contemplated rewriting the intro for, but she had no wish to ruin his life. He had been through enough. She nodded. Anyway, there was a bigger story surely to be told today...

She looked across at the man gulping down the last of the water. Then, from inside his jacket, he took two envelopes and handed them to the senior of the young men, who opened them and glanced inside. He looked around the room and Jan quickly had to look down at her mobile. She saw them talking but could not hear the conversation.

'I won't count it,' Jason said to Saul. 'It looks all here. Good job, old man.'

'OK. You can go now,' said Tom, now concentrating on Jason, having been temporarily distracted by the odd couple in the other corner. 'And you can leave us alone.'

'Not quite,' said Jason. 'He was right about us splitting up. But two seems to work, doesn't it? We got away with it with those coppers. But they'll have been in the flat since then. Asked around. I reckon they're now looking for three men. He comes with me. We're getting a taxi to Heathrow.'

'No, Jason,' said Tom. 'This isn't right...'

'After what happened at the flat, they'll know who owns it,' said Saul. 'And they will probably be able to identify me.'

'I'm just thinking about getting out of this park and into a taxi. You're going to help me do that. We'll worry later about what happens next.'

'But Heathrow? They're going to be all over it.'

'Biggest airport in the world. Easiest place to get a plane out quickly and get lost in.'

'Please, I'm really struggling now,' said Saul. 'I need to get to the hospital...'

'Come on, Jason, for fuck's sake,' said Tom growing angry.

'The man's done what you asked. Let him go. He's got his cancer treatment.'

'And he has unfinished business with me,' said Jason, drawing the knife from his pocket so that both Tom and Jason could see it. Across the room, Jan also caught a glimpse.

'Jesus. Fuck. He's got a knife,' she whispered to Rashid.

Rashid could not help looking round, stirred and stunned by all three parts of Jan's statement, but Jason had placed the blade back in his pocket. 'It's not right drawing Deena into this,' he said again.

'She's a police officer. It's what she does,' Jan insisted. 'She will want to be in on this. And we've told her to stay outside for now. Wait for back-up.'

Suddenly the door to the cafe opened and Deena and her colleague Darren stood there for a moment taking in the scene and getting their breath back. They had been on the other side of the park, the south-east corner near Great Portland Street, still getting no joy with the bloody purple hoodie picture, when Rashid had phoned. They had made it as quickly as they could, running up York Bridge, turning left on to Inner Circle, inside five minutes. They were ahead of the special unit that Frank was hastily mobilising and briefing from his car.

She saw Rashid, who stood up, concern in his eyes. 'Where are they?' she asked, a worried tone to her voice. Jan tried to stay seated and calm but it was too late. Jason had seen the two police uniforms and was out of his seat wielding the knife, its blade glinting in the hot sun streaming through the window. He pulled Saul to his feet with him, holding the point to the side of Saul's neck, the panic in his eyes transmitting itself to his raised voice.

'Fuck off, all of you,' he yelled. 'Keep back.'

There were screams from the half dozen tourists left in the cafe as they ran for the door, among them the young couple, having disentangled themselves. The kids serving at the counter were now hiding under it. Deena stood rooted to the spot with Darren. Rashid and Jan were now standing at their table, transfixed by the scene unfolding in front of them. All watched the knife make an indent in Saul's skin without piercing it. Saul's face was red, droplets of sweat running down from his forehead.

Tom would remember later that the last straw for him, for some red-rag reason, was watching a bead of sweat run down Saul's neck and lodge itself in the indent made by the knife point.

Jason's eyes were fixed straight ahead, watching the startled, frozen gathering. As Deena called out for him to take it easy, he was distracted from Tom a couple of yards away to his left, shifting his weight from foot to foot as he wondered how to react. Tom had been angry, Jason had recognised that, but ever since he had refused to let Saul go and placed his final treatment in jeopardy, a rage that required Tom to act had been building. He had wanted this resolved peacefully, his loyalty torn between family – the brother who had saved his life and helped bring him up in the absence of a father – and justice. That fraternal loyalty, he was finally concluding, as the knife at Saul's throat pierced his own denial if not yet the man's flesh, was being shockingly abused with each shameful episode. Now, he knew, his debt towards Saul was the greater. Any pain left in his bandaged arm was subsumed by adrenaline.

The door to the cafe opened again to reveal Frank, whose driver had turned around when his boss had received the text from Jan and dropped him outside, on Inner Circle.

'You fuck off as well,' Jason shouted, 'whoever you are.'

'I am a senior police officer and we all need to relax here,' said Frank.

'There'll be no fucking relaxing until you get me a taxi to an airport and a plane out of here.' It sounded ridiculous, a line from a movie, but such was Jason's desperation that he uttered what he had heard.

'That's not going to happen, son,' said Frank. 'Half the Metropolitan Police are going to be here any minute.'

Ten tense seconds of silence were ended by Tom speaking out. 'This, people, is my brother, Jason Judd. He is the man who murdered five people in that Mosque on Monday. My name is Tom Judd and I drove him there, I am deeply sorry to say. I didn't know what he was going to do but I took him. I can't deny it. This man is Saul Bradstock. He made the mistake of trying to help me. To find a peaceful way to end all this.'

Jason interrupted him. 'Shut up, Tom. Shut the fuck up.'

Tom looked at Saul, who almost imperceptibly nodded, urging him to keep going.

'I have found out things this week that I never wanted to know. But also things that I've waited a long time for someone to tell me. I have been cursed and blessed. I am sorry for those five innocent men and ashamed of my brother. And myself. I am grateful to this man who has cancer and needs to get to a hospital.'

'And won't fucking make it if you don't fucking shut up.'

'Jason, it's over,' Tom said. 'Put down the knife.'

Jason instead pushed it more firmly into Saul's neck, the point nicking the skin and drawing a drop of blood. Saul winced and Tom moved forward a yard.

'Don't you fucking dare,' said Jason but at another tiny nod from Saul, Tom dared. He sprang forward and took down both Jason and Saul, the knife scoring Saul's neck and drawing more blood before disappearing somewhere under them in the melee.

Within seconds, Rashid was across the room, shouting: 'Stay back, Deena.' Darren was not far behind. Jason soon pushed Tom's slim frame off him, rolled over on top of him and began punching his brother in the face, but Rashid and Darren were swiftly on him, dragging him off then subduing Jason between them.

It took some doing but Darren, shouting instructions, guided Tom and Rashid into helping restrain Jason. Deena was suddenly there to handcuff him as Darren held Jason's head to the floor with the flat of his right hand. Jason's screamed obscenities soon ceased as he struggled for breath and Deena, remembering procedure and her training, informed him that he was being arrested on suspicion of the murder of five men at the Regent's Park Mosque on Monday.

'You do not have to say anything,' she went on, ignoring Jason's appeals for her to fuck off. 'However, it may harm your defence if you do not mention when questioned something which you later rely on in court. Anything you do say may be given in evidence.'

Across the room, Jan turned to Frank. 'I think you have your man,' she said.

'And,' he replied, 'I think you may have a bit of a story.'

'You might just be right', she said with a smile before adding: 'The girl PC, Deena... She's a star, that one. And I think she wants to be a detective.'

Frank returned the smile and the door burst open to admit a posse of armed officers. Frank directed them to calm down, then told them to take the kid in handcuffs into the van. Kicking, screaming, he was dragged outside. On his way, he turned to shout at his brother.

'You've been a weak mug, Tom. You've done everyone's dirty work for them.'

'Including yours,' Tom shouted back. 'But no more, eh?' He turned his attention to Saul, now lying on his back, blood trickling from the wound in his neck.

'Well done, Tom,' Saul said, breathing heavily between sentences. 'You're a brave lad. And I don't just mean physically. Never underestimate the moral courage of what you did today...'

'Stop talking,' Tom replied. 'The cut doesn't look too bad. We'll get you some help.'

Five yards away, Deena, still charged with the intensity of the moment, turned her anger on Rashid. 'Don't you ever tell me to stay back again,' she said.

'But we asked you in the text to stay outside. It could have been dangerous for everyone, not just you.'

'Look, this is what I do and who I am. It might have been worse if I'd stayed outside. We would have been in a hostage situation then. We brought it to a head.'

'OK, OK. I get it. I understand,' said Rashid.

'Thank you,' she said. 'Now I need to go back to the station and sort the paperwork, OK?'

'Fair enough,' said Rashid, disappointed. 'I guess some of your lot will want to speak to me again and then I've got Friday prayers.'

She got only a few paces before turning back 'You might have told me about that purple hoodie,' she said.

'Sorry. It only crossed my mind when the journalist was interviewing me again yesterday. I didn't know it was a big deal.'

She turned to go again, then quickly turned back again and said more softly, 'I might be due some time off after this. I'd like to hear more about that story of the Grand Mosque in Paris. Who knows, maybe even visit it some time. What do you reckon?'

'I'd like that,' said Rashid, smiling.

'Nice work, constable,' came Frank Phillips's interruption to the scene as he made his way over to Saul and Tom to tell them that they would have to be taken in, and charged, for their roles in it all. Later, quietly, privately, he would add that they could expect some leniency when the details came out and given how it had ended.

'I'll make sure they know this was your collar,' Frank added to Deena. She raised her eyebrows, squeezed Rashid's hand fleetingly and joined Darren outside.

There, Jan was on her mobile. She looked up to see Deena smiling at her. She flashed a smile in return before looking back down, pacing around and continuing her conversation. Deena shook her head and listened for a moment.

'Yes, everything, Ivan,' said Jan. 'They've got him and I've got everything. First person. Front page, turning across the whole of the front of the bloody book. Six, eight, ten pages. And I want that interview with the Muslim kid in there across two pages.'

She paused to listen to her News Editor trying to dictate to her what he wanted. He barely got through a sentence.

'No, I am the one calling the shots here and I am sure the Editor will agree with me,' she said insistently. 'I'll put a new intro on it, about the ex-police cadet Muslim who helped catch the Mosque murderer, and it runs in full. Who's it going to be phoning the Editor? You, to make his weekend at Chequers by giving him and the PM the glory-glory news that the paper has cracked this case, or me, to get him to phone you?'

There was another pause. 'Good. I knew you'd see sense. I'll be in the office in half an hour.'

She cut off the call and saw Deena beaming at her. 'Sometimes you have to tell people what they think,' said Jan.

'Thank you,' said Deena.

'No, thank you. And good luck with your career.' They hugged.

Ten yards away, an ambulance arrived.

'HELP. PLEASE, SOMEBODY HELP,' came the words suddenly, piercingly shouted, from inside the cafe, interrupting the triumphalism. Deena and Jan turned, alert and anxious. Paramedics hurried from the back of the ambulance past them and into the cafe. Deena and Jan followed.

There, they were confronted by Tom kneeling over Saul, tears rolling down his cheeks.

'It's in his back. At the base.'

Two paramedics turned Saul gently so that the right side of his lower back moved a few inches off the ground. He groaned, now knowing what it was that had caused the searing pain he had complained of to Tom. The handle of Jason's British Army knife, forgotten in the struggle and the relief of its aftermath, now protruded, with some five of the seven inches of the blade embedded below Saul's rib cage. Later it would be established that the blade had pierced his right kidney, causing the fatal blood loss so quickly.

'Oh God,' said Tom when he saw the knife's handle and the leaking blood. Deena and Jan raised hands to mouths. Rashid hung his head. Frank made anxious eye contact with Jan.

'OK, stay with me, sir,' said one of the paramedics and they began to get to work. Saul's croaky voice interrupted them.

'Tom,' said Saul, his voice rasping as he stuttered out the words. 'I have a feeling I'm not going to write that novel now. Shame. I know what it might be about finally.'

He smiled. Tom laughed as he coughed out his tears.

"Sshh,' he said, 'take it easy. The paramedics will take care of you.'

'Do one thing for me, Tom, yes? Please ring Rachel...'

Tom nodded.

'Look in my jacket pocket,' Saul added. There, Tom found a set of keys.

'My flat keys,' said Saul. 'They're yours. When they've realised the truth of everything.' His voice was by now barely a whisper but he sought to raise it a little. ' Everyone hear that?' All in the silent room had.

'No. Don't go, Saul. Please,' Tom pleaded.

'And Tom...'

'Yes? What?'

'Remember what the Boss said, yes? That it ain't no sin to be glad you're alive.'

NOTES AND ACKNOWLEDGEMENTS

This book began life in 2014 when I finally decided that it was time I wrote the novel I had been promising/threatening for many years. Initially I would pen a few chapters on holidays until my wife Vikki Orvice suggested I took some time out from writing non-fiction for a living so that I could write fiction for fulfilment. She would, she said, help subsidise me. For that, and many other things, I will forever be grateful.

Vikki died of cancer, aged 56, in February 2019, a year and a couple of weeks after she organised the launch party for the novel at Primrose Hill library in North London, a lovely little venue and in the heart of where much of the action of the book took place. It is a night, a memory, that I will forever treasure as so many friends and backers of this book, created through the crowd-funding publishers Unbound, helped me celebrate my fiction debut. The names of those who generously contributed and who have my thanks follow these acknowledgements.

As the book took shape, I found that the character I most enjoyed writing was Jan Mason, the national newspaper reporter with an old-fashioned belief in traditional and noble methods of legwork and using contacts built up down the years, even if sometimes she needed to be, shall we say, tactically cute if she was going to get a story that was for a greater good. So much so that I actually wanted to write about her again. The idea took hold within me that she could even be the protagonist in a series of novels.

Unbound granted me the rights back for what was titled with them *THE OUTER CIRCLE*. I decided to set up a new company, V Books, to reprint, with the new title of *OUTER CIRCLE*. I wanted it to become the first in the Jan Mason series of cases and stories and to rebrand, partly also to bring it under the umbrella of the publishing company named after Vikki who did so much to encourage my fiction-writing career.

It has a new cover, by the brilliant Steve Leard, and that too is homage to V, who was a trailblazing sports journalist, the first female football writer to be hired to the staff of a tabloid newspaper in 1995 indeed, and who became the athletics correspondent of *The Sun*, the London Olympics being the highlight of her career. The colours on the front are those of the Olympic rings. The figure on the back is Vikki, on her phone on Primrose Hill. The shot was taken by my daughter Alex, a professional photographer and now my partner in V Books, when we were mulling over cover ideas back in 2017.

In its previous incarnation, the book enjoyed a good reaction and I am grateful to those buyers and readers of it. There are only a few minor alterations for this new edition (Jim became Frank, for example, which I thought suited him better). I could perhaps have rewritten here and there but I wanted the book to be authentic as example of my writing from that time. It is who I was and the writer I was, even if I feel I have since developed. I remain very proud of it. I do hope old readers who might have returned will feel they have been rewarded with the new material at the back of this edition – the first three chapters of the next Jan Mason story, *DON'T TALK,* that represents book two in the series – and that new readers will have come to enjoy reading Jan as much as I enjoy writing her.

She is, of course, based on Vikki, who began her career in Fleet Street as a news reporter on the *Daily Mail.* She is sparky and clever, ingenious and resourceful, just as V was. I confess that writing her is a way for me to keep her in my heart and mind. And the great thing is that wherever I go, wherever I write, Vikki goes there with me.

As well as my thanks to Alex for her support, both morally and practically, my gratitude goes also to my son Jack. It has been such a boon to have them so close to me again. Many more people have also helped me since Vikki passed and they will duly be given the acknowledgement they deserve in *DON'T TALK*. For now, I want to focus mainly on V, for this was very much her book as well as mine.

Finally, I would like to thank two great men without whom none of my life these past 33 years would have been possible: Bill W and Bruce Lloyd.

SUPER PATRONS

Tony Adams, Richard Arlett, Michael Aylwin, Darren Barker, Elizabeth Birchall, Mary Bolam, Graham Burke, Seth Burkett, Steve Claridge, Paul Cocks, Luke Conboye, Andrew Cooke, Paul Crosbie, James Devers, Rachel French, Adam Gemili, Margaret Graham, Alan Jopling, Dan Kieran, Janet King, Shirley Clift & Jeroen Knops, Bruce Lloyd, Toni Minichiello, John Mitchinson, Jimmy Mulville, Niels Aagaard Nielsen, Jean Orvice, Fred Orvice, Vikki Orvice, Justin Pollard, Alex Ridley, Barbara Ridley, Bob Ridley, Jack Ridley, Sacha Sachag, Melanie Sharpe, Simon Sharpe, Prof. Ian Smith, Emily Thoubboron, Moira Thoubboron, Emma Visick, Richard Visick.

PATRONS

Sandra Armor, Philippe Auclair, Lionel Birnie, Daragh Breen, Neville Custance, Christopher Davies, Stephen Eames, Lawrence Elbourne ,, Vernon Grant, James Gregory, Paul Harding, Henrietta Heald, Martin Huckerby, Matthew Jefferies, Judy Kane, Jonathan Legard, Richard Lewis, Diane Mackie, Mike McMonagle, Nastasya Parker, Richard Rae, Josephine Ridley, Lee Sharpe, Elizabeth Sparke, Lee Stansfield, Victoria Stubbs, David Tavener, Richard Todd, Deepti Unnikrishnan, Ed Warner.

COMING
AUTUMN 2022:

A NEW JAN MASON STORY

DON'T TALK

Read on for the first three chapters....

SUNDAY

1

THE DOCUMENT was staring at her, daring her to sign. And it was so tempting. Especially at this time of night. Especially with the bottle of red in its drained state. She lifted it from the coffee table and raised it to her eye level, closing one and focussing with the other to gauge whether she might just squeeze one more glass out of it. Hard to tell with its dregs slooshing from side to side. Maybe. She shouldn't make a decision just now. Not like this. But she'd been putting it off for a month and had to decide by Friday. Perhaps a few drinks would speed up the process, she'd reasoned after a day off when she'd walked in Hyde Park to try and come to a conclusion. If a clear head hadn't worked, maybe *in vino veritas* would be a better strategy.

Let's weigh up those pros and cons again, Jan thought. First and foremost, the money. A year's salary. Not bad. Particularly as she was now the highest paid news reporter on the paper. Or Chief Reporter at Large, don't you know. She could pay off what was left of the mortgage on this flat with half of it. Then she'd have something concrete to show for her career, quite literally. A two-bedroomed flat in Maida Vale. Not bad. She'd bought when the area was still relatively cheap and could make a good profit if she fell on hard times.

She could also take some time to rethink her life and what she was going to do with it now. People did that when they got to their 50s, right? She could travel to all those places she'd fantasised about for years: Machu Picchu, the Iguazu Falls, Ayer's Rock. And Wakefield. Yes, she could see more of her mother. Suddenly the mellowness of her mood was punctured. Seeing more of her mother. Should that be a pro or a con, she wondered, and smiled.

Maybe after a month or two's jet-setting, she could set herself up as a freelance. She still had a good name in the business. A big name, even. Reporter of the Year in the British Newspaper Awards when she'd been one step ahead of the police in catching the man who had burned five Muslims to death with a flamethrower at the Central London Mosque just after the London Olympics.

The London Olympics. My God. A whole decade ago, she thought. Really? A melancholy came over her to which only *Who Knows Where the Time Goes* by Sandy Denny would do justice and she called it up on her Spotify. It had been a while, she had to admit as the haunting song came through her Sonos speaker, since the words BY JAN MASON would have all other media scrambling to follow up what was written beneath it. The game had changed even more, too. Even more being tied down to a desk, rewriting. More 'churnalism', fewer staff. She'd continued to be professional, turning a few decent tales, about an errant politician or a human interest special on a missing child, but nothing quite as stunning or earth-shattering as that successful, inspired and painstaking tracking down of the ex-squaddie now serving life for murdering those innocent Muslims. Nothing where she'd been the one setting the agenda, being proactive.

She'd had a good run, she told herself. She'd known the best days of what was once called Fleet Street, loved the cut and thrust, savoured the sounds and smells of the newsroom that were gone for good. She'd done her best to fight the good fight for the ethics and values of print against the wild west of the internet – ink versus link – and she'd seen, felt, her combativeness wane. She'd tried to embrace the new technology, could see its value in the divulgence of fingertip information, as well as supplying instant songs and dating website faces to be rejected, but she had no love for its exclusion of the human touch.

And how much longer could she keep up her side of the battle against the news editor Ivan Vickers, known amongst the reporters as TGV – That Gobshite Vickers? He hated her elevated status on the paper that was deserved no longer, he reckoned. Too big for boots that were smaller these days was the word that came back to her. Then there was the fact that the editor with whom Jan had come up through the ranks, and who had given her the current role, was gone, to be replaced by a bright young thing from the group's London evening paper. And once a new editor came in with a mandate to make changes, anything could happen. Vickers was clearly biding his time, awaiting his moment to strike.

Best, Jan reckoned, to get her retaliation in first. To go on her terms rather than be beaten by Vickers and suffer a humiliating exit. Anyway, if she didn't take voluntary redundancy this time around, it would probably be compulsory next time. And she'd be first in line as a high-earner when youngsters who did what they were told and were more tech-savvy came so much cheaper. The terms wouldn't be this good again. And while freelancing was a rough old world, with too many ex-staffers chasing too little work, she would have the reputation and financial cushion to soften the landing. Given her status, she might even land a column somewhere.

And let's not forget finally sustaining a relationship, she considered. She might actually meet someone properly, on a holiday or at a social event, rather than in desperation online. Even with that it had been a while since she'd found someone she liked and then none that had lasted more than a couple of evening dinners and regretted nights together. She looked back – what, 16, 17 years? – on the needy, needs-must relationship with Frank Phillips, a police contact she'd used too literally, as positively stable.

"I have no fear of time," sang Sandy, to a 'yeah right' before Jan stopped the music. In the background, the TV picture with no sound on was flashing out the opening titles of the BBC News. She leant forward from the sofa and commanded volume from the remote. The lead story was about a vote in Westminster that would be taking place tomorrow. New immigration bill. She recognised the far right figure on screen offering a soundbite in the taster headlines about the country needing to look after its own. How come Peter Carew looked so distinguished but sounded so crass? *The people's politician, my arse,* she thought. She was more concerned about what a weak lead this was, though. Even for a Sunday night, leading on some Westminster vote that was going to happen tomorrow, however important the issue, was dull stuff. Couldn't anybody find a story any more? A proper story. *News is people,* she always remembered from her training. A juicy murder that resonated with the public, maybe. A series of them, perhaps.

She signed the document that had gone from staring to winking at her and she would hand it in to human resources when she started her late shift tomorrow. It would be day one of a new life. But first tonight, she'd finish the bottle. Definitely one last glass in there.

MONDAY

2

FRANK would look back and remember the words, and they would return to him insistently like an earworm from a catchy pop song, certainly well beyond the sleepless hours that would torment him through that coming night. And just when he thought he'd heard everything in this room. Or rooms like it.

"I might have been in what you people call blackout... I may need to go to the police..." the guy said. *"I think I might have killed her."*

The meeting of Alcoholics Anonymous had proceeded like any other here before those chilling words were spoken, before *he* had arrived. The crypt of the church was its usual dingy self, at its centre a candlelit circle of plastic chairs ready to embrace a set of souls in need of shelter from their solitary storms.

Frank stirred the one spoonful of sugar that was the legacy of his lingering craving for sweetness into his cracked mug of tea and took his seat. He always liked the one nearest a door, just in case. His police training had taught him to look for an exit in the event of emergency. He had always, anyway, needed an escape route as his relationships had confirmed. It had all been very messy with Jan during that once-upon-a-time of his drinking when they'd been ports in a storm for each other and it had left him with a legacy in his sobriety of being a bolter when it came to getting close to women.

The new guy Sean, wiry and wary, was already seated, next to his friend Aesha. Neighbours in South London, Frank had discovered last week, the one in his late 20s, the other early 20s. This was just Sean's second week since quitting the drink after nervously communicating his desire, even need, to stop at his first meeting this time last week. Recognising him despite the dimness, Frank shot him a smile as he settled into the unyielding chair and Sean smiled weakly back.

"How you doing this week?" Frank asked.

"Fine," he replied. "Yes, fine thanks."

"You do know fine stands for fearful, insecure, neurotic and exhausted," Frank said.

Aesha, more at ease having been coming a few months and her skin smoother and hair sleeker as a result of being sober, placed her hand on Sean's knee and laughed loudly. "Then, I for one genuinely am fine," she said.

"OK, me too," said Sean, a jittery tone to his voice, grateful to be given permission to say how he really felt.

"Welcome to our club," Frank replied. "I've been coming for 15 years and I still feel like that some days."

"Wow. 15 years," Sean said with the awe of the newcomer, before a thought came to him. "And you still have days like the rest of us?"

"It will get better," Frank replied. "But you won't be immune from all the feelings that brought you here. If you do stick around, though, you'll learn to cope through the bad days without the need to get pissed."

Sean half-smiled again, just as the meeting's secretary Roberto, a city trader known as Italian Bob in the meetings, banged an empty tin on the coffee table in front of him to signal the 7.30pm start time.

"Welcome everybody to the Monday night meeting of the Blandford Road group of Alcoholics Anonymous," he said. "My name is Bob and I am an alcoholic."

"Hi Bob," the meeting chorused.

In a mature, authoritative voice, Bob read the preamble, about AA being a fellowship of men and women who share their experience, strength and hope in an attempt to solve their common problem and help others to recover from alcoholism. The only requirement for AA membership, he added, was a desire to stop drinking.

He then called upon Erroll, a stalwart of the group in his early 40s, to read the Twelve Steps before handing over to the woman sitting next to him who was tonight's 'chair', the speaker who was to address the gathering.

"My name is Jennifer and I am an alcoholic," she announced.

"Hi Jennifer," came the customary reassuring and welcoming unison from the other five people in the room. Tonight was a quiet meeting. It was a cold, rainy and forbidding November night outside and the traffic for a televised Premier League football match a mile or so away at Chelsea had deterred a few.

Jennifer summed up her drinking – "I drank too much, too often, for too long," – before delivering the detail that newcomers always needed so they could check themselves out and identify with the other people here. Or decide they weren't as bad as these people. That detail told of secret stashes, amounts consumed; whether it was beer, wine or spirits.

Twenty minutes in, having switched from her drunkalogue to the change that her two years of abstinence had brought about and her improvement as a mother of two young kids, the somnolent, safe and serene atmosphere was suddenly interrupted by the clanking of a door handle and the creaking of the heavy portal.

All heads turned to see a man pause in the threshold to take in the scene. Almost reluctantly, but knowing it needed to be done, he closed the door behind him and took a few steps towards the centre of the room. He waited again, as if having second thoughts.

"Come in. We don't bite," said Italian Bob, adding quickly, "Any more." The room laughed to ease their own tension and offer encouragement to the man to take the half a dozen or so more paces to the circle and one of the half dozen vacant chairs.

It was a man. They could make that out at least as he moved slowly towards the candlelight. In his mid to late 30s, maybe even 40, perhaps. Drink ages people. A few strands of hair escaped from a hoodie worn under black puffer jacket and his dark facial hair was somewhere between heavy stubble and unkempt beard. He wore black jeans and, incongruously, expensive suede boots. Frank would remember those later. When you sit at an AA meeting, looking down at the floor deep in thought as people tell their stories, you get to notice their shoes.

The man stood still for a moment before Frank rose from his seat and walked over to him.

"Can I get you a tea?" Frank whispered and the man nodded, looking down the whole time. Frank guided him towards the hatch of the crypt's kitchen, where he retreated from the pool of light, as if a wild animal confronted by fire, and Jennifer finished up her talk, about these days realising that she was good enough, as a person and in her job, and no longer needed to be the perfectionist who always fell short, and fell into a bottle as a result.

"I need to be real and not ideal," she said, to nods of recognition.

Frank returned with the mug-carrying man, still hanging his head in what Frank surmised was shame, and sat him down. The guy was clearly agitated. He sipped the tea with hands shaking around the mug. He looked to be in that state of internal conflict of everyone in their early days in AA, Frank thought – wanting to flee but needing to stay.

Bob the secretary thanked Jennifer for her talk, picked up on several statements that had resonated with him and opened the meeting for 'sharing'. One by one they spoke, at varying stages and ages of recovery and articulacy, telling of their day and the state of their lives currently. The good and the bad, the gratitude, the fear, the anger, the shame and the joy.

After a while, there was just one person left who had not spoken. The silence in the room endured for a minute or so, its tension heightened by the dimness, before the secretary became the one who felt the responsibility to fill it the most keenly.

"Would you like to tell us your name?" Bob asked.

The man looked up, then around, now aware that he was the one being spoken to. He shook his head.

"Anything you'd like to share with us?". There was another pause before Bob added: "This is a safe place."

The man drew in a deep breath and began.

"I don't know where to start," he said, his voice well-spoken but trembling. "I think I need to stop drinking." His eyes darted around the room. Nodding heads urged him on.

"She keeps on at me about my drinking. Or used to keep on. I'm not sure what comes, or came, first. Me drinking and her on my case or her on my case and me drinking."

Sean laughed nervously but soon stopped when suddenly the man fell silent. Sean could feel, if barely see, a glare piercing the half-light.

"She took up with another man," the man added after a moment. "I got very drunk. I might have been in what you people call black-out, I think… I may need to go to the police. Or not. I don't know."

There was a long pause. His audience, rapt and silent, had by now been taken hostage by his story.

"Either way, whatever came first," he continued slowly. "I think I might have killed her."

He looked around the room again. This time there were no nods. All he could make out was the whites of a series of stunned eyes.

Having shocked them verbally, the man now stunned them physically by rising quickly from his seat and rushing for the door, the swift clanking of the handle and the squealing of its hinges contrasting with the tortuous noises of his entry.

His copper's instincts awoken after the initial shock, Frank leapt to follow him and ran through the open door, up the steps from the crypt and into the darkness of the West London street.

There was no sign of the man. Frank had been those few seconds too long in his astonishment. He took in the pavements for a second, up towards Fulham Road and down towards the King's Road. Empty. He heard a roar from Stamford Bridge in the distance, before descending back into the meeting.

The numbed silence of the room that Frank had left was a chatter of voices on his return, wondering what the hell had just happened. They stopped when he appeared.

"Nothing. He's disappeared," said Frank.

"Well, there's still five minutes left of the meeting," said Bob, a tremor in his voice, trying to restore protocol to a meeting unlike any that any one of them had ever attended before, no matter the length of their sobriety. "Shall we sit down?"

After they had gradually taken their seats again, Bob asked if anybody had anything else they wanted to share.

"Plenty," said Frank. "But maybe after the meeting, eh?"

Bob nodded and passed a mug around the room for donations towards room rent, tea and coffee. The men jangled the change in their pockets to find a pound coin. The women reached down into their handbags for their purses. All felt they were in slow motion, such was their shock.

The mug having been returned to the table in front of him, Bob wrapped up the meeting.

"One final thing," he said. "Can I remind everyone of the importance of what this says." He held up in the light of a candle a yellow card bearing a slogan in black capital letters that had been sitting on the table in front of him, facing the meeting, throughout the last hour. It read:

WHO YOU SEE HERE
WHAT YOU HEAR HERE
WHEN YOU LEAVE HERE
LET IT STAY HERE

3

JAN swiped left after left on her dating app to pass the time. It had been a while since she'd swiped right. The last time she did, she'd engaged the guy in a conversation only for him to back off pretty quickly once he found out she was a journalist. Mind you, he only just beat her to it. She was going to terminate the conversation at the next boast about how much he made as a city trader.

Waiting for Mr. Right was not an option for Jan, mainly because she was old enough and wise enough to know there was no such person. She'd worked that out, what, at least 15 years ago after realising that she and Frank had been ships in the night rather than the soulmates she'd hoped for. She stayed on the dating app for the reason many people seemed to believe in God, a tinge of faith that grew with age. Just in case there was something in it.

"Nothing decent on the menu tonight?" came a voice behind her. Jan hastily shut off her phone and turned to see Tracy Moreton, the deputy news editor, behind her, buttoning her coat and ready to leave for the evening to go home to her lovely young bloke who worked as a fitness instructor and their sweet toddler of a son.

"Don't worry, I won't tell," said Tracy and smiled. Jan, busted, couldn't help smiling back. She got on well with Tracy, who had been at the paper just six months and was a breath of youthful fresh air.

"So, keep your voice down then," said Jan, whispering. "I don't want him knowing." Her eyes darted towards Ivan Vickers some ten yards away. The news editor was like Jan only in not having anyone to go home to so often stayed on late. Jan did not want him having any knowledge about her private life, even if there wasn't much of one. Knowledge was power over her.

"You hand in your redundancy?" Tracy asked, her voice now lowered.

"Um. No. There was nobody in HR when I went and I didn't want to just leave it on a desk."

"Right. Well, you know I wish you wouldn't, don't you?"

"I know. But I've thought it through now," said Jan. "Worked it all out last night. I'll put it in tomorrow."

"Great shame, Jan. They don't make reporters like you any more."

Jan thanked her and Tracey departed, leaving Jan to return to the waiting that she normally did at this time of an evening on the news desk, scrolling through the websites. In the old days, she would have been impatient for the first editions to drop. These days, she was killing time until 10pm when the national newspaper sites began carrying the stories that would lead the printed versions tomorrow but needed to get out there tonight to satisfy the rolling news lust that newspaper executives insisted existed. Existed beyond TV and radio stations waiting to follow it all up, that was. Waiting for the arrival of possible stories that might be worth filching was soulless, hack work but it had to be done.

The trademark Vickers bark interrupted the lull that always descended at this time of day. The paper's first edition had been put to bed, most reporters had left their desks in the news room – or their work stations in the hub, in modern parlance – leaving just a few duty staff seeing out time on their shifts, as Jan and some sub-editors were now. Once, there would be change after change to editions with late-breaking stories but cost-cutting meant fewer staff and fewer page changes. Besides, the website could monitor anything beyond midnight. The major vote going on in the House of Commons on the bill to tighten immigration laws was being handled by the politics guys in the Westminster press room. Only Sport, down the end of the editorial floor, was still busy here with anything live. She could see a few blokes with their feet up on the desks watching the Chelsea game.

"Anything?' Vickers demanded.

"Nothing yet," Jan replied.

To the younger reporters, Vickers remained a fearsome, snarling figure; a man who made daily life a dance on burning coals and who had a habit of ruining evening plans by sending those he wanted to punish out on wild goose chases. Some years back, after a young woman reporter whom he'd fancied had told him that she was going to the theatre with her boyfriend that night, he had sent her to doorstep a couple whose young daughter had been murdered in Lowestoft.

He'd had to give up pulling stunts like that on Jan after the Mosque murders story. It had been brilliant, old-fashioned legwork, hitting the streets, using all her contacts inside Scotland Yard, following leads. Going where the story led her. She'd also given the editor and even the proprietor a time to remember at that Park Lane hotel as they basked in the glory of their dominant mid-market tabloid winning Newspaper Front Page and Website of the Year.

And, transcending peer envy, she'd also earned the gratitude of all the traditionalists in the profession who still believed in the time-honoured skills of cultivating contacts and chasing tales, rather than tails, amid the daily grind of 'content-providing' from press releases and stories robbed and recycled from other media outlets. She'd struck a blow for journalism, indeed, at a time when the old Leveson report, phone-hacking and more rabid political posturing against the written press had seen a sharp decline in trust – and sales – of newspapers. The big pay rise and the promotion had also been gratifying, she couldn't deny that.

As a result of her spell without a jaw-dropper of a tale though, Jan knew from conversations over a few drinks with other reporters and Tracy that Vickers was sensing a chink in her armour. Time had told her that with his practiced nose of a print industry predator, he could smell vulnerability. She'd overheard him in the pub telling Tracy that he hated big-time reporters. Not as controllable as the youngsters. Jan knew he wanted her taken down a peg or two. He'd even quietly told Tracy to suggest to Jan that she'd be doing herself a favour by taking the redundancy package.

"Worth a couple of calls to see if anything's happening?" Vickers enquired reasonably enough but with a passive-aggressive subtext, as opposed to the more usual aggressive-aggressive that he felt at liberty to use on the less favoured. Once upon a time, when she was still a rookie Yorkshire lass come up to the smoke to try her luck, and still to anyone junior to her currently, it would have been: "Well, make some fucking calls then."

She picked up her mobile and hit the button for the Metropolitan Police press office. Danielle, the junior only to be expected on the other end of the phone at this time of night, picked up.

"Hi Jan," she said. "What's happening?"

"Thought you might tell me."

"Very quiet," said Danielle. "We like cold, damp nights with football on the telly keeping everyone indoors."

"Come on Danielle. Must be something going on. Please tell me there is. Unlike you, I hate quiet nights."

"You know you'll get something via the wires or a press release when there's anything you need to know."

Jan's hackles rose. Danielle knew that she had to show civility to such a senior reporter from some an influential newspaper but Jan sensed in her less respect than her track record deserved. Or perhaps it was Jan's paranoia as the fear of becoming yesterday's hero was insinuating itself into her more and more, with this redundancy preying on her mind.

"Danielle. That is the sort of standard reply you give others. This is Jan Mason you're talking to. Darling of the Met? Remember?" She hoped Danielle did, or at least that somebody had related the legend.

"You know we can't be too cosy these days, Jan, be fair. Not since Leveson. Give me a break."

"Well, I'll be very nice about you to your boss if you find anything decent," Jan said.

There was a pause on the end of the phone as Danielle pondered.

"There might be something." she said.

"Yes, go on…"

"No real details but there has been a call-out to a possible serious crime at an address in Chelsea."

Jan's ears pricked up. She looked up from her doodle and across at Vickers.

"OK…"

"A neighbour phoned in having heard what she thought might have been a scream. An old lady. Uniform found a youngish woman dead in a ground floor flat."

"Dead as in murdered?"

"We're not sure yet. But could be."

'Could be' was good enough for Jan but it was the 'address in Chelsea' part that excited her. The paper was always interested in murder, like any other media outlet, but there were murders and murders. No getting away from it, her Middle England readers were more interested in high-end, aspirational rather than council estate. In any human interest news event, the first question on the editorial floor of a mid-market tabloid was always "How much is the house worth?" If the victim was attractive, so much the better.

Jan got the address from Danielle and cut short the call. Her mobile pinged again straight away. Someone had swiped right on her dating profile. She ignored it, muttering "not now".

Then came the ringtone. Her brother Robert's name and face appeared on her screen. She was in two minds about answering but work, more specifically the lure of a tale, won out. Easily. Anyway, he was probably only ringing for a catch-up, as they did once a week, about this time of night, often on a boring Monday night. Unless it was about Mum. But she couldn't deal with that now, anyway. She would ring him tomorrow night. She hit the 'decline' icon.

"Got to go," she said to Vickers, closing her laptop, stuffing it into her voluminous pink leather shoulder bag – hard to lose, easy for people to remember her – and walking over to a stand to retrieve her prized Burberry raincoat, not too eagerly so as not to overexcite him.

"What you got?" he asked.

"Not sure yet. I'll let you know. If anything."

"What about the desk? I've not got a duty reporter now?"

"I'm sure there's people you can ring if anything breaks," she said as she put on her coat. "People whose lives you can ruin like you used to do mine."

"For fuck's sake, Jan. You can't just piss off."

"Oh I think I can. My title is still Chief Reporter At Large," she replied as she disappeared towards the lift in the centre of the glassy Thamesside building's atrium.

Something had kicked in – old instincts, adrenalin – and the scent of a story was in her nostrils. It may be nothing, but then, she told herself, no ticket, no lottery win. If she was going to go down, albeit with a sizeable redundancy payment as consolation, she was at least going to be remembered as going down with guns blazing.

ALSO BY IAN RIDLEY

THE BREATH OF SADNESS: ON LOVE, GRIEF AND CRICKET

Ian Ridley's beautifully crafted memoir shows there is no right or wrong way to grieve, and yet grieve we must. A moving insight.
JULIA SAMUEL, author of Sunday Times bestsellers Grief Works and This Too Shall Pass.

A fine meditation on life, love, death and grief forged during a gentle summer of county cricket.
MICHAEL ATHERTON, former England cricket captain.

If there's ever been a more honest, intimate, visceral, unflinching account of grief than this, well, I'd be very surprised.
CHARLIE CONNELLY, THE NEW EUROPEAN.

A heart-rending read. What Ridley has written in his wonderful book is a love letter to the game.
JIM WHITE, THE DAILY TELEGRAPH.

I have been immeasurably moved by it.
VANESSA FELTZ, BBC RADIO 2.

A love song. Like all the best such tunes it is a sad one, yet also, in the end, life-enhancing.
ALEX MASSIE, THE SPECTATOR.

Beautifully produced. A book that will bring comfort to many in that same sad but often inevitable place. Humanity is at hand.
JOHN HOTTEN, WISDEN CRICKET MONTHLY.

Candid and ultimately life-affirming. One of those rare books that takes you on a journey you didn't want to have to take but feel privileged to be on.
STEPHEN KELMAN, BOOKER PRIZE SHORTLISTED AUTHOR.

A wistful rumination on love and loss. Ridley balances fond recollection with candid admissions.
SHOMIT DUTTA, THE TIMES LITERARY SUPPLEMENT.

Ridley's quiet reflection in the solitude of county grounds is a backdrop to an extremely candid and brave – harrowingly so, at times – study of his own grieving process.
MATT DICKINSON, THE TIMES.

A beautiful memoir. The Breath of Sadness is about music, food, books, hotels, holidays, films, flowers, cards, messages and presents. The things you remember; the things you find put away in drawers, the things that break your bloody heart.
PAUL EDWARDS, THE CRICKETER.

Ridley writes with feeling on mourning a loved one in a book that finds companionship with two similar ones written by the surviving spouse: A Grief Observed by C S Lewis and the more recent The Year of Magical Thinking by Joan Didion.
SURESH MENON, THE HINDU

Honest, brave, magnificent and true.
JAMES RUNCIE

Lightning Source UK Ltd.
Milton Keynes UK
UKHW010625300123
416164UK00007B/1228